"What information are you withholding?"

"The fact that I would rather like to kiss you again," Devon blatantly confessed.

"How much punishment do you think I deserve, monsieur?" Jasmine asked, keeping the tremor in her voice at bay.

Devon's shoulders shook at the rebuke. "My mistake. You did mention that a kiss would be something I'd never have the privilege of taking from you again."

"*Oui*," Jasmine agreed. "You are wasting your time."

"I'll probably need a tetanus shot. Moreover, I don't suppose with you being the Ice Queen and all, any man is going to find it easy to thaw you out."

"The ideal temperature for my body is ninety-eight degrees," she answered, feeling a tightening of the muscles in her stomach. "One of your kisses wouldn't even get my pulse to rise."

Devon took two steps toward her. "What about your heart?" Undeterred, he reached out and touched her bottom lip. "The last time I kissed you, it melted."

One tug was all it took to pull Jasmine back into his arms. Before the moment could take shape, the pressure of Devon's lips was on hers. Jasmine's response took her by complete surprise. She hadn't so much thawed as evaporated with the touch of his fire. Who was this man who had the power to turn her from ice into a steaming mass of ultrasensitive vapor?

Duel of Hearts

Sonia *Icilyn*

ARABESQUE

BET☆ BOOKS

BET Publications, LLC
http://www.bet.com
http://www.arabesquebooks.com

ARABESQUE BOOKS are published by

BET Publications, LLC
c/o BET Books
One BET Plaza
1900 W Place NE
Washington, DC 20018-1211

All Kensington Titles, Imprints, and Distributed Lines are available at special quantity discounts for bulk purchases for sales promotions, premiums, fund-raising, and educational or institutional use. Special book excerpts or customized printings can also be created to fit specific needs. For details, write or phone the office of the Kensington special sales manager: Kensington Publishing Corp., 850 Third Avenue, New York, NY 10022, attn: Special Sales Department, Phone: 1-800-221-2647.

First Printing: November 2005

10 9 8 7 6 5 4 3 2 1

Printed in the United States of America

As always, for Parissa

Chapter One

"She's eighty-two years old," an elderly black woman wearing a cream-colored hat told another woman standing on the sidewalk beside her. They were in front of a newly whitewashed house and seemed somewhat curious about its owner, who was standing by her front door, cheerfully waving her farewells to a cluster of guests. "Do you know, in all the time I've been coming to these church luncheons," the woman added for clarity, "I've never known her to break wind."

"Lilian!"

Lilian chuckled. "It's true, Martha."

"I heard they used to call her 'Miss Uppity,' back in the 1960s," remarked Martha quite casually, wearing a pale blue floral dress. "Of course, that was on account of her being married to that preacher from back home."

"Pastor Henry Charlesworth," Lilian added. "Did you know he had an affair with Miss Gracie, the organ player's daughter? They tried to hush the whole thing up until they found out the poor girl was pregnant."

"I heard all about it," Martha said conspiratorily. "Miss Gracie Manning was sent to New York and was hastily given in marriage to Pastor Erskin Rutherford and had her baby there."

"A girl," Lilian recalled.

"No, it was a boy," Martha contradicted. "He was named Ralston Rutherford and I heard that Henry Charlesworth went to New York almost every Easter and Christmas to see him."

"Whatever became of the boy?" Lilian inquired curiously.

"He grew up, got married to a Puerto Rican girl, and had a boy of his own," Martha clarified. "Devon Rutherford, they called him. And guess where *he* is now."

"Where?" Lilian asked with arched eyebrows, certain she was about to hear something spectacular.

"Right here in Birmingham," Martha proclaimed on a scandalous note. "Living right here in Handsworth Wood at that house with Miss Uppity."

"No!" Lilian gasped, wide-eyed. "Dame Carmilla Charlesworth's dead husband's grandson is living in her house?"

"She's calling him her godson," Martha gossiped for emphasis. "Since Pastor Henry passed away and the boy's parents are also dead, I think she felt an obligation to look after her late husband's family."

"It's shameful," Lilian mocked, her mouth unhinged. "And in the name of propriety, too."

"Pastor Henry and Dame Carmilla did have a boy of their own, you know. He's called Porter Charlesworth," Martha continued, hardly noting the black taxicab that had pulled up to the curb.

Instead, the two women, having been guests at the house, waited patiently on the sidewalk and watched as the other guests were slowly making their departure. They were all dressed in bright-colored hats, printed dresses, pastel-colored cardigans, and holding stylish handbags that complemented their shoes. The small congregation had attended the tea often held by Carmilla Charlesworth at her home after church services. This particular Sunday was no different, except for the arrival of a new guest who gingerly stepped from the taxicab.

She was a young woman, dressed in a pair of red tailored trousers and a white blouse that displayed her ample cleavage. Her hair was short with corkscrew curls in a shade of nutmeg brown that was not too dark against the soft caramel color of her skin. Martha and Lilian noted the young woman immediately, more because of the four Louis Vuitton suitcases that the driver unloaded from the cab. Lilian and Martha gave the woman a curious gaze, then continued their conversation.

"Porter's entitled to half her inheritance, but this godson is entitled to some, too," Martha declared in a higher, more shrill tone. "They say Pastor Henry Charlesworth left a sizeable sum in his will for Devon Rutherford after he sold all that prime real estate he owned in Jamaica before he died."

"I wonder what Carmilla Charlesworth thought of that." Lilian chuckled, as though the news had tickled her fancy.

"Not so Miss Uppity now, is she? Turning her nose up at everybody since she became a dame for her contributions during the war by the queen," Martha complained. "She'll always be remembered as—"

"My grandmother," the young woman who had stepped from the taxi suddenly intruded. "*Excusez-moi,* but that *is* who you were talking about, isn't it, the lovely madame over there?" She indicated with a nod of her head the eighty-two-year-old woman standing on the top step outside her home with a charming smile on her face.

"You are?" Lilian inquired, noting the French accent.

"Jasmine Charlesworth," the young woman said, while popping a tablet of chewing gum into her mouth. "And you two must be heathens, *oui*?"

"What?" Martha gasped.

"Talking about my grandmother like that," Jasmine said in a spirited tone. "And on a Sunday, too. You both should be ashamed of yourselves." She looked at her suitcases and tilted her chin. "Well, don't just stand there."

"You're expecting us to carry those for you?" Lilian asked, her mouth agape.

"*Oui, bien sûr*," Jasmine said.

The two women did not understand.

"Yes, of course," Jasmine amended in English. "Unless you'd like my grandmother to know what you were both saying about her and my late grandfather, who must be tossing in his grave right now. They do say a dead spirit often avenges filthy talk against a loved one."

Martha's mouth twitched. "Well, as long as they're not too heavy," she conceded, nudging Lilian with her arm.

"Hop to it, *sil vous plaît*," Jasmine ordered, immediately dismissing the two women in her mind and alighting on the first of six wide steps that led directly to the house.

It was a hot day in mid-June. She felt alive with renewed vigor and the joy of seeing her grandmother again. The last time Jasmine had visited was a year ago after visiting her parents who lived in France. Her father had taken a job with a construction company there when Jasmine was two years old. Her mother, being a nurse, had joined the midwifery team at the Port-Royal de Paris Hospital, where she still worked.

In previous years, Jasmine had only seen her grandmother at Christmastime, but since leaving home and traveling the world working as an au pair, she had been able to visit a little more often. And what she had learned about her grandmother in her advancing old age was that Carmilla Charlesworth liked to play bridge, dance on occasions, and enjoyed a good glass of bourbon before bedtime. Hardly the hobbies of an elderly Christian woman born in the Caribbean, she thought. But everyone had their vices and her grandmother was no different.

Jasmine planted a large smile on her face as she worked her way through the human maze of her grandmother's friends until she faced the woman who was the queen bee among them all. Carmilla hardly looked any different from when Jasmine had last seen her. There was the usual full head of white hair in an Afro, the maple syrup complexion that was slightly sprinkled with freckles, and the set of beaming pearly-white false teeth that made her grandmother's smile seem like a ray of sunlight. And, as usual, Carmilla was dressed in a Chanel suit. The lilac-colored skirt and jacket met Jasmine's gaze as she reached the top step and raised her brows in delight.

"*Bonjour*, Gran-mama!" she greeted loudly in anticipation.

Everyone stopped talking immediately. Suddenly,

Jasmine was the center of attention. She swung her black Fendi bag over her shoulder, took the gum she was chewing out of her mouth, strategically placing it on a tissue that was dangling aimlessly from the hand of one of the guests, and leaned her weight against the heels of her black four-hundred-dollar Jimmy Choo mules. Jasmine beamed as she stood waiting for her grandmother's usual show of affection.

"Jasmine!" Carmilla said, her hazel-colored eyes widening in amazement.

"That's me," Jasmine said, displaying a childlike smile.

Carmilla's brows furrowed slightly. "What do you want?"

"Is that the way to speak to your only granddaughter after I have traveled all the way from New York to see you?" Jasmine breathed childishly.

"If you're here with that boar of a man you came here with last summer, you can turn right around again—" Carmilla started.

"No, Gran-mama, it's just me," Jasmine exclaimed, annoyed at her grandmother's reference to her ex-boyfriend. "Jax Cajero and I have parted company."

"You waited a long time to do that," Carmilla accused.

"You were right and I was wrong," Jasmine admitted calmly. "I'm glad I listened when you said a woman should only love a man with three-quarters of her heart and keep a quarter back for herself, because he didn't deserve half of me. *Je suis désolé.*"

"You're sorry!" Carmilla repeated, hardly believing the apology because it was made in French.

Jasmine's bottom lip trembled. "Oh, Gran-mama."

Carmilla reached out and embraced her grand-daughter. "Welcome home," she said in acceptance of her granddaughter's wounded expression, while Lilian and Martha struggled to pick up Jasmine's suitcases from the sidewalk. "Come inside," she consoled compassionately. "I want to hear every-thing that's happened."

"Tea?" Carmilla asked, ten minutes later as they were seated in the expanse of her living room. "Or do you need something stronger?"

"A whiskey and dry will do the trick," Jasmine said, seating herself on a print-covered chaise-lounge that was situated close to the large open glass doors that overlooked her grandmother's garden.

The room reflected modern-day Europe. Greek tapestries hung on the silk-covered walls; French chairs were scattered around a handwoven rug; and a hand-carved stone fireplace was decorated with an array of alabaster vases holding Danish tulips taken from the back garden. Even the cab-inet, where Carmilla plucked a bottle of Scot-land's finest spirits, pouring a liberal amount with ice into a glass, was a vintage Napoleon III biblio-theca piece. But that had been a gift from her son, Porter.

"So what did happen?" Carmilla probed, hand-ing over the glass before parking herself into a chair facing her granddaughter.

"Just like you said when I visited last year. The man's a rat." Jasmine swallowed a mouthful of whiskey. "Actually, he is more than that, Gran-mama. Jax Cajero is a thief."

Carmilla Charlesworth did not flinch. Instead, she politely folded her hands against her knees and listened. "Go on."

"Remember I told you he worked as a manager of a hotel in New York?" Jasmine began. "Well, when the rooms were empty, he would search them and remove items that the clients would not miss immediately. I mean, later they would find that things were missing, but that would be when they returned home and unpacked their bags."

"He told you about this?" Carmilla inquired, surprised.

"*Oui*," Jasmine proclaimed, almost in disbelief. "He bragged about it, Gran-mama. He even gave me a brooch and now I don't know if it has been stolen."

"Do you still have it?"

Jasmine stared vacantly at her grandmother. "It's in my luggage."

At their mention, Lilian and Martha tumbled into the room and deposited her Louis Vuitton bags onto the polished wooden floor. Until that point, Jasmine had forgotten she had asked the two women, both in their sixties, to bring in her luggage. It had clearly taken them both a good ten minutes to get from the sidewalk and into the house with the four bags. Panting and wiping the sweat from their brows, they threw Jasmine an acknowledging nod.

"We'll just leave these here," Lilian said on a final note.

"*Merci beacoup*," Jasmine said, applauding. "I'll see you two ladies in that place where we all go in repentance of our sins."

"Church," Carmilla inserted, knowing that her granddaughter was being derisive. She directed her gaze from Jasmine to the two women. "What's going on?"

"Nothing," Jasmine promised, taking a fortifying sip from her glass.

"Nothing," Lilian and Martha said in unison. "We'll be leaving now, Carmilla. We'll see you next Sunday."

"Why were Lilian and Martha carrying your cases?" Carmilla demanded, concerned as she watched the two women scurry from the room.

"Gran-mama, you do fuss," Jasmine said, prevaricating, while placing her empty glass on a coffee table nearby. She rose to her feet. "Now, am I taking the master bedroom?"

"Jasmine, you're sleeping where you always do, in the back room that overlooks the pond," Carmilla reminded her. "There are fresh sheets on the bed. All you need to do is open the window."

"If you say so, Gran-mama," she acknowledged, as she walked over to where her cases were positioned. She heard the front door slam and felt a gust of wind sweep past her. Leaning forward, Jasmine picked up her vanity case and the smallest among the other three cases before straightening her shoulders. "I'll just take these upstairs."

"Do you need help with the other two?" a rich American baritone suddenly inquired.

Jasmine stared at the newcomer who had entered the room. Whoever he was, she instantly guessed his age to be thirtyish, maybe a bit more. He was a tall man, at least six feet, with brown skin the color of roasted chestnuts and an Afro cut close to his head. His mustache was trimmed in such a way that it outlined his lip like a pen. There was just enough of it to delicately edge the shape of his top lip. Beneath his lips a square chiseled jawline finished the features of a rather friendly looking face. The bushy dark brows were raised slightly in anticipation of her answer. But all Jasmine could really see was the deep-set sparkle behind his soul-searching brown eyes.

"If you're offering, I'm not complaining," she answered the enigmatic stranger.

He was dressed quite formally in a Jean-Paul Gautier navy blue suit with a pale gray silk tie against a pristine snowy white shirt. Polished black crocodile shoes were on his feet, and a car key snuggled in the palm of his hand suggested he had parked a car out front. There was something about the way he stood, his frame slightly leaning in her direction, that instantly tightened the muscles in her stomach. As Jasmine's senses leaped to attention, she wondered who he was.

"Devon," Carmilla said by way of introduction, remaining seated. "I'd like you to meet Jasmine, my granddaughter."

"Pleased to meet you." He nodded, sweeping an appraising gaze across Jasmine's own features.

"*Enchanté*," Jasmine answered. "My grandmother has never mentioned you before, Monsieur . . . ?"

"Rutherford," Devon supplied. He quickly filed to memory the corkscrew curls of her brown hair, the cherry-shaped face that appeared just as sweet, her perfectly arched brows, her small nose, and the simple curve of her frosted-colored lips. Devon considered the shade of lipstick far too outlandish for the young woman's caramel complexion, but she seemed nice enough. Red trousers, white shirt, high-heeled black shoes. He liked her style. He liked her slight French accent, too. "Carmilla has talked of you on several occasions," he added. "I presume you're staying for a while?"

"I haven't decided how long," Jasmine answered, her own curiosity piqued. "Where are you from?"

Devon chuckled lightly. "New York."

"Another New Yorker, Gran-mama?" Jasmine derided on a low note. "Must we? *C'est trop?*" she repeated in French for emphasis.

"Must we what?" Devon asked, confused.

"My grandmother was very disapproving of a New Yorker I brought to the house last summer," Jasmine explained without hesitation. "And now that I've put him and all his troubles behind me, here's another one of you. Total infestation. Gran-mama, I told you they're everywhere, like ants."

"I assure you, I'm no ant," Devon said, offended. "I'm your grandmother's godson."

"Yes, he is," Carmilla admitted, "so you be nice to him, Jasmine."

"Godson?" Jasmine repeated, taken aback.

"I am a godmother to three children," Carmilla expanded. "There are two girls back home in Jamaica, and Devon right here."

"Oh," Jasmine said.

"My granddaughter grew up in France," Carmilla remarked sternly. "She can be a little difficult."

"Only in the nicest sense, Gran-mama," Jasmine said, indicating her suitcases with a nod of her head. "When you're ready, monsieur?"

Devon picked up the remaining two cases and arched his brows. "Which room?"

"I did book the master bedroom," Jasmine intoned lightly, "but it appears that has already been taken, so I'm assuming the broom cupboard is vacant."

"Sorry?" Devon said, confused.

Carmilla chuckled. "She'll be taking the pond room."

"That's right," Jasmine said, following Devon from the living room. "I'm the stray fish that's swept in with the tide."

"Dinner is at six-thirty." Carmilla's voice echoed into the hallway as Devon and Jasmine began to take the long winding stairs. "And don't forget to call your father."

"*Oui*, Gran-mama," Jasmine hollered back.

Jasmine took the stairway in silence until they had both reached the top step, where she absorbed the new decor and paintings that hung on the walls behind her. Carmilla had obviously improved on the house since she had last been there. It was characteristic of the Caribbean, the walls being freshly painted in shades of indigo and sea blue. Large buckets of green palm plants were randomly positioned to add accents. At the top of the stairwell, a huge portrait of the family loomed, seemingly staring right at her.

Jasmine remembered when it had been taken. She was but ten years old. Carmilla was seated in the middle with Andre, Jasmine's younger brother, sitting on Carmilla's knee and Jasmine at her side. Her father, Porter, and her mother, Patti, were nearby. Standing above Carmilla was Jasmine's grandfather, Pastor Henry Charlesworth. He was such a striking man, she thought. Strength and wealth were chiseled in every angle of his face. He had been dead seven years now. The awful news had come shortly after the celebration of her twenty-first birthday.

Carmilla had remained a tower of strength ever

since. With her being widowed at seventy-five, not many had thought she could cope living alone in such a big house. Jasmine's father even toyed with the idea of putting his mother into a nursing home because he steadfastly refused to leave France, but Carmilla remained defiant. This was the house she had lived in with her husband for over fifty years. It was a rarity to find someone of her background in Britain—the daughter of a rich middle-class Jamaican surveyor and a Scottish immigrant civil engineer—having been one of the first black servicewomen to survive the Blitz in World War II unscathed.

"If I'm in the pond room and the broom cupboard is off-limits, where in the house am I to find you?" Jasmine suddenly asked Devon Rutherford.

"I'm on the top floor, in the attic," Devon answered, leading the way ahead down a long corridor.

"You know, in Victorian days, mad people were always found in the attic," Jasmine mused. "Of course in castles, they were found in dungeons, shackled probably." Devon's stride faltered slightly, and Jasmine noted it with glee. "Did you ask for the attic?"

He stopped completely. "Are you suggesting I'm mad, Miss Charlesworth?"

Jasmine chuckled. "No. I couldn't possibly stay in this house if you were."

Devon stared at her, unsure of what he was dealing with, then resumed walking again. "Your grandmother said you lived in France?"

"I was born here in England," Jasmine began, attempting to measure Devon's large strides, finding that she had to practically skip to keep up. "Then when I was two years old, my parents jumped ship with my brother and I, and we crossed the Channel to France. We've lived there ever since."

"Which part of France?"

"I grew up in an apartment building overlooking the Champs-Elysées in Paris," Jasmine boasted. "My father bought it for a pittance years ago, but now it's worth a small fortune."

"Did you work in Paris?"

"I used to be an au pair."

"What do you do now?"

"Nothing," Jasmine ended abruptly.

Devon grew alarmed. "Nothing?"

"I like the echo," Jasmine said. "You should do that more often."

Devon reached the room. He dropped the two suitcases outside and faced Jasmine with a steely expression. He noted how seductive her eyes appeared with their mink-brown glow that seemed too generous for a woman so cold. "This is where you'll be," he said.

"I know," Jasmine answered. "I recognize the door."

"I can see you're quite plucky," Devon remarked in a firmer tone. "I imagine this little trip to see your grandmother is a vacation for you. But you will not be idly whiling away the hours. There is a lot of work to do here."

"Work!" Jasmine protested.

"I can see the word sounds alien to you," Devon continued.

"Look, monsieur," Jasmine started, looking directly into Devon's eyes. "You can't tell me what to do. I'm my own woman. I have my own mind. You stay out of my hair and I will do you the courtesy of staying out of yours. This is my vacation, so let's keep it that way."

Devon chuckled and Jasmine realized she did not like the sound of it. It was almost as though he had already decided that her response held little weight. There was something quite aggressive about Devon Rutherford, she decided, as she watched him open her bedroom door. He possessed a subtle arrogance. And his very manner appeared as though he had full command of time and space.

"Enjoy your vacation while you can," he told her on picking up her two suitcases and dropping them with a certain degree of politeness in her room. "No doubt I'll see you at dinner?"

"I'm human, I have to eat," Jasmine mumbled with a hint at sarcasm.

"Until then."

"Au revoir," she chided.

He left the room and Jasmine stuck her tongue out at him as he closed the door. She dropped the two bags she had in her hands and flung her Fendi shoulder bag onto the bed. The room hadn't changed. The walls were still white. The carpet, slightly threadbare, was a paisley print in a shade of green and the four-poster mahogany double bed was of the same wood as the two wardrobes and dressing table at the other end of the room. She walked over to the window and stared out in the distance at the small pond her grandmother loved. That hadn't changed either. The only thing that had changed was her.

Jasmine sighed and turned from the window, swiftly recalling her hasty retreat from New York. It hadn't been planned. Not at first anyway. Her leaving Enrico "Jax" Cajero had been a slow, painful, emotional transition from foolhardy, happy-go-lucky to reckless and dysfunctional. And when the end came, she could not wait to leave. She could not even envision dealing with Enrico and so had taken the easy way out, ending their relationship in the lobby of his apartment building in the Bronx. An image of the past twenty-four hours permeated her mind and with it came the painful memory.

"First of all, we're through," she had shouted into the ground-floor intercom that linked to Enrico's apartment. "We don't sleep together and we don't live together."

"Jasmine, let's talk about this," his seductively Latin voice had pleaded from the other end. "I'll be right down."

"Secondly, you rotten little hood rat," she hollered, so incensed that she was almost driven to tears, "don't call me. I'm not going to marry you."

"Jasmine." His voice had been urgent. "Where are you going?"

"Why would I want to tell you that, you miserable . . . lowlife?" she fired back.

"Because you're my hood chick," Enrico said lamely. "I need you."

"And thirdly," Jasmine demanded with a note of satisfaction in her voice hearing Enrico Cajero's pleading tone, "don't try and find me, Jax. Au revoir."

And just like that, she had lifted her manicured finger from the intercom button, picked up her suitcases, and left the building. There was no use waiting around for the hustler-in-disguise-as-an-upstanding-citizen to materialize from the elevator and try to delay her departure. She headed

straight for a yellow taxi, deliberately left her cell
phone in the backseat of the cab after ignoring
three calls from Enrico, and handed her one-way
ticket to a flight attendant at J.F.K. Airport. Now
that she was back in Birmingham, in England
where she belonged, Jasmine felt safe again.

Dinner was an informal affair, at least for Jasmine. She padded into the dining room of her
grandmother's house with wet feet, a yellow-
colored towel over her damp hair, a deep pink-
colored terry cloth robe wrapped around her
naked body, and ignored the seductive power of
the tall man seated at the table with her grandmother and two other guests. Without so much as
an awkward flicker of her eyebrows, she instantly
joined the small party with a wide grin dancing
across her lips. Deliberately positioning herself
across from Devon Rutherford, who had changed
into a white polo shirt and tailored gray-colored
pants, Jasmine announced her presence in her
usual manner with one simple question.
"Can someone pass the salt?"
Carmilla Charlesworth, always accustomed to
having her dinner table arranged with polite for-
mality, raised her gray eyebrows immediately. "Jasmine, aren't you missing something?"
"My napkin," Jasmine declared openly, while
scanning the long mahogany table.
It was filled with traditional Caribbean food. A
large bowl of brown rice and peas, boiled corn on
the cob, jerk chicken, roasted sweet potatoes and
yams, fried sliced green bananas, with a tray of fried
plantains, marinated and fried goat fish, and

Jasmine's favorite, sweet suet dumplings. In front of her was a bowl of steaming hot soup that she couldn't wait to eat.

"I have guests," Carmilla said, twitching her lips.

"I know. And I'm here at six-thirty p.m., just like you asked, right on the button," Jasmine reminded her lightly.

The two elderly male guests seated at the table both chuckled as though the entire situation was screamingly funny. "Carmilla, this must be your charming granddaughter," the man with the green bow tie drawled in a Caribbean accent that indicated he came from one of the small islands. He was an amiable man dressed in a black suit, with a round dark face, dimples on both cheeks, and a patch of white hair behind a receding hairline. He turned toward Jasmine and added, "I'm Councillor Arthur Wood and on my left is the Right Honorable M.P. Bernard Augarde. What's your name, honey?"

"Jasmine," Devon Rutherford remarked, with steel in his tone. "And I believe Miss Charlesworth has forgotten herself and was just passing through to the kitchen to pick up something."

"*Oui*, a spoon," Jasmine breathed, scanning the cutlery in front of her. "Someone's neglected to place mine on the table and I can't very well eat cowfoot soup without one."

Councillor Wood gallantly picked up his own spoon. "Here, use mine," he offered, throwing her a courteous smile. "I'm sure Mrs. Bately, Carmilla's housekeeper, will find me another one."

"You're very kind, *merci*," Jasmine accepted, taking the spoon and noting how Devon's lean, muscled frame caused the chair he was in to shrink at the shrug of his body.

"Here's the salt," Bernard Augarde eagerly offered, with an even bigger smile. He looked like a hirsute animal with a mass of gray hair on top of his head, a full white beard trimmed neatly around a square chin, and a chest as wide as a sumo wrestler's. "Now you don't need to worry your little head over nothing." He gazed approvingly at Carmilla with a sparkle in his deep brown eyes that made his broad nose seem as big as his purple-colored lips. "Your granddaughter is delightful, Carmilla. You must bring her along to my barbecue party in July."

"If I do," Carmilla stated sternly, "I'll have to make sure she wears clothes."

Jasmine laughed. Arthur Wood and Bernard Augarde were the only ones who joined her. And so they ate with Carmilla's guests doing much of the talking.

Devon Rutherford kept silent throughout, throwing Jasmine very subtle disapproving glances that bounced off her flawless caramel-brown skin. He considered her too forthright, too brazen in her opinions, too. He had heard about the formidable Jasmine Charlesworth, but he hadn't expected her to be quite so . . . beautiful. Even the picture of her at the top of the stairs with her family when she was a child had captured none of her energy.

"Tell me," he suddenly interceded, feeling a primitive urge to tear her away from the attentions of the two older male guests. "Why did you leave New York?"

"They forecasted a hurricane, or was it a tornado?" Jasmine answered, in her usual nonchalant fashion. "And I thought I'd better get out of its way. I didn't want the horrible thing wrestling with me."

"Of course not," Councillor Wood agreed sweetly. "When I visited Grenada in September last year, my wife and I got caught in the middle of Hurricane Ivan. They say it was a category five, which is rare for the island where I was born. Then it headed up toward Florida and struck there, too."

"There were four storms altogether," Carmilla added. "Frances, Charley, Ivan, and Jeanne."

"My own mother's house was left in complete ruins," Councillor Wood continued, recalling when the hurricane had cut a devastating swath through the Caribbean. "We've still been doing rebuilding work for her. She'll be ninety-one years old next week."

"I shall have to try and catch up with her," Carmilla joked.

"Well, Carmilla, you are quite remarkable, you know," Bernard Augarde noted in admiration. "To have survived after Pastor Henry Charlesworth passed away and to have your darling granddaughter and godson here with you." He turned to Jasmine. "I knew your father, Porter, when he was a boy, though he was not as spirited as you."

"My father can only play with one ball," Jasmine breathed, taking a quick peek at Devon. "I know how to juggle."

She could see that Devon seemed a little annoyed that the topic he had wanted to discuss about her life had taken an unexpected detour. And yet, Jasmine could also detect that he seemed . . . attracted to her. She had seen that predatory look in too many men's eyes in the past to ignore its potency. She realized she knew nothing about him. Until overhearing Lilian and Martha, she had not heard mention of this man's name before. Why had her grandmother kept him under wraps?

"Tell me," she said suddenly. "Why did you leave New York?"

"My godmother invited me," Devon answered with a raspy texture evident in his Brooklyn accent.

"How long have you been here?" she continued.

"Nine months," he answered.

"When are you going back?" Jasmine probed, smiling coolly into the hard face and fiery eyes that met hers in combat.

"I'm not," Devon told her. "When are you going back?"

"I'm staying for very much the same reason you are," Jasmine said.

"How about a glass of apricot brandy?" Carmilla offered, quickly detecting the level of animosity growing between her granddaughter and godson. "We can go and sit out in the garden. It's a lovely evening."

Jasmine declined, rising from her chair. "I think I'll go to my room. The dinner was lovely, Granmama."

Besides, she told herself, Devon Rutherford was not one of the bright-eyed and bushy-tailed men she was accustomed to. His voice had rubbed against her like sandpaper and carried a shadow of wry dissatisfaction that would leave even the most secure of women feeling apprehensive. He was disturbing her karma. And after everything she had gone through in the past twenty-four hours, this was the last thing she needed.

"You can't possibly be depriving us of wondering what lay beneath that robe you're wearing," Devon suddenly and unexpectedly remarked in dry protest, causing the councillor's and the M.P.'s brows to rise.

Jasmine's eyelashes flickered. "I'm inclined to believe you'd like me to disrobe," she responded, looking straight at Devon seemingly offended by his lurid suggestion.

He caught her eye and Jasmine's locked onto his. Their gazes held. He admired the length of her eyelashes. She found his were far too generous for a man. He charted her chiseled cheekbones. She noted the curve of his square jawline. He absorbed the shape of her lips. She decided his lips looked too thin beneath his mustache. No, maybe too full. She couldn't quite decide because he had pursed them into a hard line. And then she felt bewitched. Jasmine was spellbound. Hooked. She tried to tear her eyes away and couldn't.

"Arthur, Bernard, are we ready?" Carmilla's voice interceded, as she rose from her own chair. "It's eight o'clock. We can just catch the sunset. Devon will get us the brandy."

And just like that, the spell was broken.

"Good night, monsieurs, Gran-mama." Jasmine smiled as she departed.

"I'll see you in the morning," Devon assured her, with a smile that held all the warmth of an arctic winter.

He was total, undiluted impertinence, Jasmine decided as she kissed her grandmother and hastily left the dining room. Reaction set in the moment she reached her bedroom and closed the door. She needed a deep intake of breath to steady her nerves. Jasmine knew she was still a little fragile after her encounter with Enrico Cajero, but this Devon Rutherford was making her feel like she could just about flip.

And wouldn't he love that? she mused, realizing now that she was up against one of those rare species of men who were cold, steely formal, and resentful of the liberated woman. She supposed he would be even more resentful if he were to discover that beneath her robe she had an enviable body worthy of lustful worship by men. *He'd hate that even more,* Jasmine thought, looking at her suitcases and wondering whether, in her haste, she had neglected to add a certain item. As night approached and her mind began to reassess her female power, she began to slowly unpack.

Chapter Two

Jasmine closed her eyes beneath her Moschino shades and sweltered under the glaring sun. Her skin was generously coated in shea butter, her nails were freshly painted in a rich shade of peach, and the yellow Gucci bikini that barely covered her slim body was adored by the symphony of birds flying overhead, twittering a harmonic soothing tune. Jasmine reveled in the peaceful bliss. She was fully stretched out on a long green recliner on the hard stone patio at the back of the house, with her head tilted back and her mind on nothing of any importance, except for the fact she had spent breakfast alone that morning.

Neither Devon Rutherford nor her grandmother was around. Betty Bately, who laid out mango and avocado slices, had simply asked her if she had a restful night and if she required a glass of grapefruit juice or herbal tea with her breakfast. Inquiring where her grandmother was, the housekeeper simply informed her that Carmilla Charlesworth was with Devon Rutherford. After breakfast, Jasmine decided to go straight into the back garden,

clad in a georgette yellow shirt and revealing her
womanly virtues to the sun.

For 10:30 in the morning, the temperature was
already seventy degrees and rising. Jasmine nestled
her limbs comfortably, allowing the invigorating
scent of the ivy that ran up the walls at the back of
the house to tickle her nostrils and imagined herself a true goddess, deserving of such wonderful
pleasure. In her own paradise, her life was trouble-
free. She was back in the parish of Handsworth
where she was born—once named Hondesworde
and then Hunesworth, after the local chieftain—
and easily slipped into the mode of "family" again.

The Old Town Hall in Handsworth was one of
the best examples of the rare "crucks" method of
timber frame construction to be found in the
British Isles. The area, well known for its race
riots and violence in the 1980s where heavy-handed
policing and drug-related problems in the Birmingham, England suburb was rife, was now one
of the safest neighborhoods with over half its res-
idents Afro-Caribbean, Asian, and other ethnic
minorities. Coming home was just what Jasmine
needed. There was nothing to worry about. No
bills. No hectic schedules. No love woes. No drama.
It was just her, the sunshine, and the birds peek-
ing at her while flittering across a flawless azure sky.

After lying in the sun a few hours, Jasmine sensed
a shadow in front of her. She opened her eyes immediately and squinted at the figure blocking the
sunlight like a rain cloud. He was standing at her
feet, staring down, his face contorted into scorn and
scrutiny. His eyes came into focus the moment Jasmine removed her sunglasses and recognized the
gaze that swept across her like a cool breeze.

"Monsieur Rutherford, *bonjour*," she said coyly. "Lovely day, isn't it?"

"If you say so," he responded coolly.

"I do," Jasmine said.

"Are you planning to stay there all morning?" he asked soberly.

"*Oui*," Jasmine quickly returned. "Have you any objections?"

"Just one," Devon answered. "You're in my recliner."

Seeing that he was not dressed in anything resembling sunbathing attire, but was in fact wearing tailored gray pants, a pale blue shirt opened at the collar, and black leather shoes, Jasmine looked up at him confused. She knew that Devon was trying to provoke her and so did not rise to the bait. Instead, she gave him a wry smile.

"Do you find me intimidating, monsieur?"

Devon's eyes bored deeply into Jasmine as she lounged, piercing her flesh with his disapproving gaze. "I believe you think you can win certain power struggles with men," he replied in a stern tone. "Which I should imagine is why you are demonstrating, quite amply, your . . . assets this morning."

Jasmine felt the instant rush of blood to her cheeks. This was not what she had expected from Devon Rutherford. He should have been cowed by her beauty. Instead, his cold-hearted arrogance made her so angry, she grabbed her yellow georgette shirt and plunged her arms into the sleeves. She rose to her feet and quickly slipped her bare feet into rubber flip-flops.

"You can have your recliner," she stammered,

daring not to look at him to avoid any further embarrassment. "I think I'll go lie by the pond."

"Wait," Devon ordered, as she started to leave. "Aren't you going to inquire about Carmilla?"

"I expect she's getting ready to run the marathon," Jasmine replied in an arsenic-laced tone, insulted that Devn should insinuate that she did not care about her own grandmother's well-being. "I'll be sure to put on my running shoes later to try and find her."

"After you've soaked up more sun?" Devon derided.

"Look, monsieur," Jasmine began, finding that her nervousness was quickly dissipating. "The sun greeted me this morning. It asked me how I am. Eventually, it invited me out. And, being a lady, I accepted. We, the sun and I, are getting on very well. It likes shining on me and I like it kissing my skin. You are an interference. *Laissez-moi tranquille.*"

"What?" Devon demanded, confused.

"I said, leave me alone," Jasmine repeated in English. "The sun and I would like to have our summer fling, alone."

"Then before you decide to enjoy any more of this fine British weather," Devon began harshly, annoyed with her snarky French reply, "I think you should know that your grandmother suffered a sunstroke a little before noon. We've had to call for a doctor. She's asking for you."

Jasmine went into a panic. "What?"

"She's in the big shed at the back of the garden."

"Well, don't just stand there," Jasmine ordered, the shock now resonating in her voice. "Take me to her."

Devon took long strides as he led the way down

the winding stone path that ran through a line of sycamore trees to the farthest part of the garden. The short walk was interrupted by Jasmine tripping over several small pebbles and cursing under her breath that she would do anything to make sure her grandmother was well again. At one point, she even turned toward Devon and launched into a childish tirade at him.

"Where were you when this happened?" she demanded, fuming.

"Unloading boxes from the Jeep," Devon returned just as hotly. "Which is more than you were doing. Carmilla told me she had a granddaughter who was stubborn and bullheaded. But I don't think anyone can ever be prepared for you. What you need is—"

"What?" Jasmine interrupted, her voice slightly raised. "Putting in my place?"

"Believe me, you're not far off the mark," Devon admitted, quickening his pace.

"You know, I've been trying to figure you out," Jasmine confessed, as she tried to still the panic in her voice. "I'm wondering whether you're really who you say you are, an old family friend anointed 'godson' for Carmilla's convenience, or someone else quite shirttail to the family, and looking for something from my grandmother."

They arrived outside the garden shed where Jasmine noted that Devon's face had contorted to the point that she nearly bit her bottom lip. She had gone too far and she knew it. Yet she felt unable to ignore what she had overheard Lilian and Martha say. It was only a snippet of family history she had caught, but the gossip that had flown across the air like shrapnel was enough to force her resolve to piece together what was going on.

"You had better be careful what you say," Devon warned, in deathly seriousness that caused a tremor along Jasmine's limbs. "Your grandmother and I have become very good friends. If I find you leveling such accusations against me again, I'll be forced to speak to Carmilla about it."

Jasmine swallowed the lump at the back of her throat. She had been put in her place, for now, she decided. But as she entered the shed and saw the first sign of her grandmother's body seated on a chair with Betty Bately waving a paper fan across her face, Jasmine grew more concerned about what exactly was going on. Who was this Devon Rutherford? What did he want? And why had he become so involved with her grandmother?

"Gran-mama," Jasmine breathed, as she burst into the shed. "I came as quickly as I could. Are you all right?"

"Just a little sunstroke," Carmilla explained weakly.

"Has the doctor arrived?" Jasmine asked, concerned. She closed the distance from the door until she was kneeling at her grandmother's feet. Though Carmilla was dressed in a flowery cotton frock, with buttons that had obviously been loosened at the front to allow the circulation of air, Jasmine could see that she still looked quite flustered. "Maybe we should call him again."

"He's on his way," Devon assured her, taking a hold of Carmilla's frail hand. "I think you should stay in here where the shade will do you good," he advised his godmother.

Jasmine immediately looked around her. The

large wooden shed was quite cool inside and was probably the best place for her grandmother right now. It was also a good shield from the sun. But there were opened and sealed cardboard boxes where she had expected to find a lawn mower, hedge cutter, and other garden equipment. There were tables, too, with colored flyers stacked among cans of food. Other boxes were labeled *chips* or *soda* and there were even bottles of liquor and wine, all of which seemed an inappropriate amount for everyday consumption.

"What is all this?" Jasmine questioned, rising to her feet to pick up a flyer from the nearest tabletop.

"They're for the ballroom," Carmilla disclosed with a shallow breath.

Jasmine was bemused. "What?"

"The Birmingham Savoy," Devon proclaimed with excitement. "It's Carmilla's brainchild."

Jasmine's mouth fell open the very instant the doctor arrived. As he opened his medical bag and reached for his stethoscope to tend to her grandmother, Jasmine's gaze instead fell on the flyer she held precariously between her fingers. It publicized the city's newest nightclub. The Birmingham Savoy was a hothouse for the development of jazz and had already become *the* place, surpassing expectations since the club's opening night four weeks ago.

It had attracted Lindy Hoppers from as far as London, Cardiff, and Glasgow, who had kept the legacy of countless dance fads alive, and the flyer was promoting the recently opened restaurant at the rear of the club, which was now taking table reservations. As Jasmine stared at the elderly woman in front of her being stabilized by the doctor, she took a steady breath and tried to ponder the amazing fact that Carmilla Charlesworth was in business.

"I need to talk to you," Jasmine told Devon Rutherford twenty minutes later as she closed her grandmother's bedroom door and met him halfway down the corridor that led to the long winding stairs.

The doctor had advised that Carmilla should rest the remainder of the day by sleeping in her room with the windows open and the curtains closed to screen out the June sunlight. It was a simple precautionary measure and they had all been assured that Carmilla would feel a lot better by sundown, provided she drank plenty of water to prevent dehydration.

Jasmine had escorted her from the shed and was alarmed to find that her grandmother had become weakened by the antihistamine shot the doctor had given her. He had explained that Carmilla's eyes were slightly watery and red, and that he could detect some slight wheezing in her chest, which was all suggestive of an allergy or hay fever. Given her eighty-two years and the fact that Carmilla was slightly congested, the doctor also prescribed tablets that Jasmine needed to pick up from the pharmacy later that day.

As she followed Devon Rutherford down the stairs and into the living room, Jasmine had afforded herself some time to think things through in her mind. She closed the living room door and remembered where her grandmother kept the whiskey. Though the clock read 1:33 p.m., Jasmine did not consider it too early in the day to pour herself a liberal glass and take a fortifying sip. Only when she felt the alcohol rush and seep into every pulsing vein did she begin to relax and look at Devon.

He had taken a seat in one of the French chairs and had thrown one long lanky leg over the other. Without a word, Devon simply sat and silently contemplated the slim, caramel-brown girl in the yellow bikini under her georgette shirt. Her shades were pulled over her forehead and her nutmeg-brown, corkscrew hair was pulled back into a pony-tail. He had to admit to himself that, even in her state of shock, Jasmine looked pretty damn fine. So fine, Devon felt the strong reaction between his legs and desperately tried to compose himself.

"Is Carmilla sleeping?" he asked, troubled by the day's events thus far.

"Yes," Jasmine answered, placing the half-filled glass on the nearby coffee table. She took a seat and faced him curiously. "I'd like to know what my grandmother was doing that caused this to happen to her."

"She was helping me sort through what I needed to pack in the Jeep to take to the Savoy," Devon explained, glancing briefly at his watch. "We use the building at the back of the garden to store what we can't keep at the club."

"Why didn't you stop her?" Jasmine demanded, finding herself becoming incensed by the mere idea that an eighty-two-year-old woman should want to spend her sunset years in such a demanding role.

"She always helps me to load and unload," Devon responded, unsure why Jasmine's eyes had suddenly become narrow and unnerving.

"I mean, why didn't you stop her from acting on this hair-raising idea that she can run a lucrative business at the age of eighty-two?" Jasmine fired back, the incredulity of it washing over her in buckets. "I can't believe you allowed my grandmother to spend her retirement fund on, what, a two-bit tin shack, probably, in a run-down part of the city where drug addicts and the homeless find shelter, no doubt? I cannot begin to comprehend the amount of work involved. There's the payroll—"

"Ten members on staff," Devon interrupted.

"The administrative costs," she continued. "Lighting, heating, the rental—"

"Carmilla owns the premises," Devon went on.

"The liquor license—"

"Which has been approved by the city council," Devon continued.

"And who distributes the flyers?"

"We have a street crew that puts them out once a month," Devon answered. "Anything else?"

She felt defeated. "Carmilla's too old to run the place," she said finally.

"Which is why I manage the Birmingham Savoy," Devon concluded.

"You're the manager?" Jasmine gasped, wondering if she was now facing a con artist who had talked his way into Carmilla's affections. Not so unlike Enrico Cajero, she thought.

Devon nodded. "I am."

"And the restaurant," Jasmine asked, "who runs that?"

"Ah . . ." Devon hesitated. "There's a chef, his assistant, and four waitresses, but—"

"No one to oversee the staff in that part of the club," she figured from the look stamped across Devon's face.

"I was going to place an advertisement in the

Nubian Chronicle this week," he explained, "but . . ."
And he hesitated. "I think it might be appropriate
that you start to earn your keep by helping out."

Jasmine's brows rose. "What do you mean?"

"I mean that you work at the Savoy overseeing
the restaurant."

"Now wait a minute," Jasmine said, searching
Devon's determined expression. "I'm here on vacation."

"Which was officially over twenty minutes ago,"
Devon proclaimed sternly. "Your grandmother has
been confined to her bedroom on bed rest and, on
my orders, will remain there for the next few days.
Mrs. Bately can look after the house quite ade-
quately and we can take care of the Savoy."

"You seem to have this all figured out," Jasmine
complained, "except for one thing. I've never
worked in a restaurant before, so you can leave me
out of your plans." She rose to her feet, intent on
leaving, but was immediately taken aback when
Devon spoke, his very tone detaining her from departing.

"Listen, shorty!"

"Shorty?" Jasmine's eyes narrowed at Devon immediately. It was unusual to find him suddenly
adopting American street slang in reference to her
gender. "Do I look like I'm from the ghetto to you?"

"Your mouth may as well be," Devon returned
rudely, his accent sounding more pronounced.

Jasmine placed both hands on her hips, not realizing that the sudden heaving of her chest was
making her bosom beneath her bikini top rise
and fall in an alluring manner. And the way her
pert little nose twitched, as she felt her anger rise
suddenly, was enough to make Devon realize that

this woman possessed a certain power that he was finding hard to resist. But Jasmine was unaware of the full effect she was having on Devon Rutherford. The only thing on her mind was putting this man in *his* place.

"I believe you're used to a certain breed of woman, Monsieur Rutherford," she began, her tone pitched. "The type who run their mouths, lick their lips, and have a mentality that can only be found on the streets. You'll have to watch me carefully, because another slip like that can have me imagining all kinds of scenarios about who you really are."

"I am exactly who I say I am," Devon remarked, his voice tight and firm. "But I have no illusions about you. I think you're a lazy, good-for-nothing little tease, who'd rather idle around all day showing off her skimpy bikini to get a reaction out of me than try and help her elderly grandmother."

He made it all sound so bad that Jasmine literally gasped. "I . . . I'll do whatever I can to assist Gran-mama," she chimed in, pulling her georgette shirt around herself and folding her arms protectively.

Devon rose to his feet and glanced at his watch again. It read 2:03 p.m. "In that case, I'll wait until you change into something more appropriate and then you can come with me to the Savoy and help out."

Jasmine was stunned. "What now?"

"We can stop by the pharmacy on the way," Devon said, already taking large strides toward the door. "I'll expect you out front in fifteen minutes."

"Why don't we make it five?" Jasmine countered. She knew she needed more than fifteen minutes

to sort through her wardrobe, find a suitable skirt
and blouse, fix her hair, apply makeup, and select
an agreeable pair of shoes. And Jasmine was also
mildly aware that she resented Devon's assess-
ment of her, too. What she hated more was just
how adept this handsome man was at cutting her
to the quick. It was not like her to find herself be-
littled so easily. Yet here she was, her resolve to
enjoy a vacation quickly shelved in favor of her
seemingly being put to good use.

"If that's all the time you need to work with what
the good Lord gave you, then I'll meet you out
front in five," Devon's voice echoed majestically.

Jasmine's mouth fell wide open as she watched
him leave. It took three short seconds for her to
catch her breath and empty the glass of whiskey
before she rushed from the room.

It was hardly five minutes, closer to fifteen, but
Devon appeared unruffled as Jasmine entered the
shiny metallic silver-colored Jeep and slammed the
passenger door. As she slapped on her seat belt, she
was acutely aware that Devon was sitting in judge-
ment of her appearance. Her midcalf-length black
skirt and short-sleeved frilly blouse in soft white silk
were just right for the summer air. And although not
designer exclusives, they were both elegant enough
for work at the Birmingham Savoy later.

She wore a minimum of jewelry—simple pearl
droplets on her earlobes and a watch—and her hair
was pinned loosely around her cherry-shaped face
with the odd corkscrew curl hanging over her forehead. Her eyes, aided and abetted by dusky eye-
shadow and black mascara, looked enormous, but

her caramel-brown complexion and full, pouting mouth were bare of all else except a little lip gloss to soften her look. And because she had not wanted to wear hosiery, she'd instead worn black open-front leather sandals on her feet. Jasmine's stray curls were dancing ever so slightly against the open car window when Devon smiled in his appreciation.

"Suits you," he said, as he turned the key in the ignition, "black and white."

Stunned by the charm of Devon's welcoming smile, Jasmine felt her spirits lift dramatically. "I've often considered becoming a nun," she said in a leading sort of way.

"You?" Devon chuckled, falling headlong into the dazzling display of Jasmine's smile. "I should imagine that there's a certain habit you can't live without, and I'm not talking about that thing you wear on your head."

"Actually, I've decided that their way of life might suit me," Jasmine returned, pulling a strand of hair away from her face as she curled her lips upward cheekily.

Devon briefly glanced across at her before pulling the Jeep into the flow of traffic. "You're not serious, right?"

It was Jasmine's turn to chuckle. "I'm joking," she confessed, finally. "But I did wonder what it would be like when my parents took me and my brother to see the Notre Dame Cathedral in Paris when I was about four years old. There was an order of nuns there visiting the cathedral, and I liked how clean and disciplined they appeared."

"Believe me, mankind needs you more," Devon breathed lightly. As he cruised gingerly onto the

A41 Freeway that ran to the city, he added, "Do you mind if I ask you a leading question?"

"As long as you're not going to steer me astray," Jasmine answered, with a wry smile.

"Your Mr. New Yorker. Is it all over?"

"Who?" Jasmine asked absently, before the memory of her past set in. "Oh, him."

"Does he have a name?" Devon probed further.

"Hood rat," Jasmine bristled, at the mere recollection of Enrico Jax Cajero.

Devon laughed.

Jasmine sighed. "Gran-mama didn't like him anyway."

"I suspect her approval matters very much to you?" Devon continued with a hint of admiration in his tone.

Jasmine nodded. "It does now. Sometimes when a woman doesn't listen and makes mistakes, she can only but learn from them."

"So . . . are you nursing a broken heart?" Devon asked.

"Me?" Jasmine was surprised at the question. "No. I'm doing okay."

"That's good," Devon accepted with a kind smile. "I wouldn't like to see you distracted once you start work at the Birmingham Savoy."

Jasmine arched her eyebrows curiously. "So which downtrodden backwater of Birmingham is this shack of a club located?" she asked, going along with the notion that by nightfall she could possibly be slaving in a restaurant with plastic tablecloths and a broken stove.

"It's in the city center," Devon answered.

"The city center!" Jasmine repeated, shocked. She had imagined an old derelict building in one of the rougher areas of the city, with a lick of fresh paint and a modestly clean image designed to attract a mix of West Indian clubbers.

"Carmilla suggested we model it on the legendary Savoy Ballroom that was once on Lenox Avenue in Harlem from the 1920s to the 50s," Devon continued. "In fact, launch night was quite spectacular."

"Four weeks ago?" Jasmine exclaimed, saddened that she had not known, nor been invited to attend. "Why didn't my grandmother tell me?"

Devon shrugged. "You'll have to ask her about that."

"Were my brother or parents there?" Jasmine asked.

"I'm not sure," Devon said, choosing his words carefully.

Jasmine didn't quite believe him, but she pursued the conversation. "So, tell me about launch night."

"We had a Cuban teacher from Harlem give basic dance lessons," Devon began. "All the guests were taught how to do the boogie back, fall off the log, the apple jack, Suzie Q, stompin', truckin', peckin', and the scarecrow. There were three guest vocalists, a live jazz band, and it was social dancing all night. We even showed vintage dance films from a projector as part of the entertainment. The local papers were splashed with stories the next day. It was great."

"And my grandmother was there?"

"She opened the night with a speech," Devon drawled, his mind going back to the lavish event. "I didn't know she used to be a Lindy Hopper in Jamaica when she was a young woman."

"My grandmother took dance classes in America when she was a child," Jasmine revealed, recalling the stories she'd been told in her own childhood. "In 1928, when she was five years old, she visited Chicago with her parents and saw, for the first time, a black vaudeville show. During her stay there, she joined the Ballet Negre. It was a distinguished black dance studio founded by Katherine Dunham, and when Gran-mama returned to Jamaica, she joined a calypso dance troupe and learned all different forms of dancing."

"Her presence pulled in a lot of old-timers who hadn't seen each other in years," Devon continued. "There was a lot of catching up to do, and the night was very much a combination of the old and new generations of swing dancers. Mind you, your great-aunt caused a ripple or two."

"Stompin' at the Savoy?" Jasmine uttered, suspecting that her late grandfather's sister had probably tried to compete with her grandmother on the dance floor. As elderly West Indian women, they both still knew how to throw down a move, she did not doubt. "I wonder if Aunt Helena was a Lindy Hopper, too," she said inquisitively.

"I would imagine Carmilla would have a lot less to say about her than that," Devon remarked, as though he was implying another meaning.

"Well, I'm happy you both enjoyed it," Jasmine conceded, realizing now that by alienating herself from her grandmother by returning to New York with Enrico Cajero, she had obviously created some animosity that probably needed ironing out. "When will we arrive at the club?"

"In five minutes," Devon told her.

* * *

"Golly," Jasmine remarked, eight minutes later as she swept through a steel back door that led into a huge catering kitchen, to a lavish restaurant, and finally to a large empty ballroom with three sparkling chandeliers dangling from the ceiling.

The floor was vast and made entirely from maple-colored wood specially treated so that it was appropriate to dance on. There were large palm plants strategically positioned to lend a certain ambience to the place. Roman-style white columns that reached the ceiling were positioned at four corners of the room, which was amply painted in a modern elegant style. At the farthest end was a bar made completely from mirrored glass, which deceptively reflected the room to be much larger. Jasmine could not even imagine the costs involved to create such elegance.

"This is the Birmingham Savoy ballroom," Devon said proudly, shoving both hands into his pants pockets, his face exalting as he looked around. "This is the result of six months of hard work."

"It's beautiful," Jasmine gasped as the full extent of the room dazzled her. It seemed her grandmother was a businesswoman with a thriving operation.

"I knew you would like it," Devon almost cooed, walking over to the bar where he placed a brown box he had carried from the Jeep parked in the parking lot. He began to unload bags of chips, cashew nuts, and pistachios, placing them on the bar counter. "The other members of staff should be arriving soon, so feel free to walk around. Get a sense of the . . . tin shack."

Jasmine's lips pursed as she decided to do precisely that. She walked from the ballroom into the restrooms where she found herself spoiled by the perfumes, toiletries, and bowl of mouth fresheners. In addition to the toiletries, the men's restroom was arrayed with cologne, condoms, and a bowl of mints. There was a similar small social lounge, too, with a circle of Chelsea-styled chairs and a guest table complete with a vase of fresh flowers, where the Savoy's guests could catch up on idle chitchat or gossip.

On leaving the restrooms, Jasmine followed the path around the dance floor to the stainless steel kitchen, fully equipped with the latest in food preparation technology. Then she casually ambled over to the restaurant, allowing her gaze to absorb the lush surroundings. She counted twenty tables in total, none yet prepared for the evening. A wall of glass separated the area from the ballroom but allowed good visibility for diners to watch the dancers strut their stuff on the dance floor.

From her vantage point, Jasmine eyed Devon stacking the chips, cashew nuts, and pistachios behind the bar counter. She noted the gallant stride in his every footstep, the dignified slope of his muscled shoulders, and realized he was indeed proud of her grandmother's accomplishment. How little she had known that Dame Carmilla Charlesworth could take an idea and make it into a working concept in her old age. By the time Jasmine had worked her way back over to the bar, she could almost feel the prickle of shameful tears emerge at the back of her eyelids.

"I can't believe Gran-mama is responsible for all this," she said, proud of everything that met her gaze. The Birmingham Savoy was clearly a place to see and be seen in. "I hadn't realized it would be so—"

"Classy," Devon finished.

Jasmine lowered her head with guilt. "You must think I'm a beastly and obnoxious person."

Devon walked from around the bar and faced her. "Actually, there were two words in my head far worse than those," he admitted, placing both hands on her shoulders. "But now that you can see just what the place is, I think you'll like it here. And," he added for emphasis, "I think your grandmother would very much appreciate your help."

Jasmine nodded, feeling the first sense of warmth from Devon reach out to her like a magnet, pulling her in. She looked up into his face and saw those soul-searching eyes again. They were friendly and accepting of her flaws, even forgiving of her foolish nature. He was tolerant beyond endurance of her bad behavior. For the first time since her arrival at her grandmother's house, Jasmine realized this man had been more than patient with her. She also realized it was a character trait she liked.

"I'm sorry if I was a little rude yesterday and for my abhorrent behavior today," she said, licking her dry lips nervously. "I do care about my grandmother and I will lend my support."

"Good." Devon removed his hands from Jasmine's shoulders and attempted to shake off the lustful aura that seemed to have cloaked itself around him. "Let me show you the office." He was about to do so when they heard the sound of voices echoing from the kitchen. "That'll be the staff."

Before Jasmine could compose herself from his touch, three men sauntered into the ballroom, chuckling. "Hey, boss," one of them shouted.

"Hey, Sonny, Wills, Gibson, come over here,"

Devon invited. "I'd like you to meet somebody." When the three black men were within close range, he said, "Guess who she is."

Jasmine had never undergone such blatant masculine scrutiny. Each man in turn, all seeming to be in their twenties, with varying shades of brown eyes, all fit and fine, and most definitely good looking in her eyes, gave her the once-over. Their appraisal was slow, tantalizing, and approving of her long, shapely legs, small waistline, ample bosom, and the cherry-shaped face that smiled shyly at them. In less than five seconds, they had become wolves on the hunt, using their predatory instincts. Noting that she was single, each man howled out a mating cry.

"Who?" they wolfed in unison.

"Carmilla Charlesworth's granddaughter," Devon introduced.

"Hello. *Hola. Salam,*" they greeted in a multilingual flurry.

Jasmine had to step back. "*Enchanté,*" she said politely.

"Listen, guys, I'm showing her around," Devon intruded, taking a hold of Jasmine's wrist. "She'll be working in the restaurant, so you'll all have a chance to see her later."

"But—" they chorused.

The heat was on. Devon's possessive grip grew tighter and Jasmine welcomed the presence of it. Then there were more footsteps. The new cloudburst of arrivals were in high heels, black skirts cut above their knees, and white shirts opened provocatively to reveal healthy, heaving cleavages. Jasmine's eyes homed in immediately on the four women. With their long manes of straightened brown hair, plucked shapely brows, and puckering red lips, their beauty struck her before the soft mellow of their voices did.

"Hi, Devon," three of them said sweetly.

"Hello, honey," the tallest one purred, showing off her red-coated paws.

Jasmine knew the moment Devon dropped her wrist that something was amiss. It was not a gradual slow action, but was akin to the quickness of someone having burned himself. Her heart leaped in such hurried disappointment she hardly knew how to deal with the reaction. The smile that crept to her lips was an involuntary motion, one that came with the practiced reflexes of a woman often left gasping in shock by the unexpected behavior of a man.

"Freya, Sue, Petronella, Alice, I'd like you to meet Jasmine Charlesworth, Carmilla's granddaughter. She'll be overseeing the restaurant."

"Hey, girl," three of the women said, chuckling.

"*Enchanté,*" Jasmine uttered, aware that the tallest of the pack had eyed her coolly.

"When was this decision made?" she inquired sternly.

"Today," Devon replied.

"Petronella has an eye on marrying the boss," Gibson suddenly whispered into Jasmine's ear. She blinked at the unexpected news as Devon placed a guiding hand on the small of her back.

"I'm just going to show Jasmine the ropes, then be with you guys a little later, okay?" he explained. "Freya, Alice, you two go prepare the tables in the restaurant. Sue, Petronella, make sure the cutlery is clean. Gibson, you go check the stock in the bar."

"We'll start in the kitchen," the other two acknowledged.

"Sonny's our African-American chef," Devon began, as the staff dispersed and went on their way. "He converted to Islam a few years ago. He's a great cook. Wills is the kitchen assistant and Gibson's from Cuba. He's the bartender."

"And the girls?"

"Your waitresses." Devon smiled. "There'll be more staff coming later."

"Another three," Jasmine said on recollection that there were ten.

"You're catching on," Devon remarked, leading the way through a door next to the bar that took them both down a short corridor and into a small back room.

It was of some curiosity to Jasmine as she followed him that Petronella seemed so much older than the other waitresses. It wasn't so much in her appearance, but more in her manner. There had been a certain maturity in her composure and a serious bearing of character that lent an air of professionalism in the way she spoke to Devon. Jasmine began to wonder if Petronella was much older than she was. A Caribbean-British woman in her midthirties perhaps. And with such poise, what was she doing working in a ballroom such as this? But then, Jasmine could well have been asking herself that very same question. She had reached a crossroad in her life. It was possible that Petronella was at that very same crossroad, too.

"So this is the office?" Jasmine said, looking around the only area of the club that was not lavishly furnished. The room was clean, tidy, and organized. A brown desk was completely clear of paper, except for a diary, telephone, pen holder, laptop computer, and other stationery items.

"The diary is to take bookings," Devon went on. "Birthday parties, anniversaries, special occasions, that sort of thing. There's a table diary in the restaurant, and each evening we need to reconcile both diaries to make sure we don't double-book the club. That's rule number one."

Jasmine looked around, more accepting of the situation. When she returned her gaze to Devon, she could hardly believe that she should suddenly wonder what it would be like to be pulled into his arms and quell that serious expression he was wearing on his face. To look into those soul-searching brown eyes and see lustful crinkles at the sides of them as they darkened with love for her. She swallowed thickly and kept her face straight.

"Naturally, I'd expect a decent wage."

"Of course," Devon responded, brisk and businesslike.

Jasmine leaned her hands against the desk and stared more directly at him. To her chagrin, since she was still bothered by what she had seen transpire between him and Petronella, a lightning bolt of jealousy struck her with a megaton force. Jasmine could not explain why she should feel that way. It was not as though she knew Devon Rutherford or had a crush on him. This was a man who had wedged himself into her grandmother's life and affections, without her ever having heard mention of his name. Within seconds, her curt nature returned with a vengeance.

"Now that I'm back in town and can keep an eye on my grandmother's investment," she began tersely, "in time, I'd like to see the accounts, just to be sure you're not playing games. I want to see this club make some serious money in the coming months."

Devon was clearly shaken. Having busied himself with opening a pile of letters he'd picked up from the main entrance door while Jasmine was making her solitary tour, he now paused in midmotion and stared wide eyed at her. "Watch it," he cautioned. "This is my territory you've walked into."

"Which I will soon be taking over," Jasmine countered, tossing Devon a combative gaze. "Let's face it, I'm Carmilla Charlesworth's granddaughter. And I think once I get to know the running of this place, inside and out, she'll leave the control of her affairs to me, *oui*?"

Devon's eyes fired at her. "Until an hour ago, you didn't know this place existed. So keep going with a wild idea like that and I'll bounce you on your ear so fast your head will hit the ceiling on your way out," he threatened. "Maybe even knock some sense into you, so let's get one thing straight." Devon braced both hands on the desktop and leaned his face forward so that he was within inches of Jasmine's nose. "This is a lucrative business and I'm not about to allow a Parisian dilettante like you to do a bit of fawning and pandering to a lonely old lady to ensure that you'll be the sole beneficiary of something you pretty much know nothing about. When push comes to shove, I think you'll find that your grandmother knows exactly what the facts are and who she can rely on."

Jasmine gulped. "And you think that's you?"

"Precisely," Devon responded hotly. "So while I go and pick up Carmilla's prescriptions and a couple of sandwiches for us both, you can go help out in the restaurant because it's going to be a long night."

The look he gave her was disconcerting. Jasmine felt flustered beneath the impassioned stare, so much so she decided to pull back and refrain from responding to Devon a moment longer. This was a new side she had not seen before. Strength, determination, and a smidgen of anger. They were destined to be at loggerheads now, she thought grimly, scolding her ill-timed foolhardiness for making such a hasty declaration. By doing so, she had made it appear that she was a gold digger after her grandmother's fortune, and that was not the truth. She would have to tread more carefully with Devon Rutherford, at least until she knew more about the secretive well he had sprung from.

Chapter Three

"How are you finding your work at the Savoy, Jasmine?" Carmilla inquired from her bed, propped up against four fluffy white pillows. Her white hair was neatly styled into small braids beneath an opaque silk scarf and she was wearing a green camisole that was not too heavy against her fragile skin. A radio was playing on low volume next to her bed, and the curtains were now open to let in the sunrise.

It had been almost a week since Jasmine had been pushed right into the deep end, laboring madly until the early hours of the morning at one of the busiest nightclubs in the city. What she had not known, but which she did now, was that the club opened every night from Monday to Saturday, with Sunday the only day of rest. The club also had its own six-piece house band, fronted by a jazz vocalist and a saxophonist, a team of four bouncers clad in black tuxedos and bow ties, and two coat attendants, all on the staff payroll. There were three hostesses, too, each earning her pay by charging visitors for lessons on the latest dance steps.

These were all people Devon had not told her about. Jasmine had begun to wonder what else he was withholding. There was no doubt he was strongly devoted to her grandmother, but to what end? Jasmine could not quite still her suspicions about him. Why should she when he not only seemed doubtful about her, but had lined up a host of other bands to play at the club throughout August and September, various quartets that Jasmine knew were going to cost a fair bit of money?

"The work's okay," Jasmine answered lamely, trying hard to hide her misgivings. Devon had been more than generous with the money he was paying her, which was enough to keep her afloat, but the late hours were taking their toll on her. She was desperately tired and though it was Sunday morning, she still felt like she had not gotten enough sleep. "Devon's shown me how to organize the diary, to use the new terminals to accept payments by credit or charge card, reconcile the order and billing receipts at the end of the night from the waitresses, and how to deal with the guests."

"Good," Carmilla acknowledged, having finished with the breakfast tray Betty Bately had brought in earlier. "I knew you two would get along."

This was the opening Jasmine was waiting for. "Gran-mama, who is Devon Rutherford exactly?"

"My godson," Carmilla breathed, gazing at her granddaughter quizzically, tilting her head to one side so that she could take a good look at her. Jasmine was lying casually across the bottom of the bed with her corkscrew hair ruffled and wearing her pink dressing gown. She looked tired for 9:43 a.m., but Carmilla saw something that was plainly obvious.

"I can see he's already set your heartstrings a-flutter. He's a fine boy, you know."

Jasmine flushed. Carmilla was as shrewd as ever and though she may have taken to bed rest over the last few days while Jasmine had been working at the Savoy, she was remarkably alert still. Carmilla's bird-sharp, hazel-colored eyes were a little moist, but otherwise keen, and her voice was calm with a hint of sincerity. Jasmine began to wonder whether Devon had said anything. He had threatened as much if her paranoia grew any more out of proportion. But it was still hard for her to grasp that Devon was someone of importance in her grandmother's life.

"I know you told me who he is," Jasmine continued sluggishly and overlooking entirely Carmilla's teasing about Devon, "but . . . well, did you know his parents?"

"I knew Devon's father when he was a boy," Carmilla confessed, "and I also knew his grandmother."

"Is she still alive?" Jasmine asked, feeling she was now getting somewhere.

"Oh no," Carmilla exclaimed sadly. "Miss Gracie Manning died six years ago, not long after your grandfather. She was widowed for many years. Her husband, Pastor Erskin Rutherford, died in 1964. They both lived in New York City."

"Did they have children?" Jasmine probed further.

"Just the one," Carmilla explained. "Ralston Rutherford, Devon's father."

"Did you know Ralston's wife?"

"Why do you ask?" Carmilla inquired.

"I was just wondering how he came to be your godson, that's all." Jasmine shrugged.

Carmilla stifled a huge yawn. "It's was your grandfather Henry's fault, that's how it all started," she began, just as there was a knock at the bedroom door. It opened. A tall shadow filled the doorway before it came into the light.

"Mrs. Bately asked that I get the breakfast tray," Devon's voice intoned, before he came into view and noted that Carmilla was not alone. "Jasmine!" Her name seemed to jump from his throat.

"*Bonjour,*" she croaked, trying to force a smile.

Jasmine could see that Devon allowed his mouth to twitch slightly, but knew he was not going to return her smile. He was not given to outward shows of emotion, except where her grandmother was concerned. She would be breathing her last breath, she decided, before she would find those dark soul-searching brown eyes lighting up with a fiery warmth for her benefit. Wearing a pair of dark blue jogging pants that emphasized rather than concealed his masculinity, he stood between her and the bed, considering Jasmine with an assessing gaze she now knew so well.

"Good morning," he announced, venturing farther into the room. "What's going on?"

"Nothing," Carmilla said, as she pointed toward her bedside table where she had positioned the breakfast tray. "Jasmine was just asking me about your parents."

"Was she?" Devon drawled.

He was now standing within inches of her dangling feet at the edge of the bed, and Jasmine was not surprised when Devon knocked her legs over, forcing her to immediately readjust to a sitting position. She faced him with the concern of a woman who was not about to take that little accident lightly.

It had been a deliberate act, though Carmilla, who noted it, seemed to imagine that Devon was merely playing with her granddaughter.

"Just like two lion cubs." She chuckled. "Both your fathers used to rollick that way."

"My father knew Ralston Rutherford?" Jasmine exclaimed, seeing that Devon had picked up the tray, but paused briefly with it before he looked across at her.

Carmilla laughed. "Oh yes, your grandfather and I visited Miss Gracie most Easters and Christmases, though we stopped going to New York after Martin Luther King got shot. Those were sad times, Ralston passing away, the Civil Rights Movement, and Vietnam. Your grandfather didn't want us to get caught up in the troubles and so Miss Gracie and I lost touch. Then, last October, her grandson contacted me."

Jasmine's gaze flickered from Carmilla to Devon. She arched her eyebrows at him instantly. "*You* contacted my grandmother?" she breathed in a deep breath of air.

"It was wonderful to hear from him," Carmilla interceded, unaware of the suspicion running rampant in her granddaughter's mind. "I invited Devon over to England and . . . well . . . you've been here nine months now, isn't that right, Devon?"

"That's right," he confirmed, keeping his gaze trained on Jasmine.

"We've talked about so many things, so many ideas," Carmilla enthused. "And when Devon encouraged me to fulfill a lifelong dream, I thought why not?"

"The Birmingham Savoy," Jasmine concluded. She fixed her cool expression on the man who was facing her. "So you being in business was really Devon's idea, *oui*?"

"Jasmine, I don't want you making a fuss about it," Carmilla warned, furrowing her brows. "That's why I didn't tell you or your parents. Besides, you forgot about me last Christmas and your family hurried back to France before the New Year. I needed to be kept busy and I knew this enterprising spirit of mine would be a great surprise to you and Porter. I can just see your father's face now, calling me a squeaking old door that needs to be kept closed. Well, I'm well oiled and open for business. As you can see, we are all coping quite well at the club."

"But—" Jasmine uttered, absorbing the defensiveness in her grandmother's voice.

"What?" Carmilla objected.

"I don't want you working at the Savoy," Jasmine insisted. She remembered just how loud the live music had been and how she had, on occasion, been shuffled around by dancing guests as she tried to move from the restaurant and across the ballroom to the bar for drinks. "You're supposed to be retired."

"Now that you're here," Carmilla hinted, "I can leave you and Devon in charge of the club and go back to tending my garden. I'm sure your father will be delighted at keeping you rooted in one place."

"Wait a minute," Devon immediately objected, noting the satisfied smile spread across Jasmine's face. He returned the tray to the bedside table and faced Carmilla sharply. "*I'm* running the Birmingham Savoy. Just me."

"Of course you are," Carmilla agreed happily. "But I would like it if you involve Jasmine a little more. My granddaughter needs a sense of direction."

"She's fine where she is," Devon chided. "Let's not rock the boat."

"*Oui,*" Jasmine agreed, seeing the angry look that homed in on her with a hint of danger. "Besides, I'm rowing along just nicely." She rose from the bed, adjusting her dressing gown and deliberately but subtly, brushing her body against Devon's as she made her way toward the door. "I think I will join you at your church luncheon this afternoon, Gran-mama," she added sweetly. "Now that I'm enjoying the boat ride."

She was hardly outside her grandmother's bedroom door when Devon was right beside her. Jasmine felt the strong hold on her wrist as he pulled her along the corridor into an alcove near the stairwell. His face was dark and unreadable. His lips were pursed into a hard line and she felt a slight resentment at being trapped in a corner with his hard, muscular body offering her no room to maneuver or escape.

"What on earth do you think you're doing?" she demanded, frantically trying to wriggle her wrist free from Devon's grip. She tried even harder to ignore the dark hair that curled lazily down his flat belly to his loins.

"I want to know what game you're playing," Devon drawled menacingly.

His grip tightened and Jasmine felt the pain of it run up her arm. "Let go of me."

"Not until you tell me what you're up to," he retorted breathlessly, using all his energy to keep Jasmine in one place.

"Nothing," she insisted.

"Liar," Devon replied. "Do you really think I'm going to fall for this pretense of you caring about your grandmother when your real intent is to try and get your sticky fingers on her fortunes?"

"My interest in my grandmother is purely out of concern for her business affairs," Jasmine responded, trying to calm herself. Her heart was beating madly, but she refused to let Devon see that she was nervous. "And let me remind you that you forced me into this job. Now that my grandmother has officially asked me to stay in it, I have every right to protect her from you."

"What's that supposed to mean?" Devon demanded hotly.

"I think you're trying to run her business into the ground," Jasmine accused with a shrug of her shoulders. "You've got far too many staff on the payroll and I find it a worry that you've hired five jazz bands to play over two months at the club when we already have a house band. It's such a great expense when you cannot guarantee to pull in the crowds."

"Every disbursement has already been budgeted for," Devon said, releasing Jasmine's wrist from his grip. "The Afro-Cuban All Stars is the first band on the Savoy's guest billing and you'll see they're gonna rock that place. I have given you no reason to think that I would ever pillage what your grandmother has left of her retirement fund. She became involved in the Birmingham Savoy solely of her own free will and the profit projections are already favorable. So get off my case."

"I'm not going anywhere," Jasmine fired back. "You heard what Gran-mama said. She wants my further involvement in the business, so if I don't tread on your toes, you don't step on mine."

For a brief moment, he looked at her. Then, to

Jasmine's complete amazement, Devon spread both his hands across the expanse of the alcove and caged her in altogether. He was really making sure she was not going to go anywhere. She was stuck precisely where she was. The piercing brown soulful eyes did not leave her face, but studied her flushed features with greater scrutiny. Jasmine knew her hair was disheveled and with not one bit of makeup on her face, at such close proximity to Devon, she imagined she was probably pale and very plain looking to him.

In reality, she looked healthy and robust. A rich copper color was whipped up in her caramel-brown cheeks and her eyes were sparkling like polished ebony. An unbidden little burst of pleasure ran through her as Jasmine became conscious of the fact that she had on very little clothing, just her lacy pink bra and knickers beneath her dressing gown. The rush took Jasmine by complete surprise, but she kept her head raised in defiance, loathing the very idea of showing the slightest ounce of weakness to this man.

"You do know that I can fire you?" Devon started firmly.

"But you wouldn't dare," Jasmine replied combatively.

"You're definitely planning to keep tabs on me, aren't you?" he challenged, bringing his head forward enough that Jasmine could not deny the clean scent of him.

"*Oui*," she declared, fixing him with her most outlandish stare. "I'll be watching you like a hawk."

Devon caught her glare and held it. Jasmine froze. All her senses screamed the moment she registered the disturbing glint in Devon's dark, forbidding gaze. Her nerves were further heightened by the predatory way in which she was caged in. It suddenly dawned on her that she was no hawk at all, but on the contrary, was Devon's prey. At least that was how she felt when she sensed the shift of Devon's head moving closer and closer.

"Don't go getting any false ideas that I'm a soft touch, Miss Charlesworth," he warned sternly. "You may be Carmilla's granddaughter, but I think you'll find in the long run that whatever you decide to do, in the end, you'll be totally responsible to me."

"And you may be Carmilla's godson," Jasmine chimed belligerently, "but I know that if I find one penny out of place, or think that you're secretly siphoning the cream of my grandmother's profits, you'll be answerable to me. I'm not going to let you get away with anything."

"Not even this?" Devon muttered thickly, as he dropped his head and planted a full kiss directly on Jasmine's lips.

Trapped firmly inside the alcove, she could not move. Instead, hot shivers of erotic excitement had taken over Jasmine's body. She felt her stomach lurch against Devon's hardened torso. She tried to still the rapid pounding of her heart, knowing it was beating in close unison to Devon's own, but every thought evaporated as her helpless lips softly accepted the possessive invasion.

A low moan echoed down the corridor. Jasmine was shocked when she suddenly realized it came from her throat. The gasp served only to make Devon want her more. He quickly surrendered to the beguiling sweetness of her mouth. He nipped the bottom lip, then sucked at the top, snatched and captured both in a fierce rapture, and just when Jasmine felt she was about to faint as a violent tremor of pleasure raged through her trembling body, Devon drew back ever so slightly. He paused long enough for one intake of air, then took her lips again with such slow, drugging persuasion that Jasmine could do nothing but sink deep into the alcove and remain captive.

Jasmine barely heard the muffled groan from Devon's mouth. She was enmeshed in a feverish, misty haze of burning, pulsing excitement. She enjoyed the darts of fire shooting throughout her veins, the wicked buzz that electrified her limbs, and the dizzy, almost sickly spell that managed to fog her mind to the exclusion of all else except the soft, trembling lips locked in a fluid motion on hers.

Why have I never been kissed this way before? a soft voice in the far recesses of her mind wept. It was not obvious to Jasmine, even though somewhere in her mind a vague image of her ex-boyfriend appeared. For the brief three seconds that he was there, she wondered what he was doing at that precise moment in New York. She thought about the heady idea that she was now feeling new lips locked against her mouth, then hoped with fervent damnation that Enrico Jax Cajero was having a bad time. . . .

The man looking at his handsome reflection in the mirror smoothed his shaven fawn-colored jawline and smiled proudly at his appearance. He considered himself a master of the game and flashed his charming white teeth as though in approval of the double-breasted purple suit, the black silk Nehru shirt, open at the neck to reveal a gold herringbone

chain, and the polished black and white cap-toe
Gucci shoes on his feet. He'd already decided he was
going to pluck a new girl from among the many that
frequented the downtown joint he was in. It was already past midnight and the Manhattan club was still
racing. He didn't want to stay until breakfast, so was
taking a leak before leaving with a pretty young
thing.

Zipping up his pants, he licked his lips and
tightened his straight brown hair into a ponytail
at the back of his head. He smoothed his dark
brows, flashed his come-to-bed green eyes, and
turned to find two burly-looking white men facing
him. It was obvious from their stance that they were
not regulars of the club. He came often enough
to know that the club had few white patrons. His
curiosity was piqued, particularly when he felt
himself pushed up against the wall and his back
muscles slap into the very mirror that he had
been admiring himself in.

"Lay off the suit," he threatened, nicely.

"The bartender tells me that you're Enrico
Cajero," the brown-eyed white man with a shaven
head remarked in an European accent. "Tell me
it's you."

"My friends call me Jax," he answered, quickly
giving them the once-over. "What do I call you guys?"

"Your worst nightmare," the other man answered
with a Dutch accent. He was by Enrico's side in an
instant, brushing a speck from his charcoal-gray
wool suit as though the Puerto Rican had left a
mark on it. "We stayed at that hotel you run downtown," he continued in a matter-of-fact manner
while adjusting his blue tie over a white shirt. "You
may remember me? My name's Mr. Van Phoenix."

He smoothed his silver-white hair and took a calming breath before unbuttoning his gray jacket. "You took something of mine."

Enrico feigned ignorance. "Me!"

"I want it back," Van Phoenix insisted.

Enrico spied the holster inside the man's jacket pocket and immediately had a recollection. "You mean the brooch." He nodded knowingly. "I didn't think you'd miss that."

"Obviously not," Van Phoenix answered sharply. "Where is it?"

"I don't know," Enrico answered honestly, unaware that the gun had been removed from its holster. He was more aware of it when it was suddenly in his face. "I . . . I . . . mean I think I might know. My ex-girlfriend has it."

"Who?"

"Jasmine Charlesworth," Enrico finally admitted. "She's in France right now, visiting her folks. I swear."

"Then, Mr. Jax Cajero," Van Phoenix uttered, tapping the gun against Enrico's nose, "you will be on the first flight to France tomorrow morning to get me my brooch."

"Why don't I just pay you guys off?" Enrico muttered, knowing that he disliked flying. "I get airsick and—" He felt his face up against the mirror. "On second thought, I can just knock myself out on a rum and Coke until the plane lands in Paris."

"Johnny the Bear here will come with you." Mr. Phoenix indicated the six-foot-five-inch, bald-headed man holding Enrico's neck.

"It's just a stupid brooch," Enrico croaked, as he contemplated the grizzly man in front of him. He was dropped instantly. He rubbed his throat. "But I'll get it back."

"You do that," Van Phoenix ordered, "because if you don't, *you* can explain to my boss how you lost the combination to a safety deposit box holding two million dollars in diamonds."

"You're making a mistake." Enrico coughed, shaking his head, confused. "I don't have no combination numbers."

"They're hidden in the brooch, stupid," Johnny the Bear revealed. "You help me get it back and maybe I let you live." He reached into his expensive jacket pocket, pulled out a handful of nuts, and cracked them in the palm of his fat hand.

Enrico gulped at its implication and simply nodded his head.

"Stop!" Jasmine pushed Devon away.

"What is it?" He seemed confused. One minute he was having the most wonderful kiss of his life, the next it was all over.

"I just felt a cold shiver run down my spine," Jasmine said, breathing uneasily.

"I was kissing you, Miss Ice Queen," Devon said, deflated, finding that his hands were still respectfully braced high against the alcove walls, his fingertips tingling with an itch to touch Jasmine's soft, tender skin.

She gazed at him blankly. She had not intended the insult and clearly did not expect one in return. The kiss had been fabulous, but Jasmine was too jolted and unprepared to explain the feeling of foreboding that had disrupted her senses. Instead, she pushed Devon's body away from her. There was no use standing around waiting for another verbal impact, not when her limbs were still trembling. Not when she just wanted to go back to her room.

"*Allez-vous-en!*" she exploded, brushing him aside.

Devon was alarmed at her sudden outburst. "Jasmine—"

"Go away," Jasmine repeated in English.

Devon didn't wait to be told thrice. "Don't worry," he breathed, taking an exaggerated step away from her. "Forget I ever kissed you, okay?"

Jasmine stared at him, feeling miserable at the dismal prospect of never knowing those lips on her again. She ran tearfully down the corridor and didn't dare look back. She didn't dare think either. She waited until she reached the safe haven of her bedroom where no one could see how troubled she was. As she closed the door behind her and leaned against the wooden frame, Jasmine felt afraid. She could not account for the sudden fear, except perhaps it was her amazement that she had kissed Devon Rutherford.

She had allowed herself that weakness. She began to wonder why. In her confusion, she also began to mull over whether she was taking on too much working at the Birmingham Savoy. Perhaps more than she could handle. She was unsure whether she had the strength to stand up to Devon Rutherford and protect her grandmother's interests at the same time. And what Jasmine was most anxious about was whether she had the backbone to protect her own.

Chapter Four

It was during the afternoon when Jasmine met her grandmother downstairs for her weekly Sunday church luncheon. Jasmine was seated at the dining table, scooping the seeds out of a papaw, when she glanced across the room and caught Devon's entrance. He was wearing navy blue trousers and a loose pale blue, short-sleeved cotton shirt, open to show the brown column of his throat. He looked stunning, especially for the warm June afternoon, Jasmine thought, as she forced herself to tear her eyes away and instead exchange a furtive glance with the man seated at the table opposite.

"I haven't seen you before," he said flirting. "Are you new here?"

"I'm Carmilla's granddaughter," she introduced, putting down her spoon to extend her hand. "Jasmine Charlesworth from France."

"Gus Thompson, from England," the toffee-colored man greeted with a handshake and a beaming wide smile. "You're a fine-looking woman."

"*Merci beaucoup*," Jasmine returned, noting that he seemed rather young to be among the congregation of elderly church guests. She guessed that Gus was probably in his early twenties, judging from the baggy pants and the Sean John jersey he was wearing and the full head of cornrowed hair. "Are you affiliated with the church?" she queried.

"I'm with the band," Gus answered. "Four brothers and I, we rock the church on Sundays."

Jasmine scanned the room. She noted Lilian's and Martha's absence. She also caught the steadfast stare that Devon shot her way and blatantly chose to ignore him. "Where are the others?"

"The rest of the band's gone home," Gus said, throwing her a casual wink. "I just came along for the food, but I sure feel like staying now."

Jasmine accepted the compliment with a cheeky smile. "You've got a smooth tongue there, brother."

"One that I'd like to kiss you with later," Gus returned, leaning his elbows onto the table. He admired Jasmine's smooth caramel-brown complexion, the cute cherry-shape outline of her face. His bright brown eyes opened wider to take in the full impact of her floral pink-colored dress. Gus was making plans. "What are you doing this evening?"

Jasmine raised her brows with a flirting tease. "My diary says I'm free."

"Actually," a male voice suddenly intruded, "she'll have to take a rain check. Miss Charlesworth and I have some work to do later."

"Devon," Jasmine gasped, swinging her chair round to face the man standing in an imposing manner behind her. "What are you doing?"

"Tactfully reminding you that since you want to accept more of the duties associated with the management of the Savoy, you will need to join me at the club later," Devon drawled sternly.

"We don't open the ballroom on Sundays," Jasmine gritted between her teeth.

"That's true," Devon said, smoothing the thin outline of his mustache as though he were making the point. "But because of the expressway traffic around the city, we take our meat deliveries every Sunday evening when the roads are quiet. That way, we don't disrupt the club or hold up the flow of traffic during the week. As you're in charge of the restaurant, I expect you to be with me so that you learn how to check and sign for the stock."

Jasmine shook her head. "On a Sunday?" she said, disbelieving.

"Sonny only likes to use halal meat," Devon continued.

"That's kind of like kosher meat, right?" Gus said knowingly. "I've heard of that."

Devon glanced across at Gus. "I'm sorry for the intrusion." He transferred his gaze to Jasmine. "I'll meet you out front at eight o'clock."

Jasmine watched him leave and immerse himself in a cluster of Carmilla's friends. While she was happy to see her grandmother looking well again, Jasmine wanted to scream. How dare Devon Rutherford interfere with her trying to get her groove on. She considered him rude. Jealous even. Devon was not the only man deserving of her attentions, but his ego seemed to suggest that he was. Why else would he make his way clear across the room and interrupt her so candidly? Jasmine wanted to turn the situation around.

"Look," she said to Gus Thompson, allowing her smile to deepen apologetically, "why don't you come along with me to the Savoy? I'm sure this delivery won't take very long, and we can go for a drink afterward."

"You sure your man won't mind?" Gus queried, sweeping his gaze over Devon's tall, muscled figure.

"Firstly, he's not my man," Jasmine exclaimed uncomfortably. "And secondly, I'm asking you, not him."

Gus smiled wickedly. "I'm up for anything if you are."

"*Bon* . . . I mean good," Jasmine encouraged, clapping her hands in delight. "Now how exactly do I finish this papaw?"

The Jeep pulled up outside the Savoy. It was 8:30 p.m. and Jasmine was surprised to find herself already feeling tired. She felt reluctant, too. It was not on her evening schedule to be presiding over a meat delivery when she would rather be at a wine bar with Gus Thompson. But Devon had insisted she join him, and throughout the entire journey they had done nothing but argue.

Earlier, Jasmine had been picking her way through the remainder of her grandmother's afternoon luncheon, deciphering the jumble of words that fell from the lips of the elderly guests. She had tried to sort out what was alcohol and what was genuine emotion, and given her own French accent and the underlying sarcasm of her style, it had been impossible to break into any lengthy conversations.

But Carmilla's face seemed transformed from her pale expression since the unfortunate sunstroke that had kept her in bed throughout the week. Her grandmother had a gift for dominating a room whenever she chose to do so, and had flitted from one person to the next with such ease that even the lingering scent of her perfume left a lasting impression. On occasion, Jasmine would join her for a fresh round of introductions as the prodigal granddaughter, no doubt, returned to the family fold. Other times, she lay low in a corner somewhere talking with Gus, whose interest in her had not abated since her leaving the dinner table after wrestling with her papaw fruit. All the while, undignified perhaps but hardly tragic, Devon kept a cool eye on her. Jasmine was no stranger to his obsession. Every so often, whatever the distance between them, she would flash her irritation back at him, though she realized Devon was too self-absorbed to notice how much he was annoying her. Finally, as the guests began to thin and the early evening drew near, Devon approached the glass doors where she was standing overlooking the back garden, getting some air.

"You'd better get ready," he prompted.

"Must I?" she complained.

"I don't want to upset Carmilla's evening," Devon threatened softly, "so we'll keep to what we have planned."

"I don't expect to be ordered around by you," she protested.

"You're in no position to dictate terms to me," Devon responded coolly.

"I'm the boss's granddaughter, remember? And don't you forget it."

"It didn't take you long to see what your chances are, did it, Miss Charlesworth?" he said grimly. "An alluring prospect, is it, to play lady of the Birmingham Savoy?"

"I'm quickly growing accustomed to how it feels to be in charge," Jasmine admitted smugly.

"Let's hope you still think so when you discover the real amount of work involved," Devon exclaimed firmly. "You'll find it very different from the high life you've lived out in New York."

"You know nothing about how I lived in America, so you've no right to criticize me," Jasmine argued quickly. "I was in a position of employment before I came back here. So you see, I'm not the kind of woman you imagined."

"Aside from the fact that you got yourself caught up with a rogue from the streets," Devon reminded her. "What were you, his little plaything?"

He knew too much, Jasmine thought. She should never have called Enrico Jax Cajero a thug. "I was an au pair, as I've told you before," she explained with a certain degree of pride in her tone. "I held down a very good job for a family in Manhattan, and when things did not work out I decided to come home. That's the truth. What I did not expect to find is you in charge of the family coffers. Is that why you find my presence here a threat?"

She noted how Devon's brows dipped arrogantly. "I think too much of Carmilla to see her exploited by anyone," he stated tersely. "The Savoy has become a big part of her life, though given her age, I know she will tire of it soon. I don't want to see all our hard work thrown away by her spoiled granddaughter who has no intention of taking the business seriously. Just because you have blood ties does not mean you can start taking liberties. Not with me, not with anyone. If you want to learn the ropes, you do as I tell you."

Pressured by the responsibility she had taken on,

and her agreement to help out at the Savoy, Jasmine joined Devon out front in the Jeep. But not wishing to wholly concede to his demands, she asked Gus to follow along. She was aware that Devon did not approve. His very actions, the shrug of his shoulders and his long expression, spoke volumes.

Eventually, Jasmine was prompted to reassert her position.

"You'd better remember who I am and to whom the Birmingham Savoy belongs," she finally taunted, as Devon put the Jeep into a lower gear and exited the A41 Freeway onto a road that led directly to the club. "As long as my grandmother is in charge, I'll be right behind you seeing that things are done properly."

"Is that so?" Devon said hotly, as he finally parked and cut the engine. "Then tell me why you're complaining about overseeing a regular Sunday delivery and why you insist that we bring *him* along." He indicated the black BMW that had pulled up behind the Jeep. "We have work to do and you want to bring on another b-boy."

"*Excusez moi*, Gus is not a b-boy," Jasmine said defensively.

"Excuse me," Devon said, anglicizing, as he opened the door and jumped from the Jeep onto the sidewalk. "I meant to say stray cat."

"Nice set of wheels," Gus's voice suddenly echoed behind him. "This baby's got some horsepower. I like your rims. Customized?"

Startled, Devon turned and faced the young man admiring his silver Jeep. "Only the best," he muttered. "What you got, twenties?"

"Twenty-twos," Gus said. "They cost some money."

Devon nodded his approval, scrutinizing the black BMW a little closer. "Nice bodywork."

"Yeah, she's a beauty." Gus smiled proudly. "Come on over and take a look. I thought about putting on some running lights, but I'd like to do some more interior work first. I got some speakers you gotta see."

As Jasmine stepped from the Jeep, she was chagrined to find that Devon and Gus had made their way over toward the BMW. As she slammed the passenger door shut, she watched them both examine the car as though it were a prized stud. Within the twinkling of an eye, Jasmine noted the comradery that struck up between the two men. The kind that excluded all else, except the car.

Her dark brows drew together in a sharp frown. "Devon, aren't you going to open up?" she asked, while approaching the back of the Jeep.

Devon raised his head, his eyes distracted. "Um . . ." He gave a slight cough and cleared his throat before reaching into his trouser pocket. "You do it." He handed over the back door keys to the Savoy. "You'll need to flip the security."

"I . . . I don't know the code," Jasmine stuttered, alarmed at how easily she'd been forgotten.

After a moment's hesitation, Devon whispered the four numerical digits into her left ear. Jasmine was immediately aware of the tingling sensation that ran down her spine as his soft American voice bounced like wisps of hair against her earlobe. It told her just how easily her body reacted to him, but she repressed any girlish illusions of allowing herself to enjoy the moment. Instead, she kept herself rigid and alert.

"The security box is right by the door," Devon

explained, turning toward Gus to find that he had lifted the car hood. "I'll be with you in a while."

His absent expression caused Jasmine to grumble under her breath as she wandered disconsolately toward the back door of the Birmingham Savoy. She was not used to being instantly dismissed. Five minutes later and furious with herself for being so feeble, she was swearing grimly as she removed an empty glass from the kitchen cupboard, before moving over to explore the contents of the walk-in freezer.

What on earth were Gus and Devon doing, upstaging her with a car? And why was she in here, about to meekly set Devon's little world to rights by accepting an early evening delivery? She wanted to give both men a hefty kick in the shins, but instead Jasmine closed the half-empty freezer and filled her glass with cold water. As she leaned against the clean bench and sipped slowly, allowing the cold liquid to wet her dry palate, her skin began to crawl with humiliation at Devon's cool, ruthless . . . rejection.

"Let me take a look at that engine," he had told Gus loudly, almost immediately after dismissing her with the keys.

Even now, his thick, husky accent echoed like blaring drums against her sensitive mind. And Gus. He had agreed to join her for a drink later. How dare he conspire to ignore her in favor of showcasing his BMW to Devon! Jasmine felt rankled. She was completely astounded by the sheer nerve of both men. *Automobiles*, she seethed, just as there was a timely knock at the back door. She placed her glass of water on the nearest workbench.

"Halal frozen meat delivery," a short, balding

Turkish man suddenly barked as he pushed the door open. Slumped over his shoulder was a huge carcass of lamb.

"*Oui*," Jasmine uttered, slightly startled. "The freezer," she said, pointing, "is right over there."

A pink copy of the Birmingham Savoy's order list was instantly slapped into the palm of her hand. Within seconds, Jasmine found herself checking the entire delivery of frozen meat. Despite summoning up all the courage at her command, she was miserably aware of a nervous lump in her stomach when, twenty minutes later, she finally found herself returning to the Jeep.

Bracing herself to face an emotional battle, she found it maddening to discover both Gus and Devon still engaged in a lengthy discussion about Gus's car. In fact, Jasmine only heard their voices. As she walked around the Jeep, she was chagrined to find both men crouched to the ground admiring the car's low suspension. Her mind boiled at their level of interest in the damned thing.

"Devon, I'm ready to go home now." Jasmine spoke out sourly, appalled at how redundant she felt.

Devon was the first to pop his head up. "You've locked up?" he asked, raising himself to his feet.

"No, I've left the door wide open for burglars to get in," Jasmine said sarcastically.

Her voice cut through Devon's distracted thoughts like a dash of icy cold water. Staring down at Jasmine's slim, desolate figure, he noted a sharpness and clarity that did absolutely nothing to bring on any shame or guilt for his neglect of her. On the contrary, Devon simply smiled and turned toward Gus. He nodded his final approval of the amazing automobile in front of him.

"I'm cool with that," he acknowledged, concluding his inspection. "I'd like to ride it sometime, but right now I gotta go check on the building. We'll hook up again, okay?"

"Sure," Gus said, heading toward the driver's seat. He waved a dismissive hand in the air as he caught Jasmine's forlorn expression. "Come down to the church anytime," he hollered. "We do rehearsals there most weekdays from three p.m. until six."

"Oh!" Jasmine gave a snort of cynical disbelief.

"Bye," he said.

"Au revoir." She sighed curiously.

As Gus drove away, Devon reached into Jasmine's hand and plucked the Savoy keys. "You wait in the Jeep," he ordered softly. "I'll be right back."

And just like that, she was alone on the sidewalk. Maybe it was his arrogant, supremely confident smile, or was it the ease in which he had stymied her entire plans for the evening that finally pushed her over the edge? Jasmine was unsure. All she knew was that when Devon reseated himself at her side in the Jeep and fired up the engine, throwing the gearbox into first, she ripped like a woman sorely let down.

"You sent Gus home, didn't you?" she accused.

"You weren't thinking he was serious about taking you out tonight?" Devon returned on a smirk. "C'mon, he's a twenty-three-year-old boy and you're what . . . thirty-five?"

"I'm twenty-eight," Jasmine fumed.

Devon chuckled as he pulled onto the road. "And you haven't discovered *men* yet?"

"Have *you* learned how to separate the women from the girls or should I be competing with a car?"

Devon chuckled again. "There have been women in my life. Nobody special."

"Why?" Jasmine asked, intrigued.

He shrugged. "No reason. I've been looking, but I just can't find—"

"The girl who fits the fantasy in your head," Jasmine finished.

"That image no longer exists," Devon confessed softly. "Sure, every man has an illusion, but in practical terms he wants a woman who can be a loyal wife and mother to his children."

"Provided she wants to end up with an old codger like you," Jasmine murmured, humiliated past reason that he had ruined her date. It was an effort just to recover from his rude condescension of her.

"Old? Me?" Devon's lips curled into a broad grin of sardonic amusement. "I'm thirty-three years old and a damned sight more experienced than the boy who just drove off in his toy."

"Just because you are still looking for a partner and have successfully managed to kiss me does not mean you have the right to interfere with my plans," Jasmine derided. "Besides, you played with his toy, too. That suggests to me you have some more growing up to do, or perhaps you deliberately looked over Gus's car to disrupt my evening?" His silence fueled Jasmine's candor. "I know you did this on purpose. You were supposed to be showing me the ropes."

"Which is hard to do since you keep reminding me that you're the boss's granddaughter," Devon recalled on a more serious note. "Technically, as I'm supposed to be the manager until you step into my shoes, you were more responsible for that delivery tonight."

"I didn't expect you to take me literally," Jasmine scolded, as she observed the late evening traffic that led toward Handsworth Wood Road.

"What choice did you give me?" Devon rebuffed. "You're in my face all the time, goading me to frustration about how you're going to take over the place. I guess that means I can take a backseat and watch you handle the whole damn show."

"I'm still learning," Jasmine conceded, detecting the anger now evident in Devon's tone.

"I can see from the stray cat I just got rid of for you," Devon rebutted, "that you really need to step up your game."

"The only person playing games is you," Jasmine breathed furiously. "Insisting that I come here at this time of night, spoiling my love life."

"You got a kiss this morning," Devon declared smoothly. "What more do you want? Crumbling at the knees?"

"I was talking about Gus," Jasmine boomed, knowing that her knees had indeed buckled beneath the persuasive motion of Devon's lips. "What did you say to make him change his mind about taking me out?"

"Oh, that." Devon suddenly tossed the Birmingham Savoy's keys into Jasmine's lap before steering the Jeep down the A41 Freeway. "I told him that, starting from tomorrow, you'll be opening up the Savoy every night, which means that your daytimes will very much be taken up with you catching up on your beauty sleep."

"You had no right—"

"I had every right," Devon interrupted, sounding half angry, half amused, as if Jasmine's earlier defiance was causing him some enjoyment. "You wanted to be lady of the Birmingham Savoy. Here's your chance."

Jasmine dissolved into silence. She'd asked for this. She had signed her own death warrant by running her mouth about looking after her grandmother's business interests. It was clearly evident now that Devon was going to work her to the bone and make her see exactly what was involved in running the place. She wasn't sure that she could do it. All Jasmine knew was that she was not about to back down.

"You don't think I can handle it, do you?" she asked, with a hint of trepidation.

"I think you'll fall at the first hurdle." Devon laughed harshly as he left the freeway. "You lack everything that Carmilla Charlesworth is made of."

Jasmine was well aware that being driven by rage and fury was not the best foot forward with Devon Rutherford or his derision of her. What she required was a cool head and the ability to make objective decisions without allowing her emotions or family ties to interfere. On the other hand, dashing in where angels might fear to tread was just the right approach for her, especially as she wanted to forget the awful memories she had left back in New York. She hadn't taken time to think hard and long about her impetuous decision. She was just going along with it.

She picked up the Savoy keys and clutched at them tightly as Devon pulled the Jeep up to the curb outside her grandmother's house. "I'll show you that I'm a Charlesworth," she spat out, as she quickly jumped out onto the sidewalk. "And when I do, you will find, Monsieur Rutherford, that I don't crumble easily, particularly when being kissed."

"Considering you didn't put enough effort into it the first time," he cruelly teased, annoyed when he recalled how Jasmine had shuddered with fear.

"That is something you'll never have the privilege of taking from me again," Jasmine told him firmly, slamming the passenger door shut. "Good night, monsieur."

Devon cut the engine and stared quietly as he watched Jasmine disappear into the house. His heart lurched forward with renewed determination. If she did not know it yet, she would soon, he vowed. He would not only steal another kiss from Jasmine Charlesworth, but was resolved he would seduce her, too. And the next time he kissed this Caribbean-French beauty, Devon promised himself it would be with such ardent passion that Jasmine would positively melt in his arms.

Chapter Five

Jasmine stared at the laptop screen. She was seated in the Savoy's nerve center, undertaking her latest duty. *I'll show you that I'm a Charlesworth,* she thought assertively. The words rummaged through her mind with such persistence she kept her gaze fixed. Jasmine was not accustomed to dealing with computers. Modern technology was never a strong point with her and she forgave herself immediately when her thoughts momentarily strayed to an impromptu conversation she had shared with the bartender earlier that day.

"For what I know of it," Gibson had said, on her probing for information about Devon, "he and Camilla took to each other like a horse to water, and which one of them thought of the Birmingham Savoy, I couldn't be sure. I don't think either of them would know it now, but as you can see, it's turned into a real gold mine, there's no denying it. Of course, black folks being like they are around here thought Carmilla had bit off more than she could chew. You really don't want to believe talk like that."

"Like the story on Devon and Petronella?"

Jasmine coerced, taking her first opportunity since working at the Savoy to expand on what Gibson had whispered in her ear on her inaugural visit.

It didn't take her long to label him the resident gossip. At best, Gibson was deceptive. A short, impossibly beautiful Cuban—in an effeminate sort of way—with a cultivated persona that seemed to accompany drag queens. He was adorable, too, but a verbose muckraker who tended the bar with a heart of gold. As far as she was able to understand from his prattle, the Birmingham Savoy had quickly become a breeding ground for buried secrets, hidden relationships, and clandestine scandals among its guests. Ever gracious at keeping the rumor mill turning, Gibson was quick to drop the latest gossip.

"Now there's a story," he exclaimed on a conspiratorial note, throwing her a sideways wink with the tipping of his chin. "You'd better watch your back, sister, because Petronella's stuck on him. I thought it wise to warn you, being Carmilla's granddaughter, 'cause she's the kind of girl who'll rather see you in hell than lose her man."

"Her man?" She refused to tell Gibson of what had happened at the Savoy the day before.

Petronella had been working efficiently and smoothly putting white cloths over the tables when she barely glanced over and caught Jasmine approaching. A tension existed between them, there was no doubt about it. But neither woman got in the way of the other. Jasmine picked up two vases of flowers from the set Petronella had already laid out on one of the tables and began to position them in the center of two tables that Petronella had already covered.

"Everything okay in here?" Jasmine had finally asked, unable to take the silence a moment longer.

"Sure." Petronella shrugged.

Thinking she would no longer be required in the restaurant area, Jasmine left and walked across the ballroom floor, past the bar, and down the corridor that led to the back office. She was hardly there five minutes when the door was flung wide open and Petronella stormed in. She kept her gaze fixed on Jasmine, who had seated herself behind the desk and switched on the laptop computer, but her face said it all. Petronella was going to stake her ground.

"I like Devon, do you know that?" she stated tersely.

"I've heard a rumor or two, not that it's any of my business," Jasmine answered coolly, leaning back into her chair to appraise Petronella.

"I heard you're from France," Petronella went on. "Why don't you do us both a favor and go back there? I don't want to see Devon get hurt."

Jasmine refused to be nettled by the snub. "As long as my name is Charlesworth, I have more right to be here than anyone else, aside from my grandmother," she replied, ignoring the footsteps outside the door. She hoped her voice hadn't carried too far when she added, "Is there anything else?"

"I'll work harder," Petronella quickly murmured. "I'll try and do my best."

Ever alert at picking up a nuance in a voice, Jasmine sensed that Petronella's sudden mellowing was not for her benefit. She was not far wrong when the tall dark figure that entered the room looked directly at her. Jasmine bit her lip, knowing that it had been Devon's footsteps hovering outside the open door.

"What's going on in here?" he demanded, glancing from one woman to the other.

They both answered at the same time, "Nothing."

Devon folded his arms and remained at the door, barring either woman's exit. "Well?"

"Oh, Carmilla phoned," Petronella suddenly inserted. "She said that I was to tell you that the transaction has been completed at the bank and that you need to call your solicitors to sign and pick up the papers."

Devon nodded. "Right."

"Wait a minute." Jasmine was out of her chair in an instant, walking around the desk until she was within a foot of Petronella. "Who gave you the authority to come into the office and use the phone?"

Petronella shrugged. "I've done it before. Devon doesn't mind, do you, honey?" she prompted.

"*I* mind," Jasmine started, weakened by the knowledge that Devon was not standing in her defense. "Your job is to see to the tables and that is all."

"Why must you both behave so childishly?" Devon breathed, annoyed at both women's conduct. "This is a nightclub, not a schoolyard."

He had reduced their bickering to two toddlers having a tantrum. "There's nothing going on that I would lose a night's sleep over," Jasmine relented, walking directly toward Devon's tall, majestic frame. "And would you please let me pass. I have work to do."

Devon stood back to let her by with an exaggerated gesture that put Jasmine on edge. She told herself that she should put the matter out of her mind, but as she brushed by him and their eyes met, she felt galled to think he could imagine her to be someone so shallow. Perhaps her earlier sarcasm had colored his view, but Jasmine refused to believe herself to be anything like Petronella.

"Don't be fooled by the candy coating," she whispered into his ear, hurt by his ridicule of her. "She's all fluff."

She went straight to the ladies' restroom and rinsed her face with cold water. It would be impossible for her to stay here, she thought. There could be many more clashes between her and Petronella like the one that had just occurred. But even so, that in itself was not nearly as upsetting as watching Devon take Petronella's side. Jasmine tried to tell herself that there was no need for personalties to come into the fray, though listening to Gibson suggested more trouble ahead.

"Petronella's already telling everybody how she's gonna get busy with Devon," he chattered, licking his lips. "That's how things are at this club. Remind me sometime to tell you what kind of people come here. A bartender always sees and hears everything about the lonely hearts, man-eaters, players, and cheaters. The Birmingham Savoy is one of those places where something is always going down. All you need to do is keep your eyes on Petronella, 'cause that baby is up to something."

"She can rest assured," Jasmine lied through her teeth, aware that her instincts were telling her differently, "I have no interest in a man who's been one of my grandmother's charity cases."

Gibson laughed. "Whoa, don't get all high and mighty now. Devon's put a lot into this club. That's why your grandmother believed in him. Without Devon, none of this would have been possible."

"Let's not forget my grandmother's part in it,"

Jasmine noted, peeved at hearing the bartender sing Devon's praises. "After all, she owns the place."

"They're partners," Gibson agreed. "But Devon's the boss."

Not anymore, Jasmine told herself astutely, as she purged the recent conversation from her mind and refocused her attention. She rubbed her brows and sighed heavily at the numbers in front of her on the laptop. Having been poor at math in school, Jasmine was determined to try and understand the ballroom's accounts. It was one of the additional tasks she had decided to take upon herself to prove her capabilities, and she had begun to scroll down the screen when the office door shot open.

"So, lady of the Birmingham Savoy," Devon Rutherford announced brazenly as he sauntered into the room and observed Jasmine seated at the desk, working diligently on the accounting program. "How are you coping?" He walked behind her and peered over her shoulder.

"Fine," Jasmine answered, as she looked at the spreadsheets, cross-legged and not noticing how far this caused her dress to slide up her slender thighs. "Just making sure you haven't cooked the books."

Outside the office door, Saturday night dancing in the ballroom went on in an unending flow. It was coming up to midnight and Jasmine was determined to finish up her work before the club closed at 2:00 a.m. Two weeks had flown by in a whirl of activity since she made her declaration to Devon. Jasmine had not only kept to her word, but was keen to prove to herself that she was more than capable of living up to her grandmother.

She was at the club at four o'clock every afternoon

to open up the building. She had learned how to run the restaurant, organize the staff rotations, sort out the paychecks, and even make the necessary deductions like pensions, taxes, and national insurance contributions. She only bit off chunks she knew she could chew, and nothing galvanized her into action more than seeing the expression on Devon's face.

He seemed astounded when she turned down his offer to ride in the Jeep, instead getting to work under her own steam by taking the bus. And equally pleased when the night was through when she took a taxi like the rest of the staff, as the ride home was a perk picked up by the club via special arrangement with the cab company. Now she was taking on office work in her spare time.

"Careful," Devon warned, unhappy at her latest accusation. Earlier last week she had accused him of choosing the wrong kind of toilet paper for the Savoy's ladies' and men's restrooms. And the week before, she had indicated her dissatisfaction with their regular vegetable delivery company, insisting that the Savoy should only serve organic greens. "Everything on that computer ledger is accessed directly into our electronic data bank," he informed her firmly.

"I need the password to go online," Jasmine breathed, scrolling along the spreadsheets. "There seems to be a discrepancy and I need to check the bank statements online."

"What discrepancy?" Devon swallowed, walking around the desk until he had a good view of Jasmine. It was one thing getting an eyeful of her slender thighs, but Devon wanted to see her face. Instead, Jasmine kept it lowered, trained on the laptop screen. She had quickly learned how to modify the way she dressed for evening work at the Savoy, he noted. As she sat at the desk working, she stood out among the drudgery of the office.

Tonight, Jasmine was in a black silk dress, with short sleeves and a low neckline, perfectly suited to greet the July guests. Devon even liked the small vintage Victorian brooch that was pinned to the left of her breast, admiring how it added to her strong demeanor. He knew that beneath the desk, she would have kicked off her three-inch-heeled shoes. He had also noted that Jasmine took strength from attempting to reach his six-foot frame. But what Devon was not prepared for was what came out of her mouth next.

"Your salary," Jasmine responded. "It doesn't appear to be listed."

"That's because it isn't," he declared, wishing she would look at him.

Jasmine raised her head. It was the first time she had seen Devon all day, and she was not prepared for the new haircut. She was also not expecting him to be dressed so formally either. Normally, Devon arrived at the Savoy in his usual black suit, white shirt, and a demure-looking tie. Now he was in a tuxedo, and even his mustache and eyebrows seemed to have benefitted from something. But she kept her focus intact.

"Why not?"

Devon noted the cherry-shaped face, arched eyebrows, soft full lips coated in red, and the dark eyes that looked right at him and felt his body react. "That's a matter between myself and Carmilla."

"You're not intending to share that information

with me, are you, monsieur?" Jasmine realized suddenly.

His senses absorbed the French accent as if it were sweet smelling salts. "No," he admitted, folding his arms beneath his chest. "But believe me, I'm not pulling a caper."

"I'm past learning to believe what men say," Jasmine confessed, while saving the data she had just looked over. "I've learned a lot about them in my last relationship, things I never learned from my father."

Devon laughed, his face changing from a dour expression to the handsome good looks that made Jasmine hold her breath for a second. "I should hope so."

"I don't mean . . . you know, about the birds and the bees," Jasmine expanded. "I'm talking about treachery . . . betrayal . . . deception." Her voice died out.

In the silence, Devon shifted uneasily. "He was rotten?" he asked, finally.

"Is that the right word, rotten?" Jasmine asked, bemused. She switched off the laptop and closed it before staring dismally into space. "Somehow, that word doesn't seem bad enough."

"You got away," Devon reminded her, intrigued at that faraway look he caught in her eyes. "That's what matters now, right? Staying away from thugs?"

Jasmine shrugged away her fleeting memories. "*Oui,*" she muttered, forcing a smile. "I've noted Gus's absence over the last two Sunday church luncheons," she added knowingly. She was also aware of Lilian's and Martha's absence for some time, too. "I've been meaning to ask you about it."

"Probably he thinks I'm strong competition and

has stepped aside," Devon remarked, smugly. "I mean, the young brother can't measure up to a man, right?"

Jasmine chuckled. "Seeing that you're dressed in all your finery," she noted. "What's the occasion, a date? The poor girl."

"The Afro-Cuban All Stars are here tonight, remember?" Devon exclaimed, slightly peeved. "Whenever we have an out-of-town band in the club, I announce them to the guests in the very best of style." He twirled so that she got the full impact of how wonderful he looked. "I put the band on an hour ago. It's red hot out there."

"Of course," Jasmine breathed, shaking her head as the night's schedule skipped her mind. She had been in the office since ten o'clock and was not alerted that the band had arrived. "Have the All Stars pulled in a crowd?"

"Come and see for yourself," Devon encouraged, smoothing his slim mustache in satisfaction. "As I told you weeks ago, it's all been budgeted for and the ticket sales have tripled."

Jasmine rose from her chair and slipped into her black Jimmy Choo heels. "Okay," she said. "Let me take a look."

She followed Devon out of the office and along the corridor that led directly into the ballroom. Jasmine had never been more startled. In front of her was a sea of men and women, feverishly gyrating and doing intricate variations of the Peabody while a mix of brass, percussion, timbales, and vocals rocked their senses. Their intoxicating joy lit up Jasmine's face instantly.

"This is amazing," she gasped, taking a good

look at the band who filled the raised makeshift platform that had been specially erected for them.

The Afro-Cuban All Stars were a thirteen-piece band that spanned four generations of musicians aged eighty-one to thirteen, though the band that night was mainly the finest in Cuba's long-retired jazz giants. The African roots music was a reflection of their collective experience, playing multiple percussion instruments and brightly lit trumpets that were paced with extravagant patience. Jasmine was already swaying to the congas and trombones when Devon held out his hand.

"Would the lady of the Savoy like a dance?" he asked softly.

"Me?" Jasmine shook her head shyly, even though her feet were already doing a casual trot that kept her body rocking. "I can't."

"Yes, you can," Devon teased, taking a hold of her left hand.

It was the first time they had touched each other in the two weeks since Jasmine began her disciplined agenda at the Savoy. But when Devon's familiar fingers clasped hers, Jasmine recognized the feelings immediately. The hot shivers of erotic excitement that tickled her nerve endings. The lurching forward of her stomach in helpless surrender. The rapid thudding of her heartbeat. These were all signs of Devon's tangible hold on her. Were he to kiss her again, at that very moment, Jasmine knew for certain she would probably faint.

But Devon's only interest was to dance, and within seconds he had pulled Jasmine into the embrace of his arms. The chandeliers sparkled like diamonds overhead as he smoothly glided her across the dance floor. While the room buzzed with faster-pacing guests raging around them to and fro, stomping up a frenzy at the Savoy, Devon and Jasmine took it slow. She looked into his soul-searching brown eyes, his gaze bored deeply into hers, and by tacit consent, they closed their eyes and bopped along with the percussion.

"You feel soft," Devon whispered against her earlobe, his voice as seductive as thick dark chocolate and equally as potent.

"You feel very warm," Jasmine returned shyly. She could smell the scent of his aftershave and savored it as a lasting reminder that this was their first dance at the Savoy.

She became aware that her whole body was pressed along the length of his and that Devon's powerful thighs were brushing between her legs as they continued to dance. Each movement bombarded her senses with highly charged signals that sent Jasmine's pulse racing. The longer they danced, the persuasive beat of the drums, Devon's hand running up and down her spine in time with the rhythm, and the lead singer's romantic voice caused an ache deep within that required soothing.

"Nice brooch," Devon commented, noting the hand-carved cameo of the profile of a woman set in an ornate suspended frame. "One of a kind. Very expensive."

Jasmine opened her eyes, recalling she had pinned to her dress the antique Victorian brooch Enrico had given to her. She had done so because it was beautiful and elegant and looked like something that dated back to the 1870s. "How much?" she queried curiously.

"About fifteen hundred brand-new," Devon answered. "Where did you get it?"

Jasmine forced down her surprise with a swallow. "A gift," she muttered.

"Any sentimental value?" he probed.

"No," she said, closing her eyes again.

She absorbed the congas and the trombone and felt the contrasting styles within her body that paid tribute to the diversity of Cuban music. The band's variety throughout the night had included classic son *montuno*, contemporary timba, swinging big band *guajira*, Afro-Cuban jazz, *danzón*, and the pure tribal rhythms of a *bakua*, such as what was seeping into Jasmine's body now.

"Can I see?"

Jasmine reopened her eyes in time to find that Devon had unclipped her brooch and was weighing it in the palm of one hand. "It's heavier than I expected," he said, moments before reattaching it to her dress. "You look lovely with it on."

Jasmine smiled. "*Merci.*"

"We should do this more often," he said, before giving her a smooch.

"We're not paying guests." Jasmine sighed pleasantly, feeling a momentary flutter of guilt. A gap in the dancers gave her a fleeting glimpse across the ballroom floor where she caught Petronella staring at them from the other end of the room. This was of no surprise to Jasmine following her earlier words with the waitress. "But we have an admirer," she added suddenly.

Devon held her closer. "Who?"

"Petronella."

Jasmine felt the rigid shift in his body as Devon altered his stance. "Great guest band," he said with a cough, as though he was removing a constriction from his throat. "You're a good dancer."

"And you must be one hell of a player," Jasmine answered cuttingly. She broke herself free from his embrace, unsure what to make of his reaction. "This dance is over."

"Jasmine, wait," Devon protested, catching her by the wrist as she hurriedly left the dance floor. "What's gotten into you?"

"How you earn your salary, that's what," Jasmine bit back, pushing open the door next to the bar. "You're right, I really must step up my game." She marched down the corridor and threw open the office door. "It's time we hired some waiters," she decided, walking right over to the desk where she picked up a jotter and pencil. "The female guests should be afforded equal rights to be served by rippling biceps, chiseled jawlines, and whiffs of aftershave instead of perfume, red lips, and long manes of hair extensions."

"You're jealous of the waitresses?" Devon remarked suddenly.

"I want them all in new skirts," Jasmine continued, as she penciled a notation on the jotter. "The new length will be cut at the knee, not raised two inches above it like we have now. This is a respectable club, not a brothel."

"You're way off base here," Devon croaked, loosening his black tie. "Your own grandmother approved the skirt lengths and white blouses."

"Which, by the way, show too much cleavage," Jasmine interjected hotly. "I want something buttoned up to the collarbone."

Devon laughed. "You're wearing a low neckline."

"That's different," Jasmine defended. "I'm . . . the boss."

"Boss's granddaughter," Devon corrected, "and don't go running with that idea too quickly because you might just get a nasty surprise."

"Like the one I just had out there?" Jasmine chided. "You and Petronella?"

"What?" Devon said.

"I've noticed how she's been looking at you since I began working here," Jasmine began. "I see her on the bus sometimes, too. She's all sweetness and nice, talkative even about her mom and her half brother, and how her mother is going to get remarried next year. It's all very unconvincing because the moment we're here, at the Savoy, I'm public enemy number one. Suddenly, she's got her claws out. You like her, don't you?"

"She's pretty," Devon confessed, feeling a certain heightened ego that Jasmine should think the waitress actually adored him.

"*Attrayant,*" Jasmine amended in French, knowing the word was descriptive of Petronella's attractive veneer, though the admission caused a coil of jealousy to seep like poison through her veins.

Devon hesitated. His instincts saw Jasmine as an immeasurably better prospect. She had a lineage he understood, a grandmother he respected immensely, and a body worthy of being made love to. In the male world, she was a typical upgrade. "But—" And he hesitated again.

"You can't keep your eyes in one direction, can you?" Jasmine mocked at his shallowness. She seated herself at the desk and kicked off her shoes. The jotter and pencil were tossed down onto the desktop. "Like I said, I've learned a lot about men.

One dance out there and it's the same all over again. Is there no end to how low a man can go?"

"When he's done murder, I expect," Devon answered solemnly.

"Well, I know whose throat I'd like to throttle with my hands right about now," Jasmine taunted.

"Mine, I suppose," Devon said hotly. "That's all you've been doing ever since I walked in here. When are you going to step off?"

"Me?" Jasmine gasped.

Devon walked right around the desk and took a strong hold of Jasmine's left wrist. He jerked her right out of her chair and forced her to face him. Her soft breasts crushed against his hard, muscled chest. "Yes, you," he stormed. "I let that slide, you accusing me of cooking the books, but—"

"I was doing my job," Jasmine interrupted in her defense, her chin raised defiantly. "You may've been paying off somebody."

Devon's jaw fell. With his steely brown eyes boring into her, it seemed as though his brain was about to explode. "What?" he gasped.

She was aware of the angry flush beneath his chestnut-colored skin covering his cheekbones and jawline, and her eyes were drawn helplessly to the strong, sensual curve of his lips. "This *is* a nightclub."

"You're way out of line," Devon scorned, dropping Jasmine's hand as if he had been burned by it. It was always the same, he thought in despair. "No matter what I do or say, you're gonna be right there, in my face? Why am I even being nice to you, Miss Ice Queen?"

Jasmine felt the sting of those three words and the shot of guilt that ran through her body. She had been full-on and knew it. She was also loath to admit that she was driven by jealousy. All she had wanted, and it didn't seem too much to hope for, was to be in Devon's arms without any female distraction from anyone. Sure, she expected women to look. After all, Devon Rutherford was an extremely handsome man with all the right attributes in all the right places. But what seemed to impose itself on Jasmine's mind was whether there had been an affair with Petronella or there was an impending one to come. And if so, where did that leave her as a woman also vying for Devon's sweet attention?

"You have no right to be calling me Ice Queen," Jasmine breathed, horrified at the disparagement. "I did not invite you to kiss me."

"That's true," Devon admitted with a nod, "but the very least you could've done was behave as though you enjoyed it. This little charade of you feeling outdone because I happen to like Petronella's company is a bit rich coming from someone who despises me."

"I don't . . . despise you," Jasmine responded, seeing the flicker of hurt behind Devon's dark, soul-searching eyes.

"No?" Devon demanded.

"Of course not," Jasmine exclaimed, attempting a smile. She walked around the desk away from Devon, trying to calm herself. It dawned on her now that she was probably carrying emotional baggage from her relationship with Enrico Cajero and was releasing it through jealousy. Whether that was the case or not, Jasmine knew she had no right to take out her frustration on another man. And so she conceded. "I'm sorry."

Devon looked across at her, disliking the distance Jasmine had put between them. He imagined that she was being self-protective, which seemed hardly possible for a woman of such amazing beauty. Even at this late hour on a Saturday night, Jasmine's features were burnished with such life and luster he hardly knew how to react to such an attraction. And the way her slim waist and shapely hips, which were accentuated by the cut of her dress, mirrored in his wandering gaze made him realize just how much he wanted Jasmine Charlesworth.

"Look," he began, taking two steps toward her, but respecting the distance she had put between them, "you're Carmilla's granddaughter and I'm her godson. If at all possible, for her sake, let's try to have some team spirit here. Let's start again, beginning first thing tomorrow at Bernard Augarde's barbecue. What do you say?"

Jasmine nodded. "I'm all for that," she agreed, not the least bit sincere about what she was saying. "I will try and keep a lid on my suspicions."

"And I will try to keep you out of my business affairs," Devon said, unconcerned whether she was offended by his steadfast determination.

It seemed an odd compromise for them to be making, given the fact that neither Jasmine nor Devon was in any real accord whatsoever. The pact in itself was testament that they still did not offer one another any leeway to develop a working relationship. Each was as bad as the other. Neither was going to back down or give in. It was as though an unspoken feud existed between them. A duel as to whose resolve—or heart— would weaken first. This was all on Jasmine's mind as she later turned down the duvet on her bed and slipped between the sheets.

Her heart sank as she thought further about staying on at the Birmingham Savoy. It would be impossible to go on fighting her attraction toward Devon. The instability was beginning to show in her behavior. She felt disheartened at having accused him of so many things, but again there was that niggling hunch, or was it fear, that Devon Rutherford was hiding something?

Jasmine wondered what on earth it could be and why this sense of paranoia existed at all. She had not thought about Enrico in such dubious terms and look at how he turned out. She had been in a relationship with a thief. Jasmine tossed in her bed as she again recalled her decision to leave New York. Enrico Cajero was dark, handsome, charismatic, and a . . . thief, she thought, dismally questioning her poor judgment. Maybe this was why she distrusted Devon Rutherford.

She closed her eyes and saw his image imprinted on her mind. It was no dream. This man invaded her every thought. Jasmine told herself that if he was someone her own grandmother trusted to live in her home, surely he should be someone she could take on and become friends with. Maybe it was time she lightened up a little, and with that conclusion firmly resolved in her mind, Jasmine slept.

"You fool," Johnny spat out in his deep European accent at the Puerto Rican seated next to him.

They were on Le Shuttle, the high-speed train that traveled at one hundred miles per hour from France to England through the underwater Eurotunnel. Both men had spent two weeks moving around Paris on an endless search to find Jasmine Charlesworth. Enrico had taken Johnny to her previous apartment, which was vacant, but where they had spoken to the landlord. A trail led to three of her friends, the third supplying a previous employer's address where Jasmine had done au pair work.

Arriving there, he was told by the parents of Jasmine's three-year-old charge that she had not been in contact, but they could provide a phone number for the agency who had recommended her. Enrico knew the French agency would be reluctant to supply any details, so was able to glean instead Jasmine's parents' address and had gone along to the apartment overlooking the Champs-Elysées, introducing himself to Jasmine's father as her American boyfriend.

It didn't take long for Enrico, with his charisma, to convince Porter Charlesworth that he wanted to surprise his daughter for her upcoming birthday by showing up unannounced with presents. The only information he needed was where she was. Porter, having heard all about Enrico Cajero at Christmas, which he had spent in England at his mother's house, quite happily provided the information Jax needed. Though it was a partial success to now know where they were going, Johnny was in no mood for any more delays, particularly when he was now in a thirty-two-mile rail tunnel hundreds of feet below the surface of the English Channel.

"How was I to know she went straight to England?" Enrico drawled, wishing the thirty-five-minute journey would soon be over. He had caught very little sleep during the train ride from Paris to Calais and was feeling quite lethargic, especially having to board yet another train to Folkestone in

England. "The agency in New York said she'd gone home, so give me a break."

"Yeah, I'll start with your fingers and then your toes," Johnny threatened harshly.

Enrico swallowed, looking dearly at his perfect fingers. "You'll get your brooch back, I promise. I told you I'm good for it. Trust me."

"The last guy to tell me that is buried in the First Municipal Cemetery in Prague," Johnny chided, slapping Enrico almost comically on the back. "Believe me, don't ever say 'trust me,' especially to Van Phoenix. He thinks T.M. means terminate."

"Got ya." Jax nodded, as he watched Johnny the Bear pop a peanut into his mouth, before rudely throwing the shell onto the floor. He looked through the window and saw nothing but pitch black. As he closed his eyes and tried to think, Enrico felt as though he'd reached the darkest part of his soul.

Chapter Six

Jasmine awoke the following morning and gave a long sigh as she soaked in the scented bathwater. The warm soapy bubbles tickled softly against her satiny caramel-brown skin as she rested her head on the inflated tub pillow, closed her eyes, and lazily relaxed. She had tied her nutmeg-brown corkscrew hair up into a topknot, plastered a clay face pack onto her face, and was now feeling the night's tension leave her body.

There shouldn't have been any strain attached to her thoughts on such a bright morning with the bathroom window open so that she could hear the summer birds singing, but Jasmine needed to reappraise her situation. Carmilla's generous intention of inviting her into the business had not only revealed an underlying tension between herself and Devon Rutherford, but she now suspected there were some staff members who begrudged her the right of inheritance to a ready-made and flourishing nightclub. Devon Rutherford certainly for one . . . and Petronella for another. Jasmine now

understood more fully the instant meaning behind
the woman's barely concealed resentment of her.

"She's gonna make sure she gets her hands on
the boss," Gibson had teased from behind the
bar, an expansion on his earlier reminder before
the events of last night. "You better keep watching
your back, sister."

And she had done that. Right up until she shared
a dance on the ballroom floor with Devon, only to
find Petronella casting a dark, gloomy shadow at
them with her eyes. Jasmine contemplated whether
it was time she moved on before matters became
more entangled. So far, she had not talked it over
with her grandmother about the length of her
visit. As vague as it all was, Jasmine began to feel
more determined that she must get around to
discussing her work at the Savoy. After all, she
had not planned to stay in Birmingham forever.

She wanted no more misunderstandings and
no more assumptions about her position, particularly now that she had struck a bargain with
Devon Rutherford to keep her nose out of the ballroom's affairs. She was still curious about the obvious affection between him and her grandmother
and why he had not wanted her to see the online
bank account details to reconcile the spreadsheets.
Yet what Jasmine realized she needed more was
clarity. By the time she stepped out of the bath, she
had made a decision to talk to Carmilla.

She felt better when she had dressed in a soft
lavender-colored georgette blouse with no sleeves and
a white close-fitting linen skirt cut at the knee with
her bare feet in a pair of white slip-on, two-inch-heel
sandals. A pair of dangling gold earrings, around
which her soft ear-length brown hair fell in a rich cas-

cade, gave her a hint of sophistication. Jasmine
added a touch of makeup and was ready to greet the
day.

"*Bonjour,*" she said jovially, as she stepped out onto
the patio where she found Carmilla seated at the
garden table sipping Earl Gray tea and gazing at her
blooming roses. She noted that her grandmother was
dressed in a Laura Ashley flowery dress with an
emerald-green linen Chanel jacket that was perfect
for the cool bright July morning. With her white hair
styled and her maple-syrup complexion splashed
with a hint of blusher and frosted peach lipstick, Jasmine wondered what Carmilla had scheduled for the
morning. "Can I talk to you about something, Gran-
mama?"

"I am going to church this morning, Jasmine,"
Carmilla returned in a tone that caused her grand-
daughter to raise her eyebrows immediately. "And
I insist that you join me."

"*Excusez-moi?*" Jasmine hesitated, surprised.

"You've been here for weeks," Carmilla remarked
sadly, "and you've overlooked one simple thing."

"What's that?" Jasmine asked, as she observed
Betty Bately approaching the table with a teapot.

"You've forgotten to call your father," Carmilla
said flatly.

"Oh, that." Jasmine sighed. "I didn't want him
pressuring me to come back to Paris."

"My son is your father," Carmilla continued, regardless. "You can't just *not* call. He needs to know
what's going on in your life."

"Like what's going on in yours?" Jasmine said,
deciding to seat herself in one of the vacant chairs
next to her grandmother. She watched Betty Bately
pour fresh tea into her empty teacup and smiled

happily at her before returning her attention back to Carmilla. "You didn't tell Papa about the Birmingham Savoy, did you?"

Carmilla flinched at the reminder. "Don't change the subject. My business affairs are entirely different altogether. I did not need my son's consent, blessing, approval, or respect for doing what I love best, dancing. You, however, need your father's respect and you need to show him the same courtesy in return if he is to ever walk you down the aisle in marriage."

"Me, married?" Jasmine laughed at the very notion. She momentarily recollected laughing at Enrico Cajero's proposals, too, before he tried to convince her that he'd been serious. "Gran-mama, you have a wonderful imagination. I shall always try and live up to your sense of humor." She turned toward the housekeeper. "My stomach thinks that my throat has been cut. What's on the breakfast menu, Mrs. Bately?"

"She'll have a hard-boiled egg, Betty," Carmilla interrupted. "It will go perfectly with her hard-boiled head."

"Gran-mama!" Jasmine exclaimed, wounded.

Carmilla sat erect in her chair. Her hazel-colored eyes bounced with concern. "Do you know how I've worried about you since you left for New York with that . . . boar you called a boyfriend?" she asked. "You didn't listen to me then, nor did Porter, come to that. He rather enjoyed listening to me last Christmas prattle about this . . . Enrico Jax Cajero's flamboyancy, but I knew better. Now look at you."

"I thought you'd allowed me space to put that

all behind me," Jasmine answered, almost sheepishly.

"I have," Carmilla explained. "Why else would I suggest that Devon take you under his wing? He's been more than tolerant with you."

Jasmine suspected that Devon had probably complained about her after all. "I'm doing my best," she insisted truthfully.

"So Devon tells me," Carmilla accepted. "But this matter of you not calling your father or your mother worries me. Porter phoned this morning. He's thinking of coming over for your birthday, now that he knows you're here in England. Of course, this will put me in a bit of a bind."

"Explaining the Savoy," Jasmine concluded. "You've always known you'll have to tell Papa sooner or later. Are Andre and my mother coming, too?"

"Porter didn't say." Carmilla grimaced, showing her pearly-white set of false teeth in annoyance. "Let's keep to the subject. You can't keep alienating your father like this. Or me. You've been flitting around the world, with hardly a word to any member of your own family, and then you show up here when your life has turned sour. I haven't forgotten anything of what you've told me on your return a few weeks ago. What have you done with the brooch?"

"It's upstairs, in my room," Jasmine answered, charting the strong features of the woman seated next to her, hardly frail in any way at all. Carmilla was a woman who had traveled the world far more extensively than the three terms of employment Jasmine had undertaken as an au pair in Greece, Australia, and New York since leaving France. "Do you want me to go get it?"

"I'd like you to pawn it," Carmilla ordered instead. "Only then will I have no more to say on the matter. By the time your father arrives, it will look better for you if you were to have a permanent position at the Savoy. You being anchored in something concrete will put all our minds and fears at ease."

"Actually, that's what I wanted to talk to you about." Jasmine hesitated as she thought back to the decision she had made earlier during her bath. "I'm not sure if—"

"Ah, Devon," Carmilla noted, as a tall figure emerged onto the patio.

Momentarily dazzled by a strong shaft of sunlight as it peeked through the leaves of a tree, Jasmine could only see the silhouette of a man outlined against the light. As he came into focus, she saw that Devon was smartly dressed in a navy blue Dolce and Gabbana suit, pristine white shirt, and gray tie, which he fixed by pinching the knot rather majestically before he seated himself opposite her and smiled.

"Good morning, Carmilla. Mademoiselle," he added cordially.

"*Bonjour*, monsieur," Jasmine uttered, feeling moody. Even so, she was unable to prevent the white-hot spark of erotic pleasure that went soaring through her trembling limbs at the mere closeness of Devon's rugged body.

"What's with the long face?" Devon asked immediately, carefully erecting his own defenses against this woman's strong attraction.

"I've asked her to join us in church this morning," Carmilla explained. "I haven't been for a few weeks and I think it's time Jasmine received a little Gospel."

"Us?" Jasmine asked, casting her eyes wayward.

"The three of us are going together," Carmilla expanded. "I've postponed my usual church luncheon until next week on account of Bernard Augarde's barbecue this afternoon. We will be leaving directly after breakfast." She sipped more tea before adding, "I expect my sister-in-law and her husband will be at the barbecue."

"Don't antagonize them," Devon warned instantly. "We agreed you'll ignore her, remember?"

Jasmine was immediately intrigued. "What's going on?"

"Red-eyed envy," Carmilla almost spat out. "It's like a cancerous disease when it exists in one's own family. It eats away at the very good nature in people."

Jasmine sighed. "What's happened?"

"Helena Charlesworth-Smith, your great-aunt, bad-mouthed me on the night we launched the Birmingham Savoy," Carmilla began in explanation. "The wench accused me of opening the ballroom because I like to drink strong liquor," she added painfully. "I was practically accused of being an alcoholic."

"No!" Jasmine gasped, recalling Devon having hinted at some form of altercation. She had assumed that her great-aunt had attempted to upstage Carmilla on the dance floor. Now Jasmine learned that it was something quite different altogether.

"She's seventy-nine years old," Carmilla continued, "and her mouth is still as big as a catfish. There's nothing worse in life than having to explain one's innocence."

"When Carmilla told her that she only owned

the premises and not the club itself, your great-aunt—"

"Called me a liar," Carmilla finished. "My own dead husband's sister. You'd never believe she was married to the mayor, would you?"

"Wait a minute," Jasmine said, confused. "Why didn't you tell Aunt Helena the truth, that the Birmingham Savoy *is* your club?"

"Because it isn't," Carmilla breathed, shrugging helplessly. "Devon owns it. The ballroom belongs to him."

Jasmine gasped, dumbstruck.

"Why didn't you tell me?" she demanded in a whisper forty minutes later. Jasmine threw daggers with her eyes at Devon, determined to get an answer. They had stepped out of the Jeep and onto the sidewalk that led to the church's entrance. She did not want her grandmother to hear the humiliation in her voice, nor did she want to give Devon Rutherford the satisfaction of knowing how much he had succeeded in dumbfounding her, a feeling that had stayed with her long after leaving the breakfast table.

"I wanted to see how far you would go," he answered under his breath, as they both followed behind Carmilla into the church building.

"Don't think you've gotten away with this," Jasmine seethed quietly, still numbed by the impact of the news.

"I already have," Devon returned. "It's my club and you're my employee. I did warn you not to run away with any false ideas because you might be in for a nasty shock."

"It's not half as bad as the shock you're going to get when I'm through," Jasmine said, seating herself beside him in a pew with her limbs still quaking at the startling revelation.

"Shhh," Carmilla demanded, while raising her head to greet the pastor.

Devon nudged Jasmine. She returned the gesture just as harshly, digging her left elbow right into his arm. Jasmine heard the mild chuckle that left Devon's lips and cringed with the knowledge that she had not caused him the slightest pain. He was enjoying this, she realized now. He had always known that he owned the ballroom, yet he had listened to her prattle, cajole, and press her case about being the boss's granddaughter. How he must have laughed at her, she thought. The ignominy was deeply wounding.

The bombshell had also jolted her into a reality that was all too clear. She was not the lady of the Birmingham Savoy. She had no rights at all to anything. Devon paid her wages, which meant she had no right to accuse him of cooking the books either. He was the proprietor of his own business account, which meant she had no right to log online at his bank. And she certainly had no right to know his salary because he owned the club. It was all weighing on her nerves to know how stupid she had been.

The pastor opened his sermon, his loud voice carrying over the acoustics of the church, as Jasmine became aware of the underhanded manner of the man seated next to her. Devon Rutherford was the one who needed a little Gospel, she thought furiously as the bellowing voice that echoed into her eardrums hushed the congregation almost instantly. It was only seconds later before Jasmine realized that everyone was holding on dearly to the pastor's every word. He was reminding his congregation of a sermon that had once been delivered by the Reverend Peter Stanford, an African-American born into slavery, who, after surmounting numerous difficulties throughout his life, became the first black pastor of an English Baptist church in the year 1889.

Jasmine found that her anger abated as she began to listen to the amazing story about the slave who had come to England and faced libel, slander, and other hardships before marriage prepared him for his calling in life. With Devon seated by her side, she was surprised to find that her attraction toward him had not lessened, but seemed amplified within the confines of the church with its high ceiling, oak beams, organ pipes, and the large podium from which the pastor was speaking.

She was immediately transported back to her childhood when she remembered her own grandfather, Henry Charlesworth, dropping such heavy, mind-gripping sermons. Again, Jasmine was filled with the niggling suspicion that some mystery was indeed attached to her late grandfather and Devon Rutherford. She needed to know more.

Facing him, Jasmine hissed under her breath, "You told me the Birmingham Savoy was Carmilla's brainchild."

"It was," Devon whispered, casting her a sharp look directly into her eyes. "She gave me the idea."

Jasmine felt positively swayed by Devon's dark, brooding glance, knowing the very potency of it touched her spirit. But she repressed the wonderful feeling that shot through her. Instead, and quite venomously, she asked, "Then why did you—" Her question was broken before its completion.

"Shhh," Carmilla hushed.

An hour later, the church band played its final hymn after the last prayer was delivered to the congregation. Jasmine did not see Gus anywhere among the young men playing the drums, bass, or electric guitars. Only when the pastor departed did people begin to file their way out and into the courtyard. Jasmine found herself resolutely following behind her grandmother, an almost invisible human being in the shadow of Carmilla Charlesworth, who was being greeted by a flurry of church members. Devon seemed the perfect escort by Carmilla's side as he walked with her, his head high, almost aristocratic, towering regally above everyone else.

Jasmine snorted at his pompous nature. This was the man who had led her to believe all manner of things. Even now, as she thought back to the many loudmouthed flauntings of her family ties to the ballroom, she was left reeling with shame at her boastful behavior. "You'd better remember who I am and to whom the Birmingham Savoy belongs," she recalled saying, the reprehensible words echoing through her ears as she stepped out into the July noon sunlight. She had convicted herself pure and simple, and it felt even worse having to endure the entire morning, first at breakfast and then in church, with the one person who had enjoyed every moment of her miscalculation.

"Why did you have me believe that the ballroom belonged to my grandmother?" Jasmine demanded in a low tone as she came up behind Devon, unable to watch him a moment longer nodding amicably at the familiar faces.

"You wanted to believe it," he answered her cuttingly.

"I wanted the truth," she shot back, hurt by his answer.

"And I wanted to teach you a lesson," Devon added without a hint of remorse. "Can't this wait until later?"

"No," Jasmine spat out. "It can't."

She was now feeling so ashamed she could only force a fading smile at the many happy faces that brushed by her as people said their farewells and left the church courtyard. Then she spotted Lilian and Martha. They were beautifully dressed for the summer weather in shades of pastel pink and blue, with wide-brimmed straw hats, open sandal shoes, and toting small bags that were a far cry from the Louis Vuitton cases she had goaded them into carrying.

"*Bonjour.*" Jasmine approached, swiftly leaving Carmilla's and Devon's side and erecting a cordial smile on her face, disguising well the shock she was under. She needed a little space to compose herself.

"Miss Charlesworth!" Lilian blushed instantly.

"Jasmine, please, Madame," she insisted.

"How is Carmilla?" Martha queried, looking over Jasmine's head. "I heard she has not been well."

"A little sunstroke not so long ago," Jasmine admitted, glancing over her shoulder across the courtyard to find where her grandmother and Devon were located. Carmilla was with a small brigade of Bible thumpers, deeply immersed in conversation, with Devon steadfast by her side. "The temperature swell to 82 degrees was too much for her. But it's cooler today and she is much better now, as you can see."

"How are you finding *him?*" Lilian asked suddenly, before quickly biting her bottom lip.

The comment did not go undetected by Jasmine. "Monsieur Rutherford?" she asked for clarification. Her own guilt and remorse rose up to torment her. "Quite frankly, I find him imperiously tyrannical."

"You too?" Lilian probed with deep suspicion. "Ever since he came into your grandmother's life, he has been nothing but controlling."

"In what way?" Jasmine asked curiously.

"He takes up all of Carmilla's time," Martha added. "We only get to see her at the church or the luncheons she has on Sundays if we have time to go along. But before he came we used to see her many times during the week."

"And he's arrogant," Lilian continued.

Jasmine didn't dare deny that. She nodded quite emphatically.

"He practically forced Carmilla into having him live at the house and . . ." Martha hesitated. "I wouldn't be surprised if he has some kind of hold over her."

It was Jasmine's turn to look at the two old ladies. "What do you mean?"

Lilian decided to come right out with it. "It's my opinion that Devon Rutherford is Henry Charlesworth's—"

"Jasmine!" Carmilla's voice broke in, shattering Lilian's last word into shreds. "It's time we were leaving."

"Coming, Gran-mama," Jasmine uttered, wondering what secret Lilian was about to disclose. She glanced across at the two elderly women. "Talk to me again when you see me," she insisted, before quickly rushing to the side of her grandmother. As she hurried toward the Jeep, Jasmine was left feeling as if she had pulled her first bucket of water from Devon Rutherford's secret well.

They arrived outside the Right Honorable Minister of Parliament Bernard Augarde's huge mansion home on a tree-lined street in the suburb of Edgbaston, thirty-five minutes later. All the while, Jasmine remained quiet throughout the trip, as her anger toward Devon had not completely abated but was still rumbling inside her empty stomach. She knew that Devon was aware of her awkward silence, because on at least five occasions he had taken his eyes off the road to glance around at her. She was in the backseat, where he noticed the forlorn expression on her face, before turning back to face the traffic again.

Finally, when Devon pulled the Jeep into the large private driveway and parked inside the estate grounds, Jasmine knew she could no longer keep quiet. The last few hours had rankled her nerves. She had tried to calm herself, but it seemed impossible to do so when Devon was behaving as though he was not responsible for the miserable way she was feeling.

"When did you decide you wanted to teach me a lesson?" she demanded after they had stepped out of the Jeep and Carmilla had taken a hold of Devon's arm. They headed toward the mansion's front doors.

For the first time, Devon began to see that Jasmine was not going to let the subject go. In fact, he had never seen her look so hurt until that moment. He should've been lapping it all up, enjoying the flagrant glory of having put Jasmine Charlesworth in her place. But Devon was not feeling so good about his actions. Throughout the entire morning, Jasmine had done nothing but niggle at him about her damaged emotions, and to his chagrin, Devon was beginning to feel a sense of pity at having caused her such humiliation, even though he was still enraged at the things she had told him.

"It was around the time you announced you were back in town to keep an eye on your grandmother's investment," he replied flatly, close to her ear so that Carmilla was not aware of the friction between them. "And then you wanted to see the accounts."

Jasmine flinched at her own ill-timed declaration. "I . . . I—"

"Dame Carmilla Charlesworth!" Bernard Augarde's deep baritone intruded, as the front doors were swung open to admit his newest arrivals. He picked up Carmilla's hand and kissed it, his eyes holding hers. "Come on through."

Jasmine recognized the deep brown eyes, broad nose, fleshy lips, and the mass of gray hair on Bernard's head and face as she made her own informal greeting. They were welcomed into the vast hallway where a waitress immediately arrived with a tray of cocktails. Taking a claret punch and offering the same to his guests, Bernard showed them through to the garden. The garden was full of people, a mix of racial backgrounds, drinking, chatting, and enjoying the bright summer afternoon. With the July sun beating down overhead, it promised to be a relaxing afternoon.

"It's not as grand as the mayor's house," Bernard said, laughing, as he surveyed all that he owned, "but of course your sister-in-law wouldn't settle for anything less."

Carmilla nodded her agreement.

"People who share the same adversaries often become friends," Jasmine was to overhear the M.P. tell her grandmother, in direct reference to the latest standoff between her great-aunt and Carmilla. "Let me introduce you to Katherine Dunham," he said in a hospitable tone. "She's an African-American originally from Glen Ellyn near Chicago and was named the first one hundred of America's irreplaceable "dance treasures" by the Dance Coalition. In 2002, she also received special recognition from Jacobs Pillow, one of the leading dance retreats in the world. I thought you'd like to meet her."

"We've met," Carmilla enthused excitedly. "When I was five years old." Carmilla would also recall that she had danced under Katherine's tutelage on her second visit to America when Katherine Dunham was a dance director for the Negro Federal Theater Project in 1938. Carmilla was fifteen and after her return to Jamaica, Katherine had moved on to work for the New York Labor Stage in 1939. "I wonder if she still remembers me. Where is she?"

"Over here," Bernard indicated.

As Carmilla was swept away, Jasmine turned and faced Devon. They were slowly walking about the lawn, milling between a cluster of people, paying no attention to anyone in particular, when she began, "About the accounts." It was in preparation to offering him an apology.

"Ah yes." Devon picked up on the topic immediately, quietly venting his fury once again. "You were feisty enough to tell me that after you had learned how to run the place, inside and out . . . yes, I think that was what you said, you would be controlling the Birmingham Savoy!"

Jasmine blinked hard as she recalled her foolhardiness. "I—"

"I should've bounced you out on your ear, like I said I would," Devon ranted, discreetly throwing a false smile at the familiar face of a blond-haired woman he recognized from across the garden. "And I was going to until Carmilla insisted you help me at the club."

"She said I needed a sense of direction." Jasmine repeated her grandmother's words for emphasis, realizing that Devon was paying more attention to what was going on around him than he was to her. "But you thought I was playing games."

"You declared you were going to watch me like a hawk," Devon reminded her, nodding a greeting to two other people. "So I let you."

"Under false pretenses and deception," Jasmine answered, galled. "When I asked you about the rental, thinking the place to be some backwater tin shack, you told me my grandmother owned the premises. Naturally, I assumed that meant the business."

"You assumed wrong," Devon said, gloating. He led the way onto a path that took them down toward a stream at the foot of the garden.

"Gibson told me you and my grandmother were partners," Jasmine stated, aware of the whirl of voices fading into the distance. "Is that true?"

"You shouldn't believe everything Gibson tells

you," Devon cautioned ruefully. "He's very good at idle talk that has no basis in fact."

"He said that Carmilla believed in you," Jasmine added, treading from the path to a grassy verge. "Are you saying I should not believe that either?"

"Your grandmother gave me the head start I needed," Devon acknowledged with a faint smile. "That's true enough. She was like a fairy godmother in many ways. Because of her, I was able to begin my life again."

Jasmine raised a thoughtful eyebrow. "Why do I get the feeling you're not telling me everything?"

"Maybe I'm not," Devon admitted, with a sudden playful smile that broadened a little as they approached a makeshift wooden bridge. As they walked along the planks to the other side, Jasmine grew nervous.

She panicked, now recalling the message Petronella had taken on the office phone from Carmilla. "What information are you withholding?"

"The fact that I would rather like to kiss you again," Devon blatantly confessed, stopping in his tracks.

Jasmine quickly glanced away and kept on walking lest Devon catch her reaction. She observed a flock of birds twittering among the trees facing her and tried to calm the flutter in her stomach caused by Devon's comment. This was the man who had only moments ago openly confessed to having taught her a lesson. The same man she had now discovered was her boss. Surely Devon Rutherford could not possibly be expecting her to reward his reckless efforts with any form of intimacy. What did this man take her for, a masochist?

"How much punishment do you think I deserve,

monsieur?" Jasmine queried, successfully keeping the tremor in her voice at bay.

Devon's shoulders shook at the put-down. "Of course, my mistake," he recalled, suddenly regaining his composure. "You did mention that a kiss would be something I'd never have the privilege of taking from you again."

"*Oui,*" Jasmine agreed, quickening her pace and not daring to look behind. "You are wasting your time."

"You're right," Devon admitted, refusing to follow her. "I'll probably need a tetanus shot. Moreover, I don't suppose any man, with you being an ice queen an' all, is going to find it easy to thaw you out."

It was Jasmine's turn to stop in her tracks. Her back felt rigid as she turned murderously and found Devon standing close to the bridge, his hands now in his trouser pockets and a fair amount of yardage between them. Behind his tall, muscular figure she could glimpse the house and the myriad of guests chattering among themselves as their feet trod across the lawn. Someone must have fired up the charcoal, because she could also see swirls of smoke rise up to meet the flawless blue sky. The smell of barbecued chicken and corn on the cob began to fill the air.

With her stomach churning not only from a craving for lunch, but from fury at being disparaged coupled with her strong attraction toward Devon, it was hard for Jasmine to reconcile what she felt most. Hunger. Anger. Or lust? In truth, she could have eaten Devon with her eyes. Determined to keep her wayward senses under control, she decided not to rise to the challenge of his brown, soul-searching gaze. Instead, she slowly retraced her footsteps until she was within five inches of him.

"The ideal temperature for my body is ninety-eight degrees," she answered, unprovoked, yet feeling a tightening of the muscles in her stomach. "One of your kisses wouldn't even get my pulse pumping."

Devon took two steps toward her. "What about your heart?" Undeterred, he reached out and touched her bottom lip. "The last time I kissed you, it melted."

"No, it didn't," Jasmine protested heatedly.

"Do you want to bet?"

One tug was all it took to pull Jasmine back into his arms. Before the moment could take shape, the pressure of Devon's lips was on hers. Jasmine's response took her by complete surprise. She hadn't so much thawed but evaporated with the touch of Devon's fire. Who was this man who had the power to turn her from ice into a steaming mass of ultrasensitive vapor?

His mouth swept over hers with a familiarity that left her breathless. Deeply provoking, intensely arousing, maddeningly tempting, his kiss completely dissolved Jasmine. She was enjoying every moment of Devon's persuasion. The way he had captured her lips as if she were bait, his sliding motion that warmed up and softened every fiber of her body, and the way his tongue ever so lightly delved into her mouth for a fleeting taste of her passion were such that she could not deny herself such perfect joy.

It was the distant burst of laughter from Bernard Augarde's guests that eventually drew them apart. Even so, the disjoining was a lengthy play of nib-

bles along the neckline, a return to the lips for another lapse into time, and then a few swaying moments of coming to terms with the realization
that they were beginning to feel something beyond
a taming of one another.

Devon spoke first. "All thawed out?" he asked.

Jasmine took a long shuddering breath. "Completely."

Having successfully stolen another kiss, Devon
said, "We should talk."

"I know."

"We should tell Carmilla," he prompted, resolved that he had still yet to seduce her.

"No."

"No?"

"She'll interfere."

Devon gently rubbed Jasmine's shoulders, his determination unshaken. "I thought her approval
mattered to you."

"It does," she answered sullenly.

"Then why—"

"My grandmother would like nothing more than
to neatly tie me up with string," Jasmine proclaimed, now realizing that working with Devon
would soon entail some unexpected and unfore-
seen complications. "She has ideas of seeing my
father walk me down the aisle."

"Marriage!" Devon exclaimed.

"You said it, not me," Jasmine joked. "So you see, I'd
rather she didn't know that we're . . . you know . . ."

"French-kissing," Devon finished smugly.

"I just don't want her getting hopeful, that's all,"
Jasmine concluded. "You understand, don't you?"

"Quite frankly, no," Devon admitted. "I respect

Carmilla very much. I'll feel uncomfortable keeping anything from her."

"It's not like we're in a relationship," Jasmine said softly. "I'm not asking you to lie, if that's what you're thinking. Just, let's keep this to ourselves, for now." She looked across at the guests. Her nose was quickly becoming invigorated by the smell of the barbecue. "Let's go back up to the house."

"Jasmine." Devon restrained her as she took her first few steps. "You're not ashamed, are you?"

"Of what?"

"I don't know." Devon shrugged, shaking his head. "Being with me, your grandmother's godson?"

"No," Jasmine responded with a half smile. She was more than aware that she had already called him a charity case, and though Gibson had scolded her for it, if Jasmine was entirely honest she would be the first to admit that it was already on her mind. "Like I said," she defended, "I don't want Carmilla getting any marital ideas."

"What about this guy you left back in New York?" Devon probed, unsure. He was suddenly filled with a heart-wrenching notion that there was some other reason why she was taking things slowly.

"The lowlife!" Jasmine spat out. "That liar is precisely where I left him, in New York, and that's where he'll be staying." She smiled sweetly, keeping control. "Let's go eat."

He respected her decision, but Devon did not like the taste it left in his mouth. "Okay."

They strolled back up toward the house in relative silence. It had more to do with the awareness that not only did they want to be together, but that their burgeoning relationship would need careful handling. At least this was the case in Jasmine's mind. Having left one situation, she was not in the right frame of mind to rebound into another, even though she could not recall responding to any other man the way she had done with Devon Rutherford.

There was also her lack of knowledge about him. Everything seemed unclear and mysterious. Lilian said he had practically forced her grandmother to let him stay at the house. Was this true and if so, why? Did Devon really have some kind of control over Carmilla? And why, given all this, did she feel so drawn to him? Even now, Jasmine gave in to the moment and allowed herself the luxury of watching Devon walk, pantherlike, in front of her. A man prowling, ready to pounce.

Jasmine inhaled a deep breath. Everything that was female inside her instinctively recognized the male animal giving her such wonderful primal shivers. They were within easy reach of the house when she was forced to divert her gaze and compose herself. Carmilla was laughing with Katherine Dunham and her local M.P., and a few of the guests had recognized Devon walking with her along the path toward the barbecue. It wasn't long before they were pulled into a curious crowd of people.

"Good walk?" someone asked.

Devon nodded. "Yes,"

"Anything worth doing down there?" another person pried, working his eyes from Jasmine to Devon.

Kissing, Devon mused wickedly. "Fishing, I expect," he answered in a hoarse breath.

"Hello again," a blond-haired newcomer suddenly intruded, walking directly toward Devon. "Remember me? Hyacinth Berkley. I visited your ballroom at the launch?"

"Ah yes." Devon smiled at the young white Caribbean woman, dressed in a long yellow dress with a pale blue silk scarf around her neck that complemented the color of her sandals. He turned toward the woman he'd just been blissfully kissing, hoping he was not betraying any sign of deep, overriding emotion. "Allow me to introduce Jasmine Charlesworth. She's Carmilla's granddaughter."

"Any relation to Helena Charlesworth-Smith?" the woman inquired suddenly.

"My great-aunt," Jasmine acknowledged with a nod of her head.

"You must be proud to have two remarkable women in your life," Hyacinth said pertly. "How does it feel to be standing next to the man who is responsible for denying your great-aunt the courtesy of using the Birmingham Savoy as a venue for the Jamaican Independence Day charity gala in August?"

"What?" Jasmine asked, confused.

"The decision was mine," Carmilla suddenly interrupted, forcing her way through the crowd to Devon's defense, having recognized Hyacinth from where she'd been standing. "I have my own personal reasons for asking Helena Charlesworth-Smith to seek some place else to hold her gala."

"I'm on the board of the charity's steering committee," Hyacinth declared in earnest, "and am helping to organize the event. We were hoping to rely on your generosity."

"That old windbag doesn't deserve any good gesture from me or my godson," Carmilla objected sternly. "She should have thought about my good intentions before she accused me of being an alcoholic."

"I'm sure as partners of the club," Hyacinth implored, "that you could both agree—"

"Mr. Devon Rutherford is the sole owner of the Birmingham Savoy," Carmilla declared flatly. "He has been these past few days since acquiring the freehold to the land and property. It was what his godfather would've wanted and he is sticking firmly to the decision we made prior to the transfer. So you can tell Helena that I am now a visiting guest at the Savoy, just like anybody else."

"But—" Hyacinth began.

"We have nothing more to say," Carmilla replied. "Good-bye, Miss Berkley."

Jasmine had remained in awe as she watched her grandmother take control. But as the matter of everything Carmilla had said began to sink in, a coillike feeling of doom crept up and wriggled its way throughout her innards. Something Jasmine had missed was beginning to slip into place. *Why do I get the feeling you're not telling me everything?* her mind struggled. It didn't seem possible for her to be learning more information than what she had been told already. Surely not. But as her mind absorbed Carmilla's comment, Jasmine felt the prickle of tears at the back of her eyelids.

"So that's what you've omitted telling me," she started, staring steadfastly at Devon, realizing he had expertly dodged the subject by offering her a kiss. "You *own* the premises, too?"

"Jasmine," he breathed, guilt mirrored across his face.

"Is that the transaction Petronella was talking about?" she gasped.

"Jasmine, it's not like that," Devon promised. "It's not what you think."

"He's right," Carmilla cut in, deciding to disclose the truth to her granddaughter at last. "I'm going back to Jamaica, Jasmine. It's time for me to go home."

Chapter Seven

"Just find the nearest hotel, now," Johnny ordered, feeling tired, restless, and hungry.

Enrico Cajero and his unwelcome companion had just departed London's underground network at Gloucester Road Station and needed shelter for the night. As Enrico scurried along, looking for the nearest building that suggested two decent beds they could camp out in, he worried further about his predicament. He was still trying to figure out where his system for scoping out bad men had gone wrong when they approached a five-story beige-colored building. Five minutes later, they were handed a key to their room. The three-star hotel had not yet adapted to electronic swipe cards, but had been courteous enough at checking them into one of the twin bedrooms that were available.

"You're still sharing with me," Johnny the Bear declared, before they took three flights of stairs on foot.

For all his six feet five inches of arrogance and boorish and menacing behavior, Johnny did not like elevators. The room itself was clean enough, offering a private bathroom, direct-dial tele-

phone, and tea/coffee-making facilities. Their
trek around Paris looking for Jasmine Charlesworth had been spent seeking respite in the
many cheap bed-and-breakfast accommodations
easily found in the big city. He was equally surprised that their arrival to another big city should
cause Johnny to agree they should get their first
decent night's sleep in more pleasant surroundings since their journey began.

"I can order up some food," he was bold enough
to say, while kicking off his cap-toe shoes and testing the spring in his bed. "What would you like?"

"To kill you," Johnny declared. He was at the
window closing the drapes. The eight-hundred-
buck embroidered green silk jacket, cream-
colored jersey, and beige silk crepe de chine cargo
pants he had picked up in Paris were wrinkled and
needed pressing. His attitude was most definitely
troublesome. "I should be in Lisbon right now, with
my girl. Because of you, I had to return with Van
Phoenix to New York to find you. Then to France
to find your ex-girlfriend. Now I'm in London
and tomorrow, we have to go look for her again in
Birmingham."

Enrico wasn't feeling too good about any of it
himself. He hadn't had the luxury of changing
clothes in Paris, and so was still wearing the same
double-breasted suit he had been forced to leave
New York in. His black hair was raked carelessly,
hardly in the sleek ponytail he usually wore, but
drooped toward the back of his neck. His last contact with a razor had been two days ago. He looked
rumpled and very much an amateur in contrast to
Johnny's distinguished international style.

"What do you want me to say?" he prodded,

watching Johnny pull a handful of nuts from his jacket pocket. "I'm a thief, just like you. I stole your boss's brooch, okay?"

Johnny cracked a nut. "What do you mean, like me?" he grunted, popping the nut into his mouth.

"C'mon," Enrico drawled, sounding a tad more confident about his situation. "I know you and that Dutchman, Van Phoenix, must've got them stones from some place you shouldn't have taken them from. That's why you want them back. Figures. What are they, blood diamonds?" he asked. "Are they stained, metaphorically speaking, with the blood of the wars that have been fought throughout Africa, which is where they came from."

"Shut up," Johnny snarled, dropping the empty nut shell to the carpeted floor.

"A blessing and a curse to the Continent, they say," Enrico continued regardless. "Murders, mutilations . . . a brutal business, but with such rewards at stake, man's capacity for savagery knows no bounds."

"I said button it," Johnny shouted, throwing his handful of nuts directly at the Puerto Rican.

"What's the deal?" Enrico inquired, attempting to escape the hangman's noose around his neck. "Drugs, artillery, explosives, tanks? I got connections. I can help you 'cause your head must be in the same guillotine as mine for the chop and—"

"Is that right?" Johnny interrupted, walking directly across the room toward Enrico. Taking a hold of his jacket, he tossed Jax like an old rag onto the nearest bed. "I ain't gonna take a bullet for no one."

"And I'm gonna help you get the brooch back. I promise," Enrico pleaded in earnest, though he was not so frightened now. They were in England where Johnny could not get away too easily with carrying a gun. Had they been back in New York, police might well have been marking out a chalked outline on the floor the following morning for another murder. "So don't kill me, all right?"

Johnny grinned mightily at the possibility. "I don't like you," he growled. "We get back what Van Phoenix wants. Anything after that is a separate negotiation."

Enrico had never felt his life in such jeopardy, but he kept his cool. "Believe me, I don't like you neither, so the feeling's mutual," he admitted caustically. "But let's be rational about this. We need to eat. I know I do."

"Yeah." Johnny nodded, rubbing his stomach while staring at the nuts scattered across the floor. "I'll take anything with a steak."

Enrico eagerly leaped for the phone while Johnny fired up a cigarette.

Jasmine's eyes misted over a little, but she blinked them clear. She didn't feel like joining Carmilla just yet, while her nerves were unsettled. Up in her room, looking through the window at the pond her grandmother loved so much, she realized how much she had begun to regard this room as her own. It had always been the place she stayed whenever she came to visit Carmilla, and she had grown to love it almost as much as her grandmother did.

Now everything felt so uncertain. Jasmine had been unable to go into work that day. She had watched from the staircase window as Devon drove away in the Jeep. Since being told the news that her grandmother wanted to go back home, Jasmine had spoken very little to either Devon or Carmilla.

Instead, she left the barbecue in relative silence after listening to their lame explanations for not having told her sooner. She had gone to bed dispirited and awoke only to remain holed up in her room all morning.

"It wasn't my place to tell you," Devon said trying to explain it to her in the Jeep on the ride home from the barbecue.

"I wanted to tell you when your parents and brother had arrived, after your birthday," Carmilla added.

"So Andre *is* coming," was Jasmine's only response.

It would be nice to see her brother again, she thought now with a faint smile. She couldn't imagine it would bother him in the slightest where their grandmother lived. Andre had never been quite as close to Carmilla as she was. His only love in life was writing songs. It was his dream to become a record producer, which was why Andre was studying music and musicology at the Université Paris IV Sorbonne in France. After his studies, he would probably enjoy the trip out to Jamaica to see his ailing old grandmother. Not her. She was devastated.

"Take the day off work tomorrow," Devon had encouraged, as she hurried into the house.

"We'll talk about this more then," Carmilla finished, seeing that her granddaughter was thoroughly distraught.

But Jasmine did not want to talk about it. She wanted to scream. How could her grandmother do this to her? And why would she want to leave England anyway? Carmilla had spent most of her life here. Okay, she had married Pastor Henry Charlesworth when she was a mere eighteen years old while in the Caribbean, but they had made England their home. Her grandmother had given birth to Porter, her father, right here in Birmingham. Carmilla had seen many of the changes within the Caribbean community over much of her lifetime. It seemed a tragedy to Jasmine that such a cultural icon, which was how she viewed her grandmother, should be leaving England.

Jasmine found herself marching from her bedroom, down the corridor, and then the flight of stairs toward the living room. It was 5:33 p.m. when she ambled, still dressed in her nightgown, into the room to find Carmilla sitting comfortably in front of the television with all the windows open, allowing the July evening breeze to sweep in. The sun had moved to the side of the house, making the air feel much cooler.

Carmilla turned her attention from the television set long enough to acknowledge Jasmine as she entered. She was already feeling quite guilty about her granddaughter's state. She had told Devon Rutherford much more than she had her own flesh and blood, and it was hardly surprising to her that Jasmine should react in the way she did.

"Mrs. Bately has left you some food in the oven before she went home," Carmilla informed her. "I hope you're not still sulking, because you haven't eaten all day."

Jasmine walked right up to the sofa on which her grandmother was sitting and stood over her, showing her distress. "Why didn't you tell me?"

"Jasmine, sit down," Carmilla instructed calmly.

"No," she protested.

"Sit, please." Carmilla patted a vacant space next to her. When she watched her granddaughter deposit herself, she placed a consoling hand on Jasmine's knee. "I have thought about this for a long time," she began slowly. "It was something your grandfather and I always said we would do."

"But he's—"

"Gone, I know," Carmilla admitted softly. "And I have made the best that I can of living here, alone, without him. It has never been easy. With your own father, my only child, in France where he has lived most of his married life, my life has become . . . an existence."

"You have your friends," Jasmine quivered.

"Yes, I do," Carmilla agreed. "Many of them, from the church. That's why I started doing the luncheons five years ago, two years after Henry passed away, to connect with people again. But it has not been enough."

Jasmine searched her mind. "There's your garden."

"Tended so well it yearns to be left alone."

"What about the Birmingham Savoy?" she said finally, her heart sinking when she suddenly remembered whose project it really was. "You at least liked the spirit . . . and vibrancy of life it gave you to be involved."

"It belongs to Devon," Carmilla proclaimed.

"Why did you sell the premises to him?" Jasmine snapped. "Why have you given him so much control over everything?"

"Jasmine!" Carmilla was shocked by her granddaughter's outburst. "It has been the most wonderful delight to have my godson enter my life. You have no idea of what he has been through. None at all."

"Then tell me," Jasmine prompted, holding back

the tears. "I want to know why you told that woman at the barbecue that my grandfather would've wanted Devon to have so much of what was rightfully yours."

"Jasmine, the Savoy building was something I purchased temporarily for Devon," Carmilla explained. "It was all done with his money. He would not take one penny of anything I wanted to contribute, even though Henry had left him a small inheritance. The building was bought ahead of his arrival in England in my name, and once the project was completed, licenses, red tape, and all the paperwork were rubber-stamped, Devon can now sign on the dotted line."

"Why?" Jasmine demanded, as though she had not understood anything. "Is it because he's an American?"

"There is some truth in that." Carmilla nodded, keeping her voice calm and equable. "There were some matters he had to deal with before he flew over to England. My acting on his behalf at the time was simply to save time."

"So you bought the building and freehold—"

"Just the building in September, last year," Carmilla answered. "I already owned the freehold after Henry died."

"And Devon came over in October, right?"

"Yes."

"Then what happened?"

"We spent some time together discussing what he could do," Carmilla explained. "He wanted to restart his life again, in England."

"Why?" Jasmine demanded again.

"Because he had been through a bad time in New York," Carmilla said firmly. "And he wanted

to meet me." She hesitated. "The only time I'd seen Devon was in 1974, the year he was born. It was on your grandfather's and my last visit to America."

"But you said the last time you visited was after Martin Luther King died," Jasmine recalled, curiously. "That was 1968."

"I know," Carmilla acknowledged. "I didn't want to talk about it. His father, Ralston, was Henry's godson. How he came into existence was a tragedy of sorts. It all happened a long time ago."

"Gran-mama, you are not making much sense," Jasmine chided her with a hint of frustration. "What's the mystery?"

Carmilla's eyes glazed over. She was transported to the past, to a time and age Jasmine knew very little about. "Your grandfather promised Miss Gracie he would always be a good godfather to Ralston, and he was. When Ralston got married, we were both there. His wife was very beautiful. We were invited to Devon's christening, too. That's when I became his godmother, before the two girls in Jamaica that I'm also custodian of."

Jasmine leaped into action. "That doesn't answer much of why Devon is here. Why he's living in this house."

"I invited him to stay here," Carmilla went on. "He's entitled to be here as much as you are."

"I blame him for why you're leaving," Jasmine admonished. "Had it not been for him making you feel you had done all that you could for a lifetime, you would be . . . at least planting more bulbs in your garden."

"This has nothing to do with Devon, my wanting to go home," Carmilla started, annoyed at her granddaughter's tone. "I was born in Jamaica. I want to go home."

Jasmine almost wept at hearing her grandmother's determination. "Daddy won't let you go back. He would—"

"Like to continue his life in France with Patti, your mother," Carmilla concluded. "And I've allowed him to do that, live his life. Now it's my turn to live mine."

"But what about the Savoy?" Jasmine pleaded again, trying to stop the tears as she looked at her grandmother. "You always told me how much you *love* to dance. You could still work with Devon, like you did before. He needs your help."

"He has you now," Carmilla said sweetly with a glint of hope in her eyes. "Why else would I have encouraged him to take you on?"

"So that you can watch him keep my nose to the grindstone?" Jasmine quipped.

Carmilla chuckled. "There is that."

"I'm a qualified au pair," Jasmine said, controlling her voice as she wiped the tears away from her cheeks. "I like working with young children. Babies. I miss that kind of work. I'd like to go back to it. This was only supposed to be a vacation. You can't expect me to fill your shoes working with Devon."

Carmilla patted her granddaughter's hand. "Of course you might want to do the work you were trained to do, but the feel of enterprise is in your blood now and it will always be there when you're ready for it, and so will I."

Jasmine felt a tremor run through her limbs. The future stretched bleakly ahead. There would always be work at the agency, she thought, though the prospect of adventurous foreign travel suddenly felt empty. All those happy families . . . and she was always alone, a little apart from the rest of the household, because of the nature of her work as an au pair, tending only to the children and sometimes more lonely than any of them would ever have guessed. Carmilla will not always be there, she realized that now, but Devon would. And yet her grandmother's conviction sounded almost like a prophecy that however much she fought against it, something stronger than herself would bring her back to Birmingham.

"I can't," she muttered.

"Devon needs you," Carmilla urged with an earnestness that caught Jasmine's attention. If she had noticed her granddaughter's face look more heated than usual, she wisely said nothing. "When I return to Jamaica, I want to be sure that you both have a future."

"Together?"

"Well, that would be up to you both," Carmilla said, hopefully. "Don't you feel anything for him?"

"Gran-mama," Jasmine bellowed, now feeling anger erupt inside her. "How can I have a life, let alone a romance with someone who refuses to tell me anything about himself? Everything about *your* godson's background is an enigma. If you're going home to Jamaica, then I'm going back to New York."

"You selfish girl," Carmilla suddenly snapped.

Jasmine was instantly silent.

Carmilla sighed heavily. "Devon witnessed a brutal murder only two months after his own parents had been killed and all you can talk about is returning to that city where you can easily become a target." She tried to compose herself. "He came here to the nearest thing he had left, me. To start his life again. Your grandfather would've wanted me to offer him all the help that I could, and I have. Devon's a good man, especially to have survived the whole awful ordeal."

"I . . . I didn't know," Jasmine replied, stunned. "What happened to him?"

"It is for Devon to tell you about his life," Carmilla remarked sadly. "His own grandmother had also seen many tragedies in her own life. For many years, your grandfather and I felt responsible for what happened to Miss Gracie. Then to lose her husband before Ralston was a grown man was another tragedy. I had every reason to help Devon, more than you know. He has not inherited anything more than my own son will receive after I have gone. The freehold to the land including the parking lot of the Savoy is all I have given him. The building and the business are Devon's own investments."

Jasmine nodded. "I'm sorry, Gran-mama."

"And so you should be," Carmilla continued. "It's bad enough having to deal with all the gossip-mongering of my own sister-in-law. No doubt, I shall back down and encourage Devon to allow her to use the club for her Independence Day gala, for I rarely hold malice with people who cannot help themselves."

Jasmine recalled her grandmother's recent altercation. "I think that would be the kindest thing," she said, not wanting to see her grandmother caught up in any sort of disagreement. "I think she will miss you."

"Helena will most likely follow me out there," Carmilla quipped. "That old battle-ax likes nothing more than to have a good sparring or two with me. We were both quite fiery young ladies when the war was over. Back then, white folks used to call us colored people. I remember when your grandfather bought this house. He was probably the first black man in Birmingham to buy one in 1953." Carmilla looked around the living room. "A whole family used to live in this one room alone. Pastor Henry rented each room to West Indians who flooded into England during the fifties and sixties, and used the money to pay off the mortgage. We never entirely had this house to ourselves until 1970, I think, when the last family moved out."

"They owe you a great deal."

"Not at all." Carmilla smiled generously. "We felt it was our duty, after the war, though the house was very cold in winter. We had never experienced cold weather before coming to England, nor had we seen snow. That fire right there"—she pointed at the modern-day gas heater housed inside the Roman hand-carved stone fireplace—"was always filled with coal. You threw some paper money into it once before we installed gas during the eighties."

"I remember when you washed the steps outside," Jasmine suddenly recalled, her mind going back to her childhood, "and that white English woman from across the street came over and threw a bucket of dirty water all over them because your steps were cleaner than hers. What a telling you gave her. How old was I? Four, I think?"

"It was on one of your visits, after your father had moved to Paris," Carmilla recalled, digging into the far recesses of her mind. "Racism never left us. I've seen a lot of it in my time. You and your father were in France when the riots hit Birmingham. So many changes, too." She sighed.

Jasmine looked around the vast expanse of the living room, trying hard to imagine what it had been like for a migrant family of three, four or even five people sharing one space. The room hardly seemed big enough to accommodate her and her own grandmother seated in front of the television. The handwoven rug and furniture made the space appear smaller and less expansive than what it was. Even so, it must've been hard to sleep, bathe, and share the same pee pot in one room.

"So many memories," she said in a whisper.

"Porter may've been an only child, but he had so many children in this house to play with," Carmilla expanded on a lighter chuckle. "That garden out there has seen more cricket games than the West Indian Championships."

"What do you think Papa would say?" Jasmine probed, trying to get a feel of whether her grandmother was making the right decision.

"He'll be relieved, probably." Carmilla smiled. "I've threatened it for many years. I think he knows it's now the right time."

"And this house?"

"Porter will know what to do with it," was all Carmilla would say.

Jasmine sighed, understanding more about this remarkable woman than she had ever done before. "I'll come and stay with you."

"It's a beach house in Negril," Carmilla immediately enthused. "Far too flamboyant for a woman of my age, but of course Henry liked it, which was why he bought it. He had no idea that he would profit so handsomely from buying so much property when he did. I couldn't bear to sell this one after he passed."

"Gran-mama, that's wonderful," Jasmine gasped. "I can now think of you as a Caribbean madame living her life of leisure."

They both chuckled and Jasmine snuggled closer to her grandmother, talking until they had exhausted themselves on the subject of the little island in the sun. Later that evening, Jasmine went to the kitchen and heated up her meal while her grandmother took a soak in the bathroom upstairs. Seated at the kitchen table, she ate alone, swirling the last potato on her plate around in the gravy left in the center before popping it into her mouth. As she did so, she felt a breeze come from the front door.

Jasmine's instincts were immediately roused. There was only her and Carmilla in the house. Betty Bately had gone home. Devon had gone to the Birmingham Savoy and was not expected back until the early hours of the morning, certainly after 2:00 a.m. when the club had closed. She placed the fork on her plate and rose slowly from her chair. Her grandmother splashing water around in her bath was a distant sound. The noise of the front door closing was much closer. Jasmine cautiously stepped into the hallway, taking furtive steps in the direction of the door, and then gasped her relief when she saw Devon emerge in front of her.

"Jasmine!" He said her name with all the seductiveness of a caress.

"What are you doing back so early?" she breathed, looking into a pair of brown eyes swimming with enough concern that she just wanted to dive into their depths.

"I wanted to see if you and Carmilla were all right," Devon explained, allowing his gaze to rove over her in a leisurely male fashion. "You were not talking to either one of us when I left."

Jasmine's heart knocked against her ribs. "I was angry, that's all," she murmured.

"And now?"

"Gran-mama and I have talked," she admitted softly. "We've straightened it all out."

"Good." Devon smiled.

Jasmine liked the way his eyes lit up at the news. "Coffee?"

"I'd love some." He followed her into the kitchen and took a seat, seeing the empty plate on the table. "You've only just eaten?"

Jasmine shrugged, reaching for the kettle to fill it with water. "I couldn't earlier. Not with . . . you know . . . Gran-mama telling me that she's going home."

"I didn't realize it would've been such a shock for you," Devon said easily. "But I suppose if you've always known her to live here all your life . . ."

Jasmine switched the electric kettle on and turned to face Devon. She thought back to all her grandmother had told her about him. "When we talked," she began, "Gran-mama told me you'd gone through a bad time in New York."

"What did she tell you exactly?" Devon asked, his voice filled with more than a hint of panic.

"Nothing much, except that I'm to ask you," Jasmine declared, detecting the shift in Devon's tone. She wanted to know everything about him. Keeping up the pretense of an unfulfilled longing was not in her nature, especially when everything she'd ever wanted in a man was facing her, there for the taking. "You don't need to get defensive with me."

"I'm not," Devon snapped. "It was one thing you probing into my business affairs—"

"Which you lied about," Jasmine said.

"Now this," he bristled.

"What?" Jasmine demanded hotly.

Devon glared at her. Jasmine could see why she was so attracted to him. He was a challenge to her. She imagined herself a challenge to him, too, which was probably why he still made bold advances toward her, like at the barbecue. Jasmine realized she was as strong a character as Devon himself. They were both the kind of people who needed strong partners. Enrico had never been enough for her, nor could she imagine Petronella to be for Devon. The waitress was far too ordinary and bland. She, on the other hand, was spirited and vivacious. A damned sight more determined, too.

"I'm going back to the club," Devon declared, rising from his seat.

"Devon, wait!" Jasmine was by his side in an instant. They stared wordlessly into each other's eyes before she spoke. "One of these days, when you least expect me, when you're totally off your guard, when you're distracted with work and your mind is not quite your own, that's when I'll get in here." She pointed directly at his rib cage, at the spot that housed his heart. "And then you'll have to tell me everything."

"Jasmine," Devon whispered. "I wish . . ." His voice faltered. His expression held such torment, Jasmine instantly found herself facing a tortured soul.

"Devon?"

She touched his cheek. Instinct guided her hand

to drop to his neck. Then she had her arms around him in a consoling embrace. Devon jerked her inward, molding Jasmine to his rigid frame as he allowed his head to rest on her shoulder. In silence, they hugged each other. Their bodies vibrated an energy force that leaped between them like a firecracker.

With Jasmine's nape within easy reach, Devon dropped a soft kiss against the velvety brown flesh and yearned to receive something equally meaningful in return. Jasmine reciprocated, touching her lips gently against Devon's jawline. She pulled away slightly and looked into his face. Devon held her gaze and then dipped his head, sliding a long lingering kiss from left to right across Jasmine's mouth in a slow ravishment of the senses. Jasmine sensed that her heart had turned right over when she felt the testing tip of his tongue, which he was using effectively for titillation. And then, as though that was all he needed, Devon pulled away.

"I've got to go back to work," he whispered close to her lips. "Cash the bill receipts and lock up the money in the safe."

Jasmine drew in a deep shaky breath. "You're right, we *do* need to talk," she said.

"When is your birthday?" Devon asked with interest.

"Friday," Jasmine answered.

He sighed. "I have to be in London tomorrow, but let's eat at the Savoy restaurant on Wednesday night," he suggested, knowing that Jasmine's birthday would probably be spent with Carmilla and the rest of her family. "We can talk then."

"Okay," Jasmine agreed, turning her head, distracted by the steaming kettle. When she returned her attention to Devon, he was gone.

Chapter Eight

"That's Justine," Gibson pointed out from across the bar where he was presiding over two orange juices while talking casually with Jasmine, who was standing on the other side. The Birmingham Savoy had opened its doors precisely one hour ago and the regulars were beginning to flow in. "She's a sly one. Always withholds information about herself, but likes to invent stories about her girl-friends to make herself feel better."

"Seriously?" Jasmine queried, almost in shock.

"Yep," Gibson confirmed, expanding his reper-toire. "Justine believes in that old adage that it's easier to gain a reputation than lose one, which is why she invents her own attachment to highly placed individuals. And there's Tracee-Ann," he in-dicated with the tipping of his chin. "Heiress to a fortune. Her father trades in Caribbean tobacco, but she's on hard drugs."

"Cocaine, heroin?" Jasmine inquired, sucking orange juice through the two straws in her glass, while spying at the woman on the ballroom floor, dancing alone.

"Both," Gibson went on, cautiously pointing out another of the Savoy's clientele. "Her over there, that's Miss Gold Digger. She'll sleep with your husband at the drop of a hat, or at the drop of his pants, whichever comes first. If he's rich and married, he's a challenge."

"Gibson!" Jasmine gasped, hardly able to believe she was listening to such gossip.

"Hey," Gibson defended, tipping his chin self-righteously. "A woman is always slapping her down 'cause she's slept with their husband. Miss Gold Digger's got so many restraining orders, she could qualify for some kind of record." He scanned the room for his next victim. "And there's Marleeka, investment broker. Nigerian. Girlfriend likes to spread herself around like confetti and likes to have a good time. You wouldn't believe she's forty, would you?"

"No," Jasmine agreed, swallowing more juice. "She's in great shape."

Gibson moved on. "The guy next to her, his name's Darren. Always arrives in a limousine, but he's lame. The girls are always complaining about him."

Jasmine raised her neatly plucked brows. "Why?"

"Figure it out," Gibson bawdily encouraged. "He's a good-looking guy, but something's not measuring up to size and it ain't the extent of his ego."

"Gibson, are you for real?" Jasmine chuckled, her mouth agape.

"That's what happens when you ask a bartender what kind of people frequent a club," Gibson responded coolly, with a sly grin and a helpless shrug of his shoulders. "We see and hear too much."

"Is there anything else?" Jasmine hardly dared ask the resident talebearer.

"Him over there, Mr. Big Tipper. Big Spender. Your usual splash-it-around town kind of guy." Gibson was discreetly pointing again. "A true believer in the cash economy, which is why he walks around with wads of paper currency in his wallet. He's got a woman at home, but keeps letting on to the ladies that he's single and get this, he engineers it so that *they* ask *him* out. That way, he doesn't have to justify to himself that he's cheating."

"Wait a minute," Jasmine breathed, astounded. "You mean as long as he doesn't do the asking, he's guilt-free?"

"Yep." Gibson nodded, taking several gulps from his glass. He swallowed.

"That's . . ." Jasmine could not find words for such deception. "Psychological—"

"It's cheating," Gibson interrupted firmly. "Ain't no other word for it. Men of his wealth and importance have their own rules. And him right there, Mr. Four-Foot-Eight-Inches. Don't ask me how he gets the ladies. He comes here with a different one every week and they're always taller than him. And that guy right there, rich as sin. Made a packet in computers, but we're all still wondering what his sexuality is. We've never seen him with anyone."

Jasmine shook her head, disbelieving. "Isn't there anyone in here that's just normal to you?"

"There's Delbert, over there." Gibson sighed, tipping his chin again. "Boring as a plank of wood with a few grids to account for his wrinkles and that's because he's the biggest gambler in town. His girl, she's a knockout. They've been together three months, but I give it two more weeks because she can pick and choose whoever she wants, period. I just can't figure what she's doing with him."

"Did it not occur to you that he might actually be treating her right?" Jasmine asked. "Faithful, moralistic, all the good stuff?"

"No way," Gibson rebuffed. "He's on a roll right now, but when the losing streak kicks in, she'll be out of there."

"There are a lot of nice couples in here. Take those two." It was Jasmine's turn to be circumspect. "I see them come in every week and he's always holding her hand. They're both sweet with each other."

"They're one in a million," Gibson said cynically. "That's how it is when you've got a title to live up to and an inheritance that goes with it. You can't afford to make any mistakes, especially if you're black. It's all about breeding."

"This is silly," Jasmine debated, indicating with a reserved nod of her head in the direction of another couple. "Those two have been staring puppy-dog-eyes at each other all evening. And look, they're married."

"Not to each other," Gibson responded flatly.

"What about those two?" Jasmine said. "He doesn't dance with anyone else."

"That's because he's an old fading rap star," Gibson drawled, as though the fact had been made obviously plain. "In his day, he would take on an entire cheerleading squad. Now he just sticks with the head cheerleader doing a jazz two-step because that's all he can muster."

"Gibson, you need therapy," Jasmine offered, sadly. "I'm going back to work."

"Not so fast," Gibson replied. "What are *you* going to do about Petronella and Devon?"

Jasmine schooled her eyes on Gibson. "What do you mean?"

"If you don't start putting some air into your tires and get cruising, Petronella's gonna drive off with your man."

"He's not my man," Jasmine insisted, though she was unsuccessful in persuading herself.

Before coming to work that evening, she had taken careful consideration in her appearance. Her makeup was perfect. There wasn't a hair out of place. All her nutmeg-brown corkscrew curls were pinned up toward her crown with only a few stray tendrils left to dangle around her earlobes for feminine emphasis. And the black sequined dress she was wearing, with its tiny straps and silky fabric that shimmered when she moved, fit every nubile curve like a glove.

She had not seen Devon all day yesterday, so it was difficult to gauge his mood since his arriving from London that afternoon looking fatigued and miserable. He had only glimpsed her briefly on his entrance into the club before disappearing into the back office. She had been left cooling her heels at the bar with Gibson in an effort to pull herself together. Though she was thoroughly amused by all the scandalmongering, Jasmine was left wondering whether her glamorous appearance had been entirely wasted.

"I saw the way Devon looked at you when he walked in here an hour ago," Gibson noted, unwittingly giving Jasmine the clarification she needed that Devon had at least noticed her. "And you're all dressed up to lure his attention. I'm wondering why you're having dinner tonight? I know something's going on."

"It's nothing you need worry your little head over." Jasmine smiled, deciding to withhold the truth, though her heart had begun to beat a little faster on hearing Gibson's candid observation. "Like I told you yesterday, we're having dinner in the restaurant to talk over some business to do with the club."

Gibson laughed as though the very idea was most definitely far from what was deemed reality in his world. "I saw the way you looked at him, too."

Jasmine leaned across the bar, intrigued. "How did I look at Monsieur Rutherford?" she asked on a suggestive note.

"Like a blooming flower showing off its petals to the sunlight," Gibson breathed teasingly. "I smell love in the air."

Jasmine was reminded that she had better say nothing about her feelings toward Devon, one way or the other. Gibson was liable to take whatever she said out of context and pass it around the club. She didn't want that, not when things were so delicate between her and her grandmother's godson. At that potent recollection, she suddenly brought to mind everything Carmilla had told her.

Devon had a past she knew nothing about, save what had been explained to her thus far. None of it sounded good. In fact, Jasmine could hardly wait to have dinner so that all the missing links in her mind could be slotted into place. She had gone to bed and awoken only to find herself spending Tuesday wondering in beguiled confusion exactly what had happened to Devon to have led him to England. New York, it seemed, held bad memories for him, too. That, at least, was something they both had in common.

But unlike her, his situation seemed dire. Even now, she could still recall the trembling of his lips the last time they had kissed. Had she been comforting Devon, she wondered, or trying to forget that she had left the Big Apple to escape the misery of being caught up in something that had no future? Enrico Cajero had been the kind of man who hurled around meaningless words like a boy trying to throw hoops. There was always a reason why he just couldn't play ball. She had come to realize that he would always be someone who preferred to weave, duck, and career his way through life looking for all the shortcuts to making it.

Devon, on the contrary, was quite different. He was a man with strategic goals, who knew he had to build good work ethics to succeed. Jasmine liked that about him. She suddenly flinched at the thought of ever accusing him of being after her grandmother's fortune. But she was trying to make amends, she told herself. She had agreed to dinner to hear Devon out. And she had apologized, too. All she needed now was to survive the meal later that evening without causing any waves.

"Carry on talking like that and I may be pressured into digging a thorn or two into one of your ribs," Jasmine objected smoothly, taking her thoughts back to their current subject. She wanted nothing more than to dip her bucket into Devon Rutherford's well and see whether it came up dry or full with past deeds, but she could not tell Gibson that. Not even Carmilla would supply anything further during breakfast these last two mornings. "Devon and I are . . . friends. Colleagues," she amended. "As far as I'm concerned, it's all mind over matter."

"Is that why you gave Petronella the night off?" Gibson asked, picking up his glass.

Jasmine raised curious brows. "Is she not working tonight?" she countered, surprised.

"Did you not know?" Gibson returned, with a
smile playing on his lips.

"No," Jasmine declared sternly. "Who gave her
the night off?"

"Perhaps you had better speak with Devon about
that," Gibson answered, draining his glass.

"I will," Jasmine confirmed, sucking the last
mouthful of orange juice through the two straws
to empty her glass. She placed it on the bar top.

"Sooner rather than later," Gibson advised, tipping his chin suggestively

As soon as he said the words, someone crept up
beside Jasmine at the bar. Ever alert to Gibson's chin
gestures, Jasmine turned her head sideways and
caught the full impact of Petronella's arrival. She
looked stunning in an azure off-the-shoulder dress,
with her hair carefully coifed and enough makeup
to accentuate the fullness of her beauty. Jasmine was
in no doubt that another clash was ahead.

"This is so cool," Petronella began, observing the
ballroom with the freshness of a newcomer. "Instead of waiting tables, I'm here as a guest with my
friends."

Jasmine forced a smile and turned toward
Gibson. "Give Petronella her first drink, on the
house," she ordered softly.

"Coming right up," Gibson responded, keeping his ears and his eyes open. "What'll it be,
Petronella?"

"Cola and rum, on ice," she answered, keeping
her gaze fixed on Jasmine, noting that she shrieked
haute couture. "Nice dress."

"Yours too," Jasmine answered, as Gibson

handed over the drink. "Very à la mode. Enjoy your evening."

"I intend to," Petronella promised, taking the glass from Gibson with a triumphant smile lighting up her face. "Like I told you, I'll work harder. I'll try and do my best to make sure you don't ruin anything between Devon and me."

Jasmine refused to rise to the challenge. Instead, she watched Petronella leave and then turned toward Gibson. "You told her about the meal I'm having with Devon tonight, didn't you?" she accused hotly. His silence was all the verification she needed. Jasmine sighed at her own stupidity in divulging anything to the bartender. "I'm going back to work."

"Mind over matter," Gibson encouraged, in a regretful tone.

"That's right," Jasmine snapped. "I don't mind that you're an idiot and *she* doesn't matter." With that answer, she walked across the ballroom toward the restaurant with steadfast determination etched in every step she took.

Jasmine's heart kicked and nestled uneasily in her chest when, another hour later, Devon was still holed up in the Savoy's nerve center. Devon had not given her a time when they would eat, but she had already instructed Wills to keep a large rump cut of beef to one side, knowing it would be the one item Devon would select from the menu. Placing a RESERVED notice on the corner table that afforded the best view of the dance floor was another task she had undertaken.

But now, an even more uncomfortable line of

thought was beginning to emerge when she looked around the ballroom and could not find Petronella. Deflated, Jasmine folded her arms across, comtemplating exactly where the two of them could be. She was back at the bar, having presided over the restaurant guests, staring at Gibson as he tended to the drinkers with an equally bemused expression on his face. How was it that Devon should demand her presence and then be late himself?

"Where's Petronella?" Jasmine demanded, throwing Gibson a deadly look.

He shrugged. "I don't know." He placed two drinks on the bar top for the paying guests, before adding, "Don't panic."

"Do I look like I'm shooting bullets to you?" Jasmine accused, trying to tame her voice.

"Frankly, yes," Gibson admitted bluntly. "And one of them just ricocheted on my head. With that hag look you're wearing right now, Devon is going to run a mile."

Let it be, Jasmine mused, before she uttered it in French. "Laissez-faire."

Suddenly, the object of her growing irritation entered the ballroom from the corridor that led to the back office. Jasmine sucked in her breath as she saw Devon's striking appearance. His tall, majestic frame towered to the point that onlookers stared in awe as he grinned, nodded his head in acknowledgment at a few familiar faces, and then rubbed his trim mustache.

"Sorry I'm late," Devon immediately apologized, as he caught sight of Jasmine standing at the bar and made his approach. With a winning smile playing on his lips, he asked, "Are you ready to eat?"

An Important Message From The ARABESQUE Publisher

Dear Arabesque Reader,

I invite you to join the club! The Arabesque book club delivers four novels each month right to your front door! It's easy, and you will never miss a romance by one of our award-winning authors!

With upcoming novels featuring strong, sexy women, and African-American heroes that are charming, loving and true… you won't want to miss a single release! Our authors fill each page with exceptional dialogue, exciting plot twists, and enough sizzling romance to keep you riveted until the satisfying end! To receive novels by bestselling authors such as Gwynne Forster, Janice Sims, Angela Winters and others, I encourage you to join now!

Read about the men we love… in the pages of Arabesque!

Linda Gill
PUBLISHER, ARABESQUE ROMANCE NOVELS

*P.S. Watch out for the next Summer Series **"Ports Of Call"** that will take you to the exotic locales of Venice, Fiji, the Caribbean and Ghana! You won't need a passport to travel, just collect all four novels to enjoy romance around the world! For more details, visit us at www.BET.com.*

A SPECIAL "THANK YOU" FROM ARABESQUE JUST FOR YOU!

Send this card back and you'll receive 4 FREE Arabesque Novels—a $25.96 value—absolutely FREE!

The introductory 4 Arabesque Romance books are yours FREE (plus $1.99 shipping & handling). If you wish to continue to receive 4 books every month, do nothing. Each month, we will send you 4 New Arabesque Romance Novels for your free examination. If you wish to keep them, pay just $18* (plus, $1.99 shipping & handling). If you decide not to continue, you owe nothing!

- Send no money now.
- Never an obligation.
- Books delivered to your door!

We hope that after receiving your FREE books you'll want to remain an Arabesque subscriber, but the choice is yours! So why not take advantage of this Arabesque offer, with no risk of any kind. You'll be glad you did!

In fact, we're so sure you will love your Arabesque novels, that we will send you an Arabesque Tote Bag FREE with your first paid shipment.

* PRICES SUBJECT TO CHANGE.

ADRIANNE BYRD

LINDA Hudson-Smith

ARABESQUE

Gwynne Forster

ALICE WOOTSON

YOU'LL GET 4 SELECT ROMANCES PLUS THIS FABULOUS TOTE BAG!

ARABESQUE

Visit us at:
www.BET.com

THE "THANK YOU" GIFT INCLUDES:

- 4 books absolutely FREE (plus $1.99 for shipping and handling).
- A FREE newsletter, *Arabesque Romance News*, filled with author interviews, book previews, special offers, and more!
- No risks or obligations. You're free to cancel whenever you wish with no questions asked.

FREE TOTE BAG CERTIFICATE

Yes! Please send me 4 FREE Arabesque novels (plus $1.99 for shipping & handling). I understand I am under no obligation to purchase any books, as explained on the back of this card. Send my free tote bag after my first regular paid shipment.

NAME _____

ADDRESS _____ APT. _____

CITY _____ STATE _____ ZIP _____

TELEPHONE (___) _____

E-MAIL _____

SIGNATURE _____

AN115A

Thank You!

ARABESQUE

Accepting the four introductory books for FREE (plus $1.99 to offset the cost of shipping & handling) places you under no obligation to buy anything. You may keep the books and return the shipping statement marked "cancelled". If you do not cancel, about a month later we will send 4 additional Arabesque novels, and you will be billed the preferred subscriber's price of just $4.50 per title. That's $18.00* for all 4 books for a savings of almost 30% off the cover price (Plus $1.99 for shipping and handling). You may cancel at any time, but if you choose to continue, every month we'll send you 4 more books, which you may either purchase at the preferred discount price. . . or return to us and cancel your subscription.

THE ARABESQUE ROMANCE CLUB: HERE'S HOW IT WORKS

THE ARABESQUE ROMANCE BOOK CLUB
P.O. BOX 5214
CLIFTON NJ 07015-5214

PLACE
STAMP
HERE

His flickering gaze roved over her in appreciation, such that Jasmine was left wondering exactly why she had gone into a panic. "I'm ready," she murmured, her voice hardly audible as Devon linked her arm through his.

Jasmine cast a confused glance across at Gibson before Devon led the way across the dance floor and into the restaurant where he noted the corner table. He pulled the chair out for Jasmine to be seated and then joined her, nodding his head at one of the waiting staff to bring over the menu. Just as easily, Devon allowed his eyes to roam once again over Jasmine's fine mien.

"You look beautiful," he breathed, nodding his approval of the black shimmering dress she was wearing against the caramel brown of her skin.

"*Merci*," Jasmine said. "And so do you."

"I picked up the suit on Savile Row in London this afternoon before driving back into Birmingham," Devon stated tersely, feasting his eyes over the menu. "I didn't have time to go back to the house."

"Very à la mode," Jasmine repeated for the second time that evening. "Fashionable."

She liked the way Devon looked in it, too. The navy blue double-breasted jacket, tailor-cut pants, and white open-necked shirt made Devon seem intensely suave, sharp, and seductive. Sexy, Jasmine concluded. The last word cut across her mind with the precision of a saboteur's knife. And Devon's face was a sight for sore eyes, too. Not the slightest hint of the fatigue she had glimpsed earlier when he entered the club.

"So," she began, having accepted his lateness, "what kept you?"

"Work." Devon shrugged, as one of the waitresses approached. "I'll have the steak with all the trimmings," he immediately told Alice. "Jasmine?"

She was crestfallen at not being given an adequate explanation as to why she had been kept waiting. "I'll have the same." She looked across at Devon and was angered that the better part of her admired the sweeping gaze of his eyes. "Was London all right?"

Devon nodded. "Very warm in the morning, but it got cooler when I started heading back."

Jasmine had expected him to elaborate on why he had taken the journey. But Devon seemed in no mood to discuss his trip.

"How is Carmilla?"

"As well as can be expected," Jasmine answered, watchful as a second member of the staff arrived and poured water into two glasses before leaving. "She's become very tactful since our discussion on Monday."

Devon found Jasmine's observation amusing. "Carmilla thought I'd be angry at what she told you," he explained, with a smile tugging at his lips, "but I told her you'd have found out about me eventually."

"Find out what?" Jasmine asked, lowering her head toward Devon, intrigued.

"That I own the club, that I'm her godson, and that . . ." Devon hesitated, making sure Freya was well away from the table. "That I'm here in England because my life depends on it."

Jasmine gasped. "Are you in trouble?"

"Not anymore," Devon said. "But there was a time when I was."

Jasmine swallowed a nervous lump in her throat and found herself reaching to take a sip from her glass of cold water. She briefly glanced around with interest, recognizing the diners in the restaurant whom she had presided over earlier, exchanging eye contact with a few before her gaze moved on. One figure caught her eye, as she began to wonder whether Devon was about to tell her something disastrous. Jasmine did a double take, then froze. Her heart leaped into her mouth. Across the ballroom, standing with a predatory stance at the bar under the dazzling chandelier lights, was Enrico. She tensed, waiting for some reaction to set in. It came with an involuntary cough.

"Oh God," she choked.

"I didn't mean to alarm you," Devon declared, concerned. "I thought it was time you knew everything about me and why I left New York."

"Need to get away," Jasmine murmured incoherently.

"Yes," Devon agreed. "It was very hard for me to leave."

"Trouble," Jasmine gasped.

She quickly refocused. It was the first time she had seen Enrico Cajero since she had in fact left New York. She had no idea what he was doing in England. Her hand shook a little and she had to set her glass down in order to gather her nerves. Devon's large hand covering hers was almost as much of a shock as seeing her ex-boyfriend again since their breakup.

"Take it easy," Devon encouraged. "Relax. I'm doing just fine. I'm not in any more trouble. I promise."

Jasmine blinked at him in amazement, then frantically returned her gaze to the bar. But the place where she had seen Enrico was now empty.

He was no longer standing there. She scanned the room, searching every niche, and when she could not see him, she glanced at Devon. His hand was now applying enough pressure to comfort her, and Jasmine could already feel the warm, soothing calm his touch transmitted.

"You were saying?" she began nervously.

Devon held her gaze. "I don't want you to be frightened," he cautioned, keeping a smile on his face. "It was something that happened and now it's over."

Jasmine swallowed. "Tell me."

Ten minutes later, when their meal had arrived, Devon was deep in conversation. "Everything went wrong the moment my parents died," he started, chewing his steak. "I'd already lost my grandmother, so when they were killed, there was no one."

Jasmine tried to concentrate, but every so often she found herself looking around the room. "How were they killed?" she asked, trying to maintain her appetite. In truth, the food was not the least bit tasty, through no fault of Sonny or Wills.

"It was a burglary that went wrong," Devon continued, his voice becoming sadder. "There were a lot of those going on in the neighborhood, in Brooklyn. My parents interrupted both the men and they fired in haste. Kids running scared. They were only twenty and twenty-two years old. They were caught. Imprisoned. But it didn't help. My folks were dead. That's when I found Carmilla's address and a few letters while sorting through the house, getting rid of clothes, shoes . . . stuff. I wrote your grandmother, introduced myself, and she replied."

Jasmine took large sips from the glass of red wine that had been placed on the table earlier with their meal "Then what?" If her voice sounded harsh, she told herself it was because she had begun to think she had imagined seeing Enrico.

"We'd been corresponding for about a month and a half, maybe two, when I witnessed a murder," he said flatly.

The glass of wine in Jasmine's hand shook. She had witnessed something, too, but seated with Devon in the Savoy, she had started to wonder if it was all going on in her head. "What did you see?" she asked, almost dazed.

"Right there, on the sidewalk, a shoot-out," Devon expanded. "I was at work and—"

"Work?" Jasmine asked.

"Accounting," Devon swiftly supplied. "Then I saw a guy shoot the other guy, right in the chest."

Jasmine's eyes zeroed in on Devon. "Oh God," she said again.

"I was subpoenaed as a witness in court when the murderer was arrested and then threatened over the phone that if I testified I'd be next." Devon chewed on the last bite of steak. "So I was swept into the witness protection program. I didn't want to change my name or identity after the case was over, so when Carmilla invited me over to England, I opted to relocate here permanently. That's why I left New York."

Jasmine's own reasons for leaving loomed over her but she was not prepared for any of what Devon had told her. "I was wondering," she said, swallowing more wine, "if we could skip dessert."

"Ouch." Devon sighed, pursing his lips. "You're thinking I'm some sort of fugitive?"

Jasmine gulped, finding her eyes had begun to sweep the ballroom once again. "No, no. It's—"

"Who are you looking at?" Devon demanded suddenly.

"Petronella's over there," she said by way of explanation. "She resents me having dinner with you tonight."

"I see her," Devon returned calmly. "She interrupted me in the office earlier while I was catching some sleep."

"Oh?" Jasmine's attention was immediately on Devon.

"I was beat when I got back from London. I didn't think you'd mind me disappearing for an hour to rest and . . ." He stalled, reaching for his wineglass to rinse down the remnants of his steak. "She came in and woke me up. Said she wanted to dance. I told her later but"—Devon allowed his gaze to stray toward Petronella—"now I'm not so sure. I'd rather spend the rest of the evening with you and fall in love a little."

Jasmine felt her heart flutter as if it were a butterfly lodged in her rib cage. Suddenly the image of Enrico Cajero was removed from her mind, replaced with the wonderful, handsome picture of the man seated in front of her. The more Jasmine looked at him, the more she came to realize that he was everything she could want in a man. Certainly and initially as a boyfriend, and maybe in time, as someone more meaningful in her life. But she was restrained by fears that were still with her, the kind that could sway any woman from giving too much away.

"I have it on good authority from my grandmother that a woman should only love a man with three-quarters of her heart and keep a quarter for herself," Jasmine said, sweetly. "What does a man do?"

"Foolishly give all of himself." Devon chuckled. "I want to make love to you."

"Devon!" Jasmine laughed, embarrassed.

"And I want us to tell Carmilla," he went on.

"No." Jasmine was adamant. "She'll want to interfere. Suggest all manner of things like marriage, children."

"And what's wrong with that?" Devon asked, confused.

"I don't want to lose my freedom," Jasmine answered sternly. "I happen to like the fact that I can move around, travel, meet people—"

"Change lovers," Devon finished. "That's what you're saying, isn't it?"

"No," Jasmine protested.

"You left one man back in New York and you're here in England, having walked into the life of another one," Devon chided. "I suppose it's quite easy to change when your freedom is being threatened. What did the last guy do, ask to marry you?"

Jasmine wanted to laugh, hysterically. The mere mention of Enrico and marriage was like trying to mix oil with water. She felt even more troubled because she could have sworn she had seen him in the club earlier. Yet over an hour had passed since the ceiling lights had flickered ever so brightly above the tall man she had seen standing at the bar, leering straight at her. Perhaps it had not been Enrico at all, she told herself convincingly. Ballroom lights were renowned for playing tricks with one's eyes. Whoever it was she had seen, he was no longer in the club and she did not want the man on her mind either.

"Do we have to talk about him?" Jasmine sighed heavily.

"Yes," Devon answered. "Unless you have something to hide?"

"Me?" Jasmine threw out a shrill, high-pitched peal of laughter. There was, of course, Enrico's marriage proposal, but she was not about to say anything about that. "There's nothing to tell. In fact, Carmilla wants me to pawn a brooch he gave me, and when that's done she doesn't want to hear mention of him again."

"What did he do, break your heart?" Devon probed further.

"He killed it. There, is that answer enough for you?" Jasmine relented, furious with the ongoing questions. "I have no love left to give, okay? Just my freedom to share with anyone who doesn't mind partaking of a little of my time."

Devon was suddenly out of his chair. "You're right, let's skip dessert," he said. "I want to make love to a heart that is alive and beating, not a dead one. There's been too much of that in my life."

Jasmine understood Devon's meaning. "Wait!" But his long strides had taken him out of the restaurant, across the dance floor, and down the corridor that led into the back office. Jasmine chased him all the way there, ignoring the wide-eyed look that Petronella leveled at her as she swept by. Jasmine was in the back office seconds after Devon had arrived there, closing the door with a thud before she took three deep breaths to get her bearings. He had dug his hands into his trouser pockets and had his back to her when she crept up behind him. When Devon turned and looked down into her face, Jasmine was smitten by the heartfelt soul-searching look that bored into her.

"Devon," she said, in a voice that had suddenly weakened. "I . . ."

He pulled his hands out of his pockets and touched her gently on the line of her waist. The soft sequined fabric tickled his fingertips as he pulled Jasmine closer. "I've thought about nothing but kissing you today," he confessed in a whisper. "I've dreamt about touching you. I've longed to hold you. To smell you." His lips moved closer. His forehead touched hers. "I want to foolishly give all of myself to you. Is it so hard for you to be crazy, too?"

"Devon . . ." Her voice disappeared.

He smothered his own name with his lips. Devon pulled Jasmine's mouth into his own and captivated her swiftly with a crushing kiss. Every nerve in Jasmine's body leaped into action. She felt renewed. Reawakened. And there was no stopping her returning the glorious feelings that were being given to her. Her arms circled Devon's neck and she didn't drift, but sank into his rugged frame.

The world flew by in an instant. Her only existence at that very point was the sweetly bruising lips on hers. Somewhere deep in Jasmine's mind, she realized she liked the very outline of those lips shaping hers. The soft pulsing flesh, the taste of wine as a lingering reminder of their dinner together, the tingling brush of Devon's thin mustache that ever so slightly tickled her top lip.

With her eyes closed, she dreamed of an everlasting kiss. The kind where pleasure and joy were never ending, as now. And when she felt her delight could not be taken any higher, Devon thrust the tip of his tongue into her mouth, elevating their desire. Jasmine moaned with the lust and passion it gave her. Was this really her, behaving just as Devon had wanted her to? Jasmine couldn't think. All she knew was that she did not want this boundless kiss to stop.

And Devon had no intention of stopping. His arms circled Jasmine's waist and pulled her into him until her body molded against his own. He liked the feel of Jasmine next to him, the beating of her heart against his chest, and the knowledge that only he could inflame such a fire. This from the woman he had once called Ice Queen. The same woman who had declared he could never take a kiss from her again. He had never felt so powerful as he did at that precise moment, taming the brusqueness of Jasmine Charlesworth.

Her rancor was replaced with a softer, more appealing side he seldom felt was ever shown to anyone, except maybe her grandmother, and even so, Carmilla was always aware of when Jasmine was trying to sweeten her mood. Devon felt the smile that tugged at his lips as he finally felt in control of the one woman he had never desired so much as he did now. In his mind, Jasmine Charlesworth was his. All he needed now was to prove to her that he wanted her for keeps.

He was doing so now, with every nip, suck, and tantalizing caress of Jasmine's neck, her eyebrows, her cheeks, her forehead, the tip of her nose, and finally in the retaking of her lips. If Jasmine had thought herself harsh and cynical about the dangers of men, she did not think so now. Enrico Cajero may have been wrong in every way, but Devon felt so right. Devon was wonderfully and gloriously the epitome of everything a man should be. When his lips finally left hers, Jasmine swayed back into reality.

"You're right," she whispered against Devon's neck as she slowly dragged her face away from his. "We should tell Gran-mama."

Devon took a deep breath of air. His heart was pounding so fast he more than needed the blast of oxygen to his lungs. His forehead touched hers. "I thought you said we should keep quiet."

Jasmine tried to refocus. Her brain was far from keeping pace with what her heart wanted. "I mean—"

The words of her surrender were hardly off her tongue when a knock at the office door interrupted their little world. Devon raised his head and pulled away from Jasmine in time to watch the door open. It was Petronella's head that poked into the room. Her cool gaze scanned everything. She saw Devon standing upright, Jasmine within six inches of him, with no sign of activity because the computer was off and the phone on its hook. The silence was pretty unhelpful, too.

"Devon, you promised me a dance," Petronella said weakly.

"I'm . . . conducting a private meeting, as you can see," Devon declared firmly. "I'll meet you in the ballroom."

But instead of politely departing the room, Petronella opened the door wider and gave herself permission to enter, closing the door behind her. As Jasmine was about to ponder the older woman's audacity, Petronella brazenly walked across the room and slapped Devon across his face. Her own face was intense as she lobbied a fierce glare at him, before throwing another one in Jasmine's direction.

"You know what that's for," she spat out.

"What in the hell are you doing?" Devon protested, rubbing his left cheek. "I'm your employer."

"And I'm trying to protect you," Petronella replied with a hardened breath.

"What?" Devon exclaimed loudly.

"You shouldn't be in here with her," Petronella burst out. "I thought . . ." She tried to take a steadying breath.

"I have a life," Devon readily told her, though he was reluctant to have any complications among the members of his staff.

"As I can see," Petronella agreed through clenched teeth. The accusatory finger pointed directly at Jasmine did not go amiss. "But the fact that she's Carmilla's granddaughter does not mean you should be reckless in this way and make a fool of yourself."

"You'd better leave, right now," Devon warned.

"*She* thinks you're one of her grandmother's charitable cases, for Chrisssake!" The words ripped out of her. "Ask her."

Devon turned to face Jasmine. "What's she talking about?"

"I didn't mean it like that," Jasmine protested, feeling it was time she muzzled Gibson's mouth as she recalled her ill-chosen words, obviously repeated. But now that the floodgates were open, she could no longer contain the gush of words she had kept in her own reservoir for Petronella. "Give up on this crusade of trying to stop what is going on between Devon and me. You're only making a fool of yourself."

Petronella's body tensed. "You're using him," she bristled loudly, noting with satisfaction Jasmine's pale expression and trembling figure. "Your only interest in Devon stems from the fact that you found out that *he* owns the Birmingham Savoy and *not* your grandmother."

"That's a lie," Jasmine almost squealed.

"Is it?" Petronella ventured calmly. She appealed to Devon. "In her eyes, you're one of her grandmother's successful projects that she's toying with. I see you as something far more than that and I just don't want to see you get hurt."

"This is not part of what you're here for, to intrude in my life," Devon said sternly. "Please leave now, if you still want your job, and tomorrow I'm going to do you a favor and pretend that this never happened."

Petronella seemed justifiably hurt, but her maturity rose to the fore. "I resign."

She left with a slam of the door.

"Femme fatale," Jasmine yelled, refusing to be intimidated by the woman who'd left the room. A scant minute later, she burst into tears. "I'm sorry," she sobbed with the shameful truth of what she had told the bartender hanging over her. "I did think you were a charity case. I told Gibson as much and—"

"I'm sorry, too," Devon declared, his American accent tinged with remorse as he walked over to Jasmine and took her into his arms again. "I imagined I could steal another kiss from you because you were Carmilla Charlesworth's granddaughter." His voice was sincere. "I want to get to know you, properly. No more deception, or lies."

"I'm willing to suspend hostilities if you are." Jasmine grinned at him, wiping her tears away, wishing that they could mean more to each other than simply work colleagues.

Their eyes met. Jasmine was right. She had long suspected that they were both equally as bad. That they were both indeed a challenge for each other. Their honesty was probably the biggest act of bravery both would ever undertake in their lives. Petronella's interference had only given rise to their darkest fear of losing something they had yet to find. Maybe being foolish, reckless, and wagering their last penny of emotional investment on searching was going to be brief, but would it be worth it? Neither of them knew.

Petronella was contemplating the very same thing, but for different reasons, when she left the office. She thought of Devon, his mustachioed smile, his face, and all his features and virile masculine attributes that were out of bounds to her. Was it worth it? Yes, it was worth it. But she loathed herself for provoking a scene, because Devon had nothing to share with her at all and she knew it.

She could hardly blame Jasmine Charlesworth for earmarking Devon as her own. What Petronella feared most was that Carmilla Charlesworth's granddaughter was a woman Devon had known in less time than he had known her. She resented the name. To her, it seemed the only thing Devon Rutherford wanted to live up to was an acceptance into the Charlesworth clan.

"I'm going home," Petronella told her friends, as she arrived back in the ballroom. "I've just overstepped my boundaries and can't stay."

Outside the club and in her coat, she tried to

plot her next step. She had impulsively given up her job because of possibly jeopardizing a relationship between Jasmine and Devon, the happy couple. It was torment enough imagining them together in that way. Such were the hazards of working with a handsome boss. Were they kissing? Hugging? Laughing at her? Petronella miserably walked around a corner and into the steel frame of Enrico Jax Cajero.

"Got a light?" Johnny the Bear asked, as he came up behind her.

Petronella stalled. The European accent caught her attention immediately. She looked into his smiling face and dug into her coat pocket, pulling out customized Birmingham Savoy matches. She stared at the packet of foreign cigarettes, then at both strangers, noting the nervous twitch of Enrico's brows. "There you go." She handed the matches over. "I work here. You guys looking for somebody?"

Enrico licked his lips. "What I'm looking for is right here, baby." He smiled, putting on the charm. "What's your name?"

Chapter Nine

They did not drop the bombshell of their relationship on Carmilla right away. Instead, Devon and Jasmine spent an inexorable amount of time in each other's company in a relaxed mood, happily talking and sharing experiences about themselves. Even Carmilla had detected something between them during breakfast, but ever tactful that she had already spoken out of turn about Devon's past, she kept whatever views were held in her mind to herself. Her only comment that morning was about her sister-in-law's forthcoming gala.

"I spoke with your great-aunt Helena," she told Jasmine, opening the topic with ease. "We've agreed to put aside our trivialities for the sake of Jamaica's Independence Day in August. On account of receiving an apology from her, I've decided she can use the Birmingham Savoy for her charity event since the funds raised will be to relieve the hurricane victims still suffering from last year's tragedy. Devon, I hope you will not object?"

Her godson was so immersed in the image of the young woman seated across from him that he was hardly aware of the reply he gave Carmilla. With Jasmine dressed for warmth against the unpredictable chill of rainy weather, the ruffled white collar of the blouse she was wearing was hidden beneath a red cashmere jacket that complemented a black slim-line skirt, providing a frame for her face, which seemed shyer than when he'd last kissed her. With her three-inch black Jimmy Choo shoes, appearing more feminine than ever, her brown hair loosely pinned up toward her crown, not too much makeup on her face, and pearl earrings dangling from her earlobes, she was not impervious to enjoying the pleasure of his company.

"Anything you say," he answered Carmilla happily.

"We'll book it in the diary." Her granddaughter smiled in return.

"Your parents will also be coming on Friday. They will be on the twelve-thirty p.m. train," Carmilla added, before sipping from her teacup. "Make sure you go along with Devon to pick them up in the Jeep."

"*Oui*, Gran-mama," Jasmine acknowledged cheerfully.

Later, at the Savoy, being together seemed much more relaxing, too, since Petronella's untimely departure. It was as though a dark cloud had been lifted from the place, and for the first time the air was clear again. Despite the brave show of flowers Devon had seen from his attic room window in Carmilla's back garden he, too, had decided to dress for warmth in a white long-sleeved polo-necked jersey over which he wore a black tailored viscose suit with black lacquered shoes on his feet. He went directly to the office to deal with the mail, leaving Jasmine to tend to her duties.

And she was a woman drifting in a world where everything seemed renewed with hope. With Petronella gone, Jasmine was aware just how much more content she was feeling. Naturally, that meant there was no longer any news for Gibson to get his teeth into. The kind of tidings where communication was often misunderstood, exaggerated, or used against someone to add substance to his day.

"No more grist for your mill?" she teased the bartender on her approach, noting that he was preparing the bar for the evening.

"There's nothing in this ballroom but grist," Gibson told her quite cynically, his chin rising a notch as she struck a nerve. "There'll be a lot of bloodletting soon."

"And who's going to be the first lamb led to the slaughter?" Jasmine queried, slowing the pace of her footsteps long enough to receive his reply.

"The one least worthy of sacrifice," Gibson revealed. "You fired her last night."

She stopped at the bar. Her eyebrows narrowed defensively. "I didn't fire anybody," Jasmine declared. "Petronella resigned of her own free will."

"And did you ask Devon why he had given her the night off?" Gibson debated suddenly.

Jasmine had forgotten about all that. Her entire day had gone by in one long flurry of budding passion. She had not found time to reflect on anything else save getting to know Devon a little better. After breakfast, they had left the house and gone to the Bullring Shopping Mall. It seemed silly now, but at the time it felt like a remarkable step forward toward a common aim of doing something together.

* * *

Devon had taken a hold of her left hand, resisting all her coy attempts to pull away as they slowly strolled through the city center mall.

"It doesn't matter if anyone sees us," he began chuckling.

"It does to me," Jasmine breathed, as a cascading whirlwind of electricity shot through her veins. "We haven't told Carmilla and I don't want anyone to see us and spread the news ahead of time."

She tried to pull her left hand free again, but with her Fendi handbag in her right hand, Devon continued successfully to fight her resistance. "Behave yourself," he commanded, deliberately weaving her through the traffic of people to where they could take a better look at the shops. "If you be a good girl, I'll buy you something."

"I don't want you to buy me anything," Jasmine insisted. "I'll only feel obligated to get you something in return."

"No, you won't," Devon objected, "because it'd be your birthday present."

"Devon!"

"Come on," he encouraged, his American accent inviting as he laced his strong fingers through hers.

There was . . . an extraordinary feeling of warmth and safety engendered in those long, strong fingers, Jasmine thought, as they walked around for about twenty minutes, picking their way through the crowd until Devon stopped outside a display window. He refused to release Jasmine's hand, but instead pulled her gently over. An array of gold, silver, and platinum watches glistened beneath the display lights. Bracelets, rings, and necklaces were placed on soft cream-colored cushions for public display. Each item was tagged with a price that caused Jasmine to arch her brows.

"Devon, everything in here is far too expensive," she complained. "I don't need another watch."

"Let's go inside," he urged.

"No." Jasmine inhaled as she caught sight of the wedding rings. They looked adorable, yet she could not understand why she felt rooted to the spot.

"I want to buy you a brooch," he told her, "to replace the one your grandmother wants you to get rid of."

"Oh," Jasmine breathed a sigh of relief. "I really don't—"

Devon dropped her hand and walked behind her, gingerly pushing the small of Jasmine's back until she had no choice but to stumble over the jeweler's threshold. It was a small shop, filled with expensive trinkets in addition to a further array of what they had seen in the display window. The attendant was a kind, middle-aged man with small eyes and an equally small beak of a nose, but with a kindly smile. On Devon's prompting, he disappeared into a back room and returned with a box embossed with the name of the store. By the time Jasmine left the shop, her throat had closed over.

"You picked this out for me, didn't you?" she choked, placing a finger against the luxurious brooch crafted in eighteen-karat gold, which was nicely pinned to the lapel of her red jacket.

"I called them this morning," Devon confessed, forming his mouth into a knowing grin. "I thought it would suit you because you're French. It's a fleur-de-lis. The name, when anglicized, means 'lily flower' and the symbol was used by King Philip the First of France in the eleventh century."

"It's beautiful," Jasmine murmured, swiftly kissing Devon's left cheek. "*Merci.*"

"You're welcome," he accepted warmly.

Something in his smile sent Jasmine's heart rippling.

Devon's voice was soft and soothing as he reached for Jasmine's left hand and lifted it to his lips, just as Bernard Augarde had done with her grandmother. The light respectful kiss gave Jasmine a shivery sensation of gooseflesh. Her hand, having strangely felt lost, was retaken, and this time she did not protest when Devon's fingers curled possessively around her own.

"Why does Carmilla want you to get rid of that old brooch anyway?" Devon inquired curiously as they began another leisurely stroll through the mall. "Is it a cursed family heirloom or something?"

"I can hardly wait for my family to come tomorrow," Jasmine said.

Devon considered her thoughtfully. "Jasmine?"

"I told you why," she replied solemnly, the remnants of whatever memory was left of Enrico Cajero coming up to haunt her. On leaving the club last night, she had not seen him anywhere, which simply told Jasmine that her mind had indeed been playing tricks with her. After all, she had left him in New York City and that's where he was right now, probably raiding the luggage of another unsuspecting hotel guest. "My last boyfriend gave it to me, and by selling it, I can forget him. There's a pawnbroker in Handsworth Market," she added nervously. "I think I'll take it down there this weekend."

"If you say so." Devon shrugged, trying not to press the issue. "But if you want to get a fair price for it, you should try the Jewelry Quarter in the city center. It's been around for centuries and the shops there might make you a better offer for it than a pawnbroker."

"How do I get there?" Jasmine inquired, interested.

"There are two sidewalk trails you can walk that will take you right in," Devon continued. "The 'Findings Trail' and the 'Charm Bracelet Trail.' Or I can give you a ride if you like."

"Sounds like a jeweler's boneyard to me," Jasmine relented, noting how old the place was. "Let me think on it."

"Okay." Devon pulled Jasmine along, deciding to enjoy every moment of her presence. "You must be very happy about seeing your mum and dad again?"

Her surliness mellowed. "You met my father last Christmas." Jasmine assumed that they both liked each other. "What does he think of you?"

"Do you need his approval, too?" Devon countered.

"He is my father," Jasmine responded.

"Well, for the record, Porter and I got on quite well," he declared softly.

"Did he say you can call him that? Porter? Not Mr. Charlesworth?" Jasmine asked, almost in shock.

"He introduced himself by his christened name," Devon stated. "Why?"

"No reason," Jasmine said quietly. "It's just that, he's always been quite formal in the past."

"How many male suitors has your father met?" Devon asked suddenly.

"Just the ones in France," Jasmine explained. "And he was far too heavy-handed with them all."

His laser-sharp gaze hit head-on. "In what way?"

"Papa would joke about wanting to see pictures of their cars, mansions, yachts even private jets." Jasmine giggled. "I suppose I was still very young and he wanted the best for me. After I finished college, I left France and went to Greece for a one-year fixed-term au pair job and liked it so much that I went to Australia for two years afterward. When I came home, my father had a few suitors in mind, so I took off and flew to New York."

"Then what?" Devon asked curiously.

"I started work for a lovely family in Manhattan, and—"

"Met the lowlife," Devon finished. "He put you on a roller coaster before you jumped off and returned to the safe haven of your grandmother in England."

"Nice and neatly put," Jasmine said applauding.

He watched her shyly drop her eyes and moisten her lips with the small pink tongue he had already tasted, and felt his breath quicken. Devon decided he would come to the subject of that ex-boyfriend later. For now, he was enjoying the time spent learning about Jasmine's life and work. "Why did you decide to work with children?"

Their eyes met and the mutual recognition was electric. "I'm not sure," Jasmine admitted, trying helplessly to still the shudder of her heart. "My mother's a *sage-femme*—a midwife. After finishing school, I came to learn that there is a great deal of support in France for people who decide to have children. The country has had one of the lowest birth rates in Europe since the mid–eighteenth century, but recently that has changed. France now has the second-highest rate, after Ireland. I think I must've logically thought a lot of babies need au pairs."

Devon's eyes shone. "Was it work you enjoyed?"

"Oh yes." Jasmine laughed. "The first child I ever looked after was a two-year-old boy called Alexandre. His parents were from Albania, but he was born in France and was registered at the Mairie. That means when he grows up, he could apply to become a French citizen like me. Although I was born in England, I've lived in France most of my life."

"Your mother, Patti," Devon probed deeper. "You never really talk about her."

"My mother's very strict," Jasmine began in explanation. "I think that's because she was always busy at the hospital. She's typically French. Her parents were originally from Haiti in the Caribbean and strongly believed in good parenthood. She would always dress me for school in a pinafore, black patent-leather shoes, and a hat, under which my hair was in tiny braids with white satin ribbons."

"I can hardly imagine you with pigtails." Devon chuckled, aware of a stirring in his loins seeing the grown woman in front of him now.

"Believe me, I looked hideous," Jasmine said. "I suppose my parents and others thought I looked ridiculously sweet."

"You do," Devon professed, with that seductive chocolate voice that made him sound almost good enough to eat.

The gravelly texture of his accent was very sexy in a toe-curling sort of way, and Jasmine tried to stop her heart from working double time by choosing to stay with the subject in hand. "My mum comes from that generation that takes great pains to ensure that their children are *bien-élevé*. Well raised."

"I suppose the schools in France are also strict," Devon expanded, admiring Jasmine's tact not to take the compliment too seriously.

"Oh yes," Jasmine agreed. "And the French government takes it upon itself to support the cost of education for every child. It's nothing like the hundreds of thousands of dollars American parents have to spend to educate their children."

"We believe in family values, too," Devon responded, "meaning your family is valued if you can take care of them yourself."

Amused by Devon's last remark, Jasmine remained feeling comfortable walking through the Bullring Shopping Mall. A little later, they had walked into the gloomy sunlight. The sky threatened rain, but they decided to have lunch out on the plaza and take advantage of the outdoors before the weather turned. With two jacket potatoes and cheese, they had seated themselves on one of the wooden benches that were scattered around for public convenience and breathed in the humid July air.

A formal smile brushed her lips. "What did you think of my mother?" Jasmine dared to ask as she forked a lump of cheese into her mouth.

"Patti . . ." Devon paused to swallow. "She looked tired. To be honest, I found it hard to understand her, you know, with the heavy Parisian accent."

"She speaks Haitian patois, too," Jasmine confessed knowingly. "Sometimes I don't understand her and she hates traveling. I guess you met Andre, my twenty-four-year-old kid brother?"

"Actually, your brother didn't come over last

Christmas," Devon revealed. "I think your mother said he was in Spain."

"Spain!" Jasmine swallowed. "I wonder what he was doing there."

"I don't know. Your parents only stayed four days and left before New Year's." Devon shrugged, then carefully scrutinized Jasmine's face. "I'd say you look like your father. But you definitely have your mother's eyes."

"You mean the squint," Jasmine joked. She took another mouthful of cheese. "Who did you most look like?"

"My dad," Devon confessed. "There's very little of my mother in me. Her name was Juanita. She emigrated from Puerto Rico to New York in in the early 1970s with her family to find work. Then she met my father. They married and had me. She secretly mourned the fact that she was advised not have any more children. Mum had a condition that made it a risk to her health."

"I'm sorry," Jasmine sympathized. "That must have been very hard for her."

"She doted on me tremendously," Devon continued. "Perhaps too much. I never left home. Never had my own apartment. I worked in the city and came home to the place we've always lived in in Brooklyn, a brownstone where my grandmother also used to live when she was married to my grandfather, Pastor Erskin."

"Miss Gracie Manning," Jasmine acknowledged.

Devon nodded. "That was her name before she married. She was just Nanna Gracie to me."

"And what work did your father do?" Jasmine inquired, delving into more of her hot jacket potato and cheese.

"Mum never worked. She stayed home with me," Devon continued, "but my father was a driver on the New York subways. He loved his job. He really did."

Jasmine heard the tremor in Devon's tone and decided to move on quickly. She wanted to ask him about the murder and the trial, but their shopping excursion seemed not the opportune time to discuss it. "We should head on to the Birmingham Savoy after we've eaten these," she suggested, glancing at her watch. "It'll be time to open up the club soon."

She never thought anything could have spoiled their first real time together, sharing their views and life experiences while filing layers of knowledge about each other, but coming to the ballroom had changed all that. Jasmine did not expect to hear any fresh revelations drop from Gibson's lips.

"What do you mean?" she demanded of Gibson on his reference to Petronella being asked to take the evening off.

"They were kissing in the . . . john," the bartender revealed, throwing the words out in a convulsion of verbal vomit. Unable to keep it all in, he added, "I saw them both with my own two eyes."

"Devon and Petronella," Jasmine gasped. "Where was I?"

"In the office," Gibson replied.

Suddenly, all her suspicions about Devon came flooding back with a tide of emotions that washed over her in waves of bitter betrayal. Why would he do this after everything she had told him about her distrust of men? Was he getting some sort of sick satisfaction knowing he had wormed his way into

Carmilla's affections and now hers? As much as she had learned about Devon, Jasmine realized there were still missing links in her mind and she was going to glue those together, right now.

Shooting Gibson a parting gaze, she tilted her chin upright and walked directly from the bar, along the corridor, and into the office. Devon had just completed a call on the telephone and was in the motion of replacing the handset into its cage when his smile broadened on seeing Jasmine's entry. She had been the bright spot of his day. He could not wait to spend more time learning about this fascinating woman.

"How's your cheek?" she asked, while cutting the distance between them.

"Damn, I forgot about that," Devon drawled, rubbing the freshly shaven side of his face that Petronella had slapped the night before. "It's not painful. Not hurting at all."

"Then let me slap the other one," Jasmine said, doing precisely that. She struck a blow for all womankind dealing with any form of double standards. "Perhaps you'd like to explain your conduct in the restroom, with Petronella."

"Who in the hell told you about—" Devon's eyes narrowed. "Gibson, right?"

Jasmine folded her arms beneath her chest. "I'm waiting."

"Did he tell you which restroom she was in?" Devon inquired, rubbing his right cheek. "Think, because that's very important."

"He said you were kissing her," Jasmine responded. That was all she needed to know.

"She followed me into the men's restroom," Devon began, annoyed. "I'd just finished taking a leak when I turned around and she was there. Before I could send her packing, Gibson walked in and she got a hold of my neck and started taking liberties."

"Are you sure that wasn't the other way around?" Jasmine accused hotly.

"I didn't enjoy kissing her if that's what you're thinking," Devon replied, knowing he could not tell Jasmine the truth about Petronella just yet. She would not believe what he had to say anyway.

"When did it happen?" Jasmine demanded.

"Before I went to London," Devon explained, "and Petronella has apologized. I told her I'd forget about it as long as she remembers that I'm her boss. I then gave her last night off to cool her heels because I didn't want her to spoil my dinner date with you."

It sounded plausible enough. "Oh." Jasmine sighed with a sense of relief that was almost tangible.

"Did our resident blabbermouth mention that . . . that I didn't want her to spoil our dinner?" Devon probed, rubbing his right cheek. "Let me guess. No, he didn't."

Jasmine was instantly remorseful. "Devon, are you all right?"

"Don't worry, I've got more teeth," he said soberly.

"I didn't mean—"

"Didn't I tell you not to pay attention to anything Gibson tells you?" he reminded her sternly.

"I'm sorry," she murmured. "*Je suis désolé.*"

"Boy, you can throw a punch." Devon tried to soothe his cheek.

"I can juggle, too," Jasmine tried to joke, but it

was thin on the ground. "Is there anything I can do?" she asked sweetly. "Like kiss it better?"

Devon immediately whimpered like a child. "Yes," he muttered. "Doctor's orders."

Jasmine laughed. "Come here, you big softy."

She fell into his arms instantly and allowed Devon to plant a firm kiss smack on her lips. Jasmine recognized the deep yearning that immediately came with it. Her body knew that it wanted to take things further, but her mind was wary and as far as she was concerned, there had to be a meeting of the two before she could submit to Devon's heated demands. His persuasion made it much more difficult because every flick of his tongue, every motion of his lips swayed her into an invisible crevice of pure pleasure where she wanted to remain, sated and delirious.

Enjoying the moment, Jasmine raised her arms and circled them around Devon's neck, seeking to push the boundaries a little further into that crevice. Passion unleashed itself from every hidden part of her soul and crept into her mouth from where she transmitted it to Devon. It was almost surreal. Jasmine was in no doubt that the back office was too confined a space for what was about to erupt inside her.

She pulled back before she got carried away. "I'd better go and see to the restaurant," she breathed, attempting to compose herself.

"I've got some more phone calls to make." Devon nodded his agreement. "The street crew needs to regroup to receive the new flyers for the guest band playing this Saturday, so I'll be going out for a while."

Jasmine more than welcomed any distance

between them right now to cool her embers. "Okay," she accepted. "I'll see you later."

"Why did you wear his brooch?" Devon's question came suddenly and so unexpectedly that Jasmine stifled a cough.

Following their blissful encounter earlier in the office—the memory of which was still causing desire to bubble just beneath the surface of her very cool persona—Jasmine had succeeded in removing from her mind all thoughts of Enrico Cajero, the man who had cast such a blight over her recent life. Her planned visit to a pawnshop that weekend would finally root out all trace of him from her existence. So Devon's mention of him now, while she had avoided all discussion about him, was the least welcoming of subjects at that precise moment.

"I liked it—once," she said at last, trying to control a fast-rising tide of anticipation.

"Hmm," was his only reply.

Devon was driving the Jeep and she was comfortably seated beside him. It was the first time since her beginning work at the Birmingham Savoy that she had allowed him to drive her home. He seemed to accept her answer as he stared out across the dashboard at the night traffic, rain-lashed with the dreary outpour while the screen wipers worked overtime to give him a clear view.

But Jasmine felt unnerved by his silence. The last time Devon had tried to inquire about her ex-boyfriend, she had burst out that he had killed her heart and that she had no love left to give to anyone. Devon's response had not escaped her either. Still, she was not going to tempt the fickle hand of fate by dwelling or delving into the past when it was all best forgotten.

"Did you find the street crew to organize distribution of the new flyers?" she queried, steering the topic.

"Yes." Devon nodded without elaboration.

Deeply conscious of the lean, muscled body sitting next to her and the slim, long fingers resting confidently on the steering wheel—fingers that only hours earlier had left her feeling warm, safe, and comfortable—Jasmine sensed a shift in Devon's mood and tried to think through how best she could deal with the situation. "What's the matter?" she was finally compelled to ask.

Since his arrival back at the Savoy, she had noticed Devon looking a little withdrawn. In his absence, she had tactfully kept Gibson at arm's length, while tending to the diners in the restaurant who had enjoyed immensely the club's resident six-piece house band fronted by their most revered vocalist and saxophonist. The dark movement of bass lines, live drums, funky guitar licks, and keyboard vibes had served to keep the embers burning that Devon had stoked before his departure.

She had watched the dancers and their floor show with a longing to be retaken into Devon's arms and be swept across that same maple-wood floor, the chandeliers above twinkling at them. The club, as was the case on weekdays, was semi-busy, which meant she had not been rushed off her feet. It was a mix of the usual midweek faces with a few new ones she hadn't seen before.

Her mind had been trained on a man wearing an expensive suit and breaking monkey nuts, carelessly dropping the casings onto the ballroom floor, when Devon returned shortly after 1:30 a.m. to close the tills and shut down the club for the night. Only when the guests had left, the musicians had packed up their equipment, and all the staff members had taken cabs home, did Devon suggest that she ride with him.

"Did you love him?" he asked quietly, so quiet the words were hardly audible.

"Love Jax?" Jasmine didn't need to think that one through. "No," she answered emphatically.

Devon moved on. "Was that his name? Jax?"

Jasmine inhaled, disliking the turn in conversation. "He was called Enrico Cajero," she explained uneasily. "Jax was a street name."

"What work did he do?" Devon probed further, putting the Jeep into a cruise gear as they drove along the A41 Freeway.

"Do we have to talk about him?" Jasmine protested, now on the defensive.

Devon threw her a sideways glance. "I know you said you'd rather not," he began, "but I want to. Please."

She heard the pleading tone and, to her chagrin, gave in. "He worked in a hotel as the general manager."

"That's decent work," Devon acknowledged, accepting her answer. "When you called him a lowlife I thought he—"

"He wasn't an honest man," Jasmine interrupted, not wishing Devon to get any false ideas about the true nature and character of her ex-boyfriend. "There were a lot of things I didn't know about him, which was why we . . . I parted company."

"How did you meet him?" Devon asked.

"Funnily enough, in a church," Jasmine declared.

"There are rodents in the church, too, and they look for nourishment in young women like you," Devon added, quite cynically.

Jasmine felt a shudder run through her, but continued regardless. "The family I was working for went to Mass every Sunday and during Communion last year Easter, when they invited me along to watch over their two infants, I met Jax." She took her mind back to that point for one brief moment. "He thought the children were mine, but when I explained that I was in New York working as an au pair, he invited me out for coffee. That's when it all began."

Devon heard an odd note in her voice. "What began?"

"A romance," Jasmine admitted softly. "By the summer, the family I was working for took a vacation to their house on Martha's Vineyard, so I invited him to England to meet Carmilla because I needed a break, too."

"And?" Devon anticipated.

"Jax was quite rude to her," Jasmine went on, looking through the windshield at the black sky that lashed rain as they got snarled in blind traffic. "We stayed for one week in June, and in my grandmother's opinion, that was one week too many."

"She never liked him?" Devon guessed.

"No," Jasmine confessed. "Gran-mama nicknamed him 'the boar.' In many ways, she was right about him. We stayed and then returned to America, and that's when I began to learn a lot more. But as always, with a woman, things seem very different when you're wearing rose-colored lenses. It took a while before the glasses came off."

"And that's when you decided to come home," Devon concluded.

"*Oui.*" Jasmine nodded, aware that she was feeling a huge sense of relief at having explained everything to Devon so assuredly and calmly. "When the family I was working for took their yearly vacation to Martha's Vineyard last month, I told the agency I'd be going home for an indeterminate period."

"Did you mean it when you said he'd killed your heart?" Devon asked suddenly.

It was another question that took Jasmine by surprise. "I really didn't want to talk about him then," she said, feeling a touch embarrassed at her outburst. "And, to be honest, it really is an imposition now. I haven't asked you any such probing questions."

"Fire away," Devon invited, as he took the Hockley Flyover that headed toward Handsworth.

Jasmine blurted out the first thought that struck her. "Why did you go to London yesterday?"

"I went to see a firm of solicitors to sign some papers to complete my ownership of the Birmingham Savoy," he stated proudly.

"Oh." Jasmine sighed, realizing that this must've been the transaction Carmilla had talked about. "Why didn't you use a firm in Birmingham to handle the work?"

"Because these are lawyers who liaise with the Home Office," Devon said truthfully. "I was initially under a witness protection program back in the States and was then transferred to the relocation program when I decided to live abroad.

There were formalities that needed to be dealt with, sensitively."

"Of course," Jasmine breathed, trying to understand. But she would never truly comprehend what it had been like. "The trial," she began, trying to envisage the cruel scenario. "Was it terribly hard on you?"

"It was not an easy situation," Devon admitted uneasily. He was not sure he wanted to talk about it, but having forced Jasmine into an area that she was uncomfortable discussing, he felt it hardly fair if he were to try and escape the one topic that he least wanted revisited on his mind. "The murderer was affiliated with a group that was known for its brutal intimidation of others and discovered that I'd been called to testify. I don't know how, but my life was in danger and I had to be taken away from everything."

Jasmine was totally sympathetic. "I can't think how harsh that must've been after you'd recently lost your parents," she said.

"I was tense for much of the time," Devon declared solemnly. "Still in mourning. No one to turn to. Had it not been for Carmilla's invitation to come to England . . ."

Jasmine's heart reached out to Devon. "Please, don't go on," she intoned sadly. She placed her right hand over his left, moments before he shifted gears. "I don't want you to relive the pain. Not ever."

Devon tried to smile, but it was weary on his lips. "I don't think I'll ever truly forget," he said, almost on a whisper. "But I do know I want to get on with my life. I want to find love. Marry. Have three or four children. I want to fill my life with all the things a man is entitled to before he reaches old age."

Jasmine admired his confidence. "And you will." She squeezed his hand, almost as though she was conveying a promise. A deep affection flowed between them that was pure adrenaline and highly potent in the way it touched their souls. "You will."

Chapter Ten

Beneath the white cotton sheets, two bodies were at play. Jasmine had told herself she was not going to enter into another relationship in a hurry, yet here she was holding on to a kiss that was stoking the mutual fires of a blazing passion. Her breasts felt tight, her nipples had peaked until they ached for a man's touch, and as though he knew it, Devon's mouth reached down and sought its new target. One brush and a lick of his tongue and the giggles began.

Once they had entered the house and closed the door behind them, it had almost been impossible to ignore Devon's sensual, erotic caresses as his fingers slid over her slim waist. When his hand crept upward toward the full curve of her breasts, she had known whatever battle she was fighting with herself was over. His timely declaration, whispered so closely to her earlobe as she had tried to wriggle out of her red jacket, was all the encouragement she needed.

"I want to make love to you," Devon told her, much more forthrightly and seductively.

"Yes," she answered weakly, in her acceptance.

They could not get to the attic fast enough. The buttons on her ruffled white collar blouse had been swiftly undone. Devon's white polo jersey was whipped over his head. His trousers, her skirt were discarded with ultraspeed. Jimmy Choo shoes flew in the air and landed next to the black ones Devon had removed from his feet. The rich shade of honey-colored hosiery equally alighted beside dark brown woolen socks that had found refuge at the bottom of the bed.

Devon's confession had sent Jasmine's pulses racing out of control, just as they were now. Covering her trembling limbs was his hard, naked body. Amid giggles, the Calvin Klein underpants had been removed just as easily as when Jasmine unclasped her lacy bra and dangled her breasts provocatively in front of Devon's face. It was all the impetus he needed to pull her into bed with him. Delight shivered through every fiber of her being as Devon whisked away the lacy knickers she was wearing.

His touch was as light as thistledown, the velvety warmth of his fingers providing a torment between pain and pleasure. Devon's mouth was sweetly kissing her soft lips as they parted, her eyes closing with the reaction that had swept its way across her skin. The warm moistness of his tongue skipped along her teeth as Jasmine lifted her full sensitive mouth to his. She could not stop the soft moan of desire that escaped her parted lips while Devon's arms slid around her and drew her closer.

Her lips clung to his persuasive invasion with a conviction of their own. She traced the shape of his own, touching Devon's white teeth before meeting the sensitive tip of his tongue. Devon's lips pressed harder with renewed excitement as he tasted the inner lining of her mouth. For a dizzy moment, he withdrew with maddening deliberation before his ardor took the place of exploration.

He kissed her caramel-brown cheeks, the delicate lids of her eyes, then allowed his mouth to move downward to her throat to find the scented hollow where Jasmine's pulse fluttered crazily. She giggled as a senseless woman in love took over, causing Jasmine to slide her arms around Devon's neck and press his face to her throat. She arched her neck to enhance the deliciously grating touch of his teeth.

Who was overpowering whom, Jasmine had no idea. All she was aware of was the caressing of her ribs, the swelling of her breasts, the tightening of her loins, and the possessive, sensational touch that was causing her to melt inside. She swiftly sank beneath the rushing tide of deep, pulsating passion. Jasmine had never felt more languid and wet. She welcomed the cool night air from the open window gently fanning their two brown naked bodies as they became caught up in a tornado of lust.

Devon ventured lower with his mouth and sought the shadowy valley of Jasmine's breasts once more. There was no moonlight, but he sensed with his tongue her tight breasts and the turgid peak of her nipples. With an ever-rising ardor, he repeated the sucking, teasing motion against the hardened flesh with his lips. A throaty giggle was repressed with a harsh moan of pure delight that leaped from Jasmine's mouth and flew out the window to mingle with the hoot of an owl.

There was nothing restricted or inhibited about their lovemaking. So many weeks had gone by with neither of them admitting their powerful sexual need for each other. They had done nothing but compete for supremacy as to who was going to be in charge of the Birmingham Savoy, so that the window of opportunity had been slow to open. Now Jasmine and Devon seemed gripped by a raw, untamed hunger to merge their raging emotions in a fiercely wild union of bodies and minds.

Jasmine's heart raced and pounded as Devon's mouth moved slowly in the dark down her quivering body, his tongue marking and exploring every secret curve and crevice that met his lips. Jasmine was once more moaning heavily and helplessly into the night, every nerve ending becoming quickly alive with the erotic nature of what Devon was doing.

"You know how to touch me," she whimpered, almost in awe.

Devon raised his head. "That's because you have an amazing body," he responded. "The kind a man likes to feast on."

Jasmine chuckled. She'd never thought of her body as the kind to be worshiped. "You like?"

"I like very much." Devon's voice echoed across the darkened room moments before he dipped his head and began a second onslaught on Jasmine's senses.

She was breathless with the retaking of her lips. Her heart did a crazy flip-flop in her chest as the nerve-tingling caress mellowed her into an almost dreamlike state. The glowing embers of delight in her stomach sparked to life with a flame so hot she was aching to be quenched of her thirst. Devon picked up on her body movements and began to work his fingers between Jasmine's legs. The delicious, sensitized torture caused her to lurch forward involuntarily, which took Jasmine by surprise and forced her to plunder the sensitive skin of Devon's neck with a harsh nip to split the pleasure. It was one of Devon's powerful thighs that kept the rest of her body rooted to the bed.

Jasmine groaned with satisfaction as Devon began to work magic with those very fingers, stroking in one direction and then the other with long scorching caresses at the very juicy core of her womanhood. And with hands framing her hips, he laid a trail of kisses down her midframe to the navel, which he circled lazily with his tongue until Jasmine was gasping at the dual gratification.

"I don't know how much longer I can hold out," Devon growled, as he felt Jasmine's first real hold on his manhood.

She had snuck in there when he least expected it and felt the hardened rod of his arousal throbbing between her fingers. With gentle pressure from her hands, she urged her way up and down the shaft, taking infinite care not to scratch Devon with her nails, though a slight soft grazing as she reached the moist tip elicited an animal sound from his throat, the kind a woman in the throes of passion longs to hear.

"Please tell me you have condoms," she almost pleaded, as she squeezed tighter, enjoying the power she possessed and exerted over Devon at that precise moment.

"Baby, I'll be right back," he whispered, springing from the bed with the agility of a black panther. Within seconds, he returned totally sheathed and ready for his third onslaught.

This time they took turns arousing each other. Arms entangled, legs entwined, bodies twisted to face each other, Jasmine and Devon rolled back and forth across the bed in a constant battle to push the boundaries of restraint to their limits. The silence of the attic was punctuated only by their giggles and moans and the sound of a hooting owl through the window.

Jasmine restlessly nestled beneath Devon and with sweat-slick limbs wet with desire instinctively lifted her hips for Devon to enter her. The touch of his hardened passion against her inner core was all she needed to yank him in. Devon was buried so deep that Jasmine sensed his struggle for readjustment. But her legs had locked around his round bottom and she started the love dance.

Devon held up his body with the strength of his hands and took each thrust steadily and slowly, almost panting for release from the ever-increasing tension that was holding them together. For him, it felt like a lifelong anxiety was finally being allowed to let loose. The tension that was with Jasmine seemed to fill her whole body like a jug of water that needed to be poured out. She eagerly needed more of Devon's thrusting brown rod to take her to the next plateau.

She was striving to reach there, too. Her hips tilted higher in an aggressive motion and her bottom rocked at an assailing pace that mirrored Devon's back motions. They were in perfect tandem with each other, just as they had been on the Savoy's dance floor. There was something indescribable about how she was feeling, about the way her body was performing, almost as though by a will of its own. Jasmine could not understand why

there was an instinct to move her hips higher.
Then, suddenly, the answer came like a thunder-
bolt.

She was blinded when a convulsion of muscles
ripped through her inner core and sent shock
waves throughout every part of her body. Jasmine
almost screamed at the unexpected flash of splintering emotions, so much so that she felt un-
wanted tears emerge at the back of her eyes. Her
heart was thudding like she'd never known before.
She was so overwhelmed that when Devon joined
her in her climax, all Jasmine could do was hold
on to him and relish the tenderness that passed between them. In the distance, the owl hooted one
last time before it went to sleep.

A gentle July dawn heralded a fine warm Friday
morning. The birds were singing and chirping in
the garden outside Devon's bedroom as though
they knew that on a pleasant day such as this, the
seed of love that had been planted was destined to
grow. Jasmine was reluctant to rise and join the rest
of the world. Her grandmother would probably be
downstairs, she mused, with Betty preparing breakfast of ackee and saltfish.

A quick look around revealed a beautiful room
with shades of blues and greens, combined with a
warm hue of yellow that was reflected in the curtains. The lime-green carpet, the pinewood furniture, and the small cane suite in the far corner of
the room were in a more modern style than her
own room. She could also see where Devon had
stamped his personal signature with a selection of

DVDs and CDs that were scattered, rather aimlessly, on the floor close to a small entertainment unit.

She shifted slightly beneath the strong arms that cradled her and was greeted by a thin mustache that had grown more hair. The two eyes above it were closed, but they twitched slightly, which made her smile when she recollected the hours of lovemaking that had gone on until dawn. Even as she licked dry lips that were still tender from Devon's kisses, her body felt prepared to take on a sixth onslaught.

Jasmine knew she had never made love like that before. Ever. Reaching the mountaintop or the highest pinnacle was something she'd never achieved with Enrico. There was no selfishness attached to Devon's touch, his kiss, or his giving or sharing of himself as there had been with her ex-boyfriend. Enrico's pleasure had only been his own. As was often the case with men that were too handsome, she told herself with newfound experience, there was always something lacking in areas not far flung from the bedroom. But Devon had needed no ego boosting. No reaffirmation of his manhood, his looks, or his capability to attract the opposite sex. He was simply a man whose determination was to make her happy.

Her eyes widened with deep fascination as she watched him sleep. He didn't snore and she hardly heard any sound from him, except in the quiet lifting and dropping of his chest. Jasmine raised herself on one elbow and fingered his Afro, which was only slightly out of place. She committed to memory the roasted-chestnut color of his skin that seemed to glisten under the rays of the rising sun intruding through the open window. She reminded herself of the square jawline infested with her kisses, which now displayed a full day's stubble, and noted the rigid full chest in front of her sprinkled with dark curls of hair that had tickled beneath her fingers throughout the night.

The white sheets over them both modestly covered the one part of Devon's anatomy that was already sending curls of excitement throughout her loins. Jasmine suppressed a lustful sigh just as Devon's eyes twitched and slowly opened. She was immediately smitten by the soul-searching gaze that bored into her. He blinked several times before raising his head slightly to lazily gaze downward. Jasmine was unaware of what had caught Devon's attention until she felt the soft bud of her nipple being pulled into his mouth and sucked on gently. Her eyes rolled toward heaven in a hazy daze when, for an instant, she lost her mind.

When her head dropped helplessly into the pillow, Devon found her lips and drugged her with a series of kisses. Weakened, Jasmine accepted every aching touch of his sweet lips. She could not imagine a time when she would ever deny this man the privilege of taking her again and again. Why would any woman want to escape being taken into oblivion by a man she adored? When Devon finally raised his head, Jasmine felt wonderfully alive and a little concerned that she could just about promise Devon anything.

"*Bonjour.*" She smiled, gazing into his eyes.

"Good morning," Devon whispered, nipping her earlobe. "Happy birthday, mademoiselle."

Jasmine felt the shudder of that nip rock her. She raised a knowing brow. "You know me too well, monsieur," she said giggling.

"I know," Devon answered with satisfaction. "Where to kiss you, when to touch you, what to do to you, and how to give you an orgasm."

Jasmine's eyes widened. "What?"

"My guess is that you've never had one before," he told her matter-of-factly. "That ex-boyfriend of yours should be put to shame."

"How . . . how did you know?" Jasmine asked, flabbergasted. She'd never felt so transparent in her life.

Devon propped himself up on one elbow and gazed down at the adorable beauty in his bed. She seemed just as fresh in the early morning sunlight as she did when dressed, only Devon knew that she was still naked beneath his white sheets. He brazenly tugged and pulled a corner of the sheet slightly away from her to reveal the fine shape of Jasmine's breast. No amount of willpower could stop him from running a lazy finger up her arm, down her chest, and around the outline of those heaving breasts.

"I just do," Devon declared. "And you're not frightened to work with me. We understand each other."

"Do we?"

He touched her nipple and felt her reaction. "Come here," he ordered softly.

He pulled her into his arms and smothered her with deep, tempting, sweetly bruising kisses. Jasmine's eyes rolled to the back of her head as she melted right there. Every thought and memory flew from her mind. She was instantly ultrasensitive to the warm body pressed against her own. When Devon slipped an invading finger into the deep portal of her core, catching her offguard, she recognized the lurching forward motion of her body and knew she was in for another treat.

The sixth onslaught was much quicker. In the daylight, there was a certain shyness attached to seeing one's flesh ragged with lust and overbearing excitement. Another condom later and she was on that high rise with her hips. This time, Jasmine had a sense of what she was doing, of what the outcome would be. She was also aware that she wriggled her bottom more readily, was lunging forward more aggressively with her thighs as though she was desperate not to lose the moment. Devon matched her flow with a belligerence of his own until the final moment pushed them both over the edge. And just as before, they hugged each other until their hearts were sated.

"*Ma chère*," Jasmine muttered in French, as she dropped her last kiss for the morning on Devon's lips before departing his bed. "I must shower and change because my parents are coming and we are supposed to pick them up from the train station, remember?"

"Just five more minutes," Devon pleaded, feeling sleepy and worn.

"No." Jasmine was happily adamant. She picked up her clothes from the floor and loosely threw on the blouse and skirt, carrying the other items in her hand as she made her way toward the door. Her last impression of Devon was his naked body modestly covered with lashings of white sheets. "I'll meet you downstairs," she said on a loud whisper, "and not a word to Carmilla."

Jasmine showered amidst a cloud of fragrant steam. She sponged French-milled soap into her skin and closed her eyes as the lathered bubbles soothed and sedated her well-being. She had not wanted to wash Devon from her body, but she was feeling a certain pang of guilty sentiment at having made love to him in the attic while in a bedroom below, her grandmother had been silently sleeping, totally unaware.

But though there was fault attached to her emotions, there was no shame. Devon's image emerged in her mind the moment she rinsed away the bubbles, stepped from the shower cubicle, and mollycoddled herself with a soft cream-colored towel. After lavishing shea butter into her skin, Jasmine dressed in an executive-cut black suit that was smart as well as serviceable, since she would be working at the Savoy later. Underneath it, she chose a white cotton blouse with cuffs that would have a more feminine look when she removed the suit jacket at the restaurant.

After slipping into black leather court shoes, she reached into her Louis Vuitton vanity case and plucked from its interior the Victorian brooch Enrico had given her. Jasmine examined the plunder and its intricate beauty, wondering if Devon was right about its worth. It felt weighty enough. She marveled at his wealth of knowledge on such a small item. If he was right, it meant she could be left with enough money to treat herself to something entirely new, like a fresh pair of shoes to commemorate her birthday.

There certainly wouldn't be any harm making a visit to the Jewelry Quarter and finding out how much she could sell the brooch for, she mused. Taking one last look, Jasmine popped it into her Fendi handbag and positively skipped from her bedroom, down the stairs. She went through the house until she reached the back garden. She suspected that Carmilla would be out there eating breakfast or maybe tending to the blooming roses close by. The bushes would need pruning soon, she further mused, as she happily stepped out onto the patio. Carmilla was indeed seated at the garden table, but Jasmine was taken aback when she recognized the man in a gray pin-striped suit by her side and the two familiar faces with him.

"*Maman, Papa!*" she gasped on a high note. "Andre!"

In the general chorus of French greetings that came next, Jasmine was conscious of several things at once. A small nudge from her mother's elbow, a wink across the table from her father, an acknowledging nod from her brother that said *yeah, she's in love*, and the realization that though her grandmother was old enough to develop a certain perception of things, the twinkling in her eyes suggested she much rather preferred to say nothing.

Jasmine felt a sense of panic. *I wonder if they know*, her mind screamed on the fringes of paranoia. With the exception of her younger brother, Andre, these were older people who probably recognized the telltale signs that resulted from a night of passionate lovemaking. Could they really see the evidence displayed across her face, or was it in the tousled display of her hair that she had painstakingly tried to tame with a fine comb? Or a certain glow in her complexion, the sparkle hidden beneath her mink-colored brown eyes perhaps that revealed too much of the inner peace she was feeling? Jasmine could not be sure.

"What's wrong?" she questioned, straightening her shoulders and observing her parents more closely. Aside from the slight thinning of her father's full head of black hair with the emergence of a few more gray strands and the neat manicure of her mother's short nails, they hadn't changed dramatically at all.

"You look great, doesn't she, Porter?" her mother announced suddenly.

"Must be the boyfriend," he answered knowingly, throwing another wink at Andre.

"Boyfriend!" Carmilla's eyes immediately lit up against the sound of her son's throaty chuckle. "Oh, Jasmine. Where's Devon?"

"Upstairs in his room," Jasmine said, deliberately taking a chair and wedging it in between her mother and father. She eyed them carefully as she seated herself, noting the fine lines in their brown faces while she attempted to read their mobile expressions. Her mother was beautiful in a natural sort of way, feminine, liberated, and not overdressed in a cream-colored tweed suit. Her father loomed tall and majestic in his chair, with his brow tilted in her direction in anticipation of her next word. But Patti simply kept a smile fixed to her face, one Jasmine knew to be suspicious. "How did you get here? I was supposed to be picking you guys up at the train station at twelve-thirty p.m."

"We took a taxi," Patti enthused, smoothing her short brown straight hair. "Your father wanted to surprise you." She handed Jasmine a square blue box, tied with a cream-colored ribbon.

"It's a bracelet," Andre disclosed without thinking. He caught himself up short when he realized Jasmine had not yet unwrapped the present. "I mean . . . you'll like it."

"It's from the three of us," Porter said, dropping a big kiss on his daughter's cheek. "Happy birthday."

Jasmine smiled as she removed the satiny blue paper and opened up a black-embossed box where, nestled on a velvety white cushion, was a slim-line gold tennis bracelet with inset zicronia rubies. With excited fingers taking delight in the new gift, she removed the bracelet and, while placing the box on the table, allowed her father to clip the jewelry around her left wrist.

"It's beautiful," she gloated, showing it off to her grandmother. She kissed both her parents. "Thank you."

Carmilla admired the bracelet's neat fit before adding, "Happy birthday, my dear. I have a gift for you, too, upstairs. I'll ask Devon to fetch it later."

Jasmine's heart skipped at the mention of his name, but she turned and faced her mother with the guise of a woman who didn't want to reveal too much. "So how was the flight?" she asked, knowing full well that her mother hated traveling.

"Tedious," Patti complained. "I'm not in favor of bottled water either, but that's all I wanted to drink."

"On the train into the city from Birmingham International Airport, she had a brandy," Porter teased.

"Two," Andre inserted.

Jasmine giggled. Betty Bately appeared at the garden table with a fresh pot of tea and Carmilla's mail. Jasmine asked the housekeeper for a plate of ackee and saltfish and watched her disappear into the house, feeling happy that her family was with her again. "I want to hear all the family gossip," she breathed.

"Andre's been doing some work in Spain," Patti began softly, picking up the freshly brewed teapot to pour a liberal amount of tea into all the empty cups. "We were just telling your grandmother before you joined us. A small record label there has offered him some work over the holidays. He worked there last Christmas and Easter this year."

"That's brilliant," Jasmine said, encouraged by her brother's progress.

"It's mostly Latino music," Andre expanded, "but it'll look great on my resume when I complete my degree next year."

"Of course," Jasmine accepted, realizing that her brother, with his caramel-brown complexion and handsome features, hadn't changed dramatically either.

"What about you?" Andre asked.

"Me?" Jasmine didn't know where to begin, especially to someone who still held all the boyish charm of a much younger man.

"You should've told me you finished your job in New York," Porter immediately scolded. His voice was not strict, rather more consoling.

"You would've told me to come home, back to France," Jasmine accused lightly, "and I wanted to stay in England for a while with Gran-mama."

"Who has just been telling me what you've been up to," Patti finished, replacing the teapot.

Jasmine felt hot blood rush into her face. She panicked. *It does show.* After all, electrifying hours of lovemaking were bound to leave their mark. "What do you mean?" she said, evading, not wishing to be taken anywhere near the subject.

"The Birmingham Savoy," Porter stated tersely. "I understand from my mother that you're overseeing the restaurant there."

"*Oui*," Jasmine muttered, hardly able to handle her relief. "I'm enjoying the work."

"What made you decide to do a job like that?" Patti asked her daughter with a good dosage of curiosity. "You were doing steady work with the agency as an au pair."

"It was Gran-mama's idea," Jasmine confessed, looking across at her grandmother. Carmilla was sifting silently through her mail, but it was clear to all present at the table that she was avidly listening to all that was being said. "She started the—"

"Notion that Jasmine needed a sense of direction," Carmilla said, taking over, immediately raising her head and ignoring a half-opened envelope. She tossed a maddening glance at her granddaughter and Jasmine acknowledged the nuance in her tone. "Devon owns the club and I suggested that Jasmine work there to develop some new skills."

"Well, I'm surprised," Porter remarked in an admiring tone. "Jasmine was never one who liked too much hard work."

"*Papa*," Jasmine murmured, as she heard footsteps out on the patio. It was Betty returning with her plate of ackee and saltfish.

"I wonder what's keeping Devon," Carmilla intoned.

"How are things with your godson?" Porter inquired on raised eyebrows.

"Much better," Carmilla replied with a wide smile as she reached for her cup of tea. "Since he opened the Birmingham Savoy, his investment has doubled. I did all I could for him, but the credit for all he has done is his own and something he deserves." She took a sip from her cup before adding, "Your aunt Helena wants to hold the Jamaican Independence Day Charity Gala there next month."

"Wonderful," Porter approved. "We must fly over again and attend."

Jasmine forked her way through her breakfast before saying, "I'll be working there later if you want to come down with *Maman* and take a look."

"I'll come, too," Andre inserted.

"We're only here for the weekend," her mother said sadly. "I'm expected back at the hospital on Monday, your father is working on a new contract, and Andre flies to Spain on Tuesday to do some summer work. I think we'll spend our time with your grandmother and visit the club in August."

"If you say so," Jasmine accepted, disheartened. But her spirits quickly lifted as she heard another set of heavier footsteps approaching.

"So, are you going to tell me about your boyfriend?" her father's voice whispered into her ear as she watched the tall frame of a man step out onto the patio.

He was dressed in black corduroy trousers, an open-necked white shirt, and a paisley-gray waistcoat that made him appear taller than his six-foot frame. Devon's hair was well groomed, too, the recent trim and morning shave accentuating the thin line of his mustache added strength to his features. His gaze crept across the small gathering before landing on Jasmine. Their eyes met. Some inner emotion flickered into his eyes but was quickly hidden. They stared wordlessly at each other.

"Ah, Devon." Carmilla instantly swallowed, replacing her cup into its saucer. "You remember Jasmine's parents?"

"Of course." He strolled over and effected a series of formal greetings with a firm handshake.

"They'll be staying for the weekend," Carmilla continued, as she watched her son fix his burgundy-colored tie against his white shirt collar before he offered Devon his hand.

"That's very nice," Devon continued, throwing a lazy leer at Jasmine.

He joined them at the table. "I'm free until this afternoon if you need driving anywhere," he offered, reacquainting himself with the Charlesworth family from France.

"Thank you," Porter said, "but I think I'd like to get some rest. Maybe chill out right here in the garden."

"Why not?" Carmilla approved. "Patti?"

"I'll stay with Porter," she answered.

"I'd like to go out and buy some CDs," Andre piped in.

"That's settled," Devon accepted, smoothing his moustache. "We'll leave right after breakfast. Jasmine?"

"I'll come along, too." She smiled, feeling betrayed that Devon had not returned the smile. "I've got a jewelry boneyard to go to."

The Jeep pulled up into the heart of Birmingham city. Devon left it in gear and cut the engine. With Andre seated in the back and Jasmine next to him up front, he didn't want to sound too alarmist when he turned and faced Jasmine. She appeared to be in a contented mood sitting next to him, her bag on her lap. In control of her poise as well as her feelings, he admired her constraint.

He, on the other hand, had been bursting with
energy since the moment he awoke and was filled
with enough force to tell his godmother about
their newfound relationship. But that energy had
been zapped by Jasmine's parting comment when
she left his bed. And seeing her at the breakfast
table with her parents was not the right moment
to say anything, but he could not hold in his disappointment any longer, not when the remark
was still resonating in his head.

"What was all that about, not a word to Camilla?"
he whispered into her ear as she released her seat
belt.

Jasmine had known something was wrong when
Devon seemed more quiet than usual during breakfast. She had also noted the daunting gaze he'd
tossed at her on several occasions. She'd thought
perhaps her parents' presence had reminded him
of the loss of his own and that having spent the
morning in each other's arms may have attributed
to a fit of nerves. It had proved incredibly hard for
her to keep her own composure intact with her
father prying for details about her love life, but
now to scramble her thoughts together under
Devon's steely gaze was a supreme effort for her. Jasmine had no reply ready. She had to clear her
throat and lick her lips before any words emerged.

"I . . . er . . . thought we'd wait," she answered
on a low tone.

"For what!" Devon exclaimed.

"Are you two arguing?" Andre intruded, leaning
forward from the backseat until he was pretty
much in their faces between the two front seats.

"No!" Devon and Jasmine said in unison.

"Then can we go?" Andre leaped into action and jumped from the Jeep.

Jasmine quickly turned to Devon. "I think Granmama already knows," she hissed, annoyed.

"What?"

"I'll see you back at the house," she concluded, picking up her bag. "We'll talk then."

"Don't you want a ride home?" Devon asked, his brows raised in surprise.

Jasmine departed the Jeep. "No." With that answer, she slammed the passenger door shut and quickly disappeared into the crowd.

She felt the prickle of tears behind her eyelids as her feet carried her along toward the city center. This was not how she'd expected her day to flow. Devon had spoken to her as though they had been living a deception that had gone on for too long, as though they were making fools of her family. But that was not the truth. She had simply wanted to wait for the right moment, perhaps after church on Sunday or during her grandmother's afternoon luncheon. The formalities were not yet set in her head. Now she felt her day was destined to be ruined.

I'll be damned if I spend my birthday in tears, she told herself, while moving through the throng of people milling around. It had been a while since she last looked around Birmingham or walked the city by foot. In that moment, Jasmine decided she would take the opportunity to see some of the landmarks, take in a little of the architecture, civic spaces, and public floral displays that created a corridor through England's third largest city. She would also enjoy a smidgen of British culture to boost her mood.

She started with some interesting enclaves and glimpses of grandeur in Birmingham's cultural hot spots. Then there was the redbrick and terra cotta Gothic fantasy of the Victoria Law Courts, the Old Square where a relief mural showed the history of the site from the thirteenth century, and Victoria Square, where the centerpiece, a nude in a fountain called *The River,* was locally known as the "floozy in the Jacuzzi."

After seeing more attractions, she was finally on Colmore Row, working her way toward one of the two historic trails Devon had mentioned that led to the city's Jewelry Quarter. Most of the buildings were second-generation late-Victorian structures. The Charm Bracelet Trail and the Findings Trail were designed to provide visitors to the city the opportunity to unlock some of its secrets. Without quite knowing where she was going, Jasmine opted to take the Findings Trail as she was closest to Newhall Street. She began the lengthy walk, noting the thirty different sidewalk slabs with plaques imbedded and made from stainless steel in the design of hallmark tags, which provided information about the area.

She momentarily paused outside a shop front and took a steadying breath. As she did so, Jasmine caught her reflection in the glass display window. With high flags of color in her brown cheeks, which she had to admit were not brought about by anger, she looked alive in a way she could not remember having seen in herself for a long time. She smiled moments before she recognized the image standing behind her. A dart of alarm speared throughout her body. Enrico's sneering expression was as cold as ice.

Jasmine spun round, eyes furiously searching for a sign of him, but Jax was nowhere to be seen. He had disappeared faster than a ship in fog. Her heart started to pound anxiously as she thought of all the possibilities that could've led her to imagine he was there. *My birthday,* her mind divulged. Telling herself not to panic, Jasmine swung her Fendi handbag over her shoulder and gingerly started walking, taking one step at a time, looking sideways for any sign of the Puerto Rican who had expertly escaped her. She was now certain her mind was not playing tricks. He was here.

The Jewelry Quarter was just around the corner. One turn was all it would take. All Jasmine could think about was getting rid of the brooch Enrico had given her. With it gone, he would have no further hold on her. Just as Carmilla had said, that would be the end of the matter. Her footsteps quickened. She looked behind her. There was no one there. But before she could join the Charm Bracelet Trail, Jasmine walked straight into a human wall and found herself looking into the come-to-bed green eyes of the man she'd left behind in New York.

Chapter Eleven

"Jasmine!" He displayed his white teeth.

Enrico's voice was calm and relaxed. His green eyes kept their gaze fixed like an iguana and his hands were slightly raised in surrender. He inched one step forward, braced for action. For one mad moment, Jasmine imagined herself a wild horse about to be appeased by its owner. She noted the way he was standing, too, anticipating the moment to throw a noose around her neck. Jax seemed unsure of himself. He could not gauge her reaction, nor could he predict what her response would be. And that's just how he was, Jasmine now realized. A man totally incapable of reading her emotions.

His appearance hadn't changed. Enrico was dressed in a purple suit that was ruffled from weeks rather than hours of traveling across the Atlantic. The black silk twill Nehru shirt he was wearing, opened at the collar to reveal the herringbone chain he often liked to showcase, seemed worn, too. She was surprised to find that the polished black and white cap-toe shoes on his feet were actually shining. It was in direct contrast to the rest of him. There was the haggard look on his face, the brown hair slicked back into a ponytail but which lacked the sleekness she once admired, and a fawn-colored stubbled jawline, unlike his smooth shave and playboy glow. To see Enrico now, it was more as though he were escaping something than trying to lasso her.

"Didn't I tell you not to try and find me?" she attacked on a fiery note.

"Jasmine, listen," Enrico pleaded, keeping his voice calm. He took another step forward. "I need to ask you something."

"No, you don't," Jasmine rebuffed, swinging her bag from her shoulder as though she were about to use it to defend herself. "Now get out of my way."

"Listen!" Enrico's voice had turned to steel. "I need to *know* something."

His sudden grip on her wrist, holding her firmly in place, was the last thing Jasmine needed. "I don't want to marry you," she said, panicked at recognizing the iron-cast nuance in his tone. "I don't love you and I don't want to be your wife." With that answer, Jasmine broke free from his strong grip and took to her feet.

She retraced the Findings Trail in a hurry, knowing Enrico was right behind her attempting to catch up. She heard his heavy panting. Felt stricken with fright that he was gaining pace. The horde of people who were browsing the shops were unmoved as she darted and wove her way through them. Perhaps they thought she was heading for a bus or was late for an appointment. Jasmine did not know which. All she knew was she wanted help and was not going to get it. The idea of screaming seemed futile under the circumstances. It was a reasonably warm July afternoon, she was on the street in stark daylight, and Enrico, playing catch-up behind her, did not look at all threatening. Her only recourse was to outmaneuver him.

She ran across the street to the other side, marginally missing a car that beeped its horn so loud, onlookers were alerted of her mad haste. A quick toss of her head saw Enrico struggling to negotiate the traffic. It was the opportunity Jasmine needed. She sidled into the nearest boutique, picked up two jackets from a rack, and headed straight for the ladies' changing room.

Inside, Jasmine panted for air. She needed to sit down and think. It was obvious to her now why Enrico had followed her. She had left New York in a hurry with no real explanation as to why she'd departed his life. In her mind, Enrico needed closure. He needed to be told why she could not marry him. She would have to be tactful. Use carefully chosen words to suggest that there was more she wanted from her life than being the wife of a hustler. That was all there was to it. Jasmine even told herself this was something she could achieve without any mention of Devon.

But as a worst-case scenario began to formulate in her head, she instantly sought refuge in one of the changing room cubicles and dropped her bag onto the hard-tiled floor. She sank her body, helplessly, onto the small wooden bench. A moment later, she realized that the catch on her black bag had snapped open. There was spillage from inside her Fendi all over the floor.

"Shit," Jasmine uttered, reaching to the floor to pick up her lipstick, driver's license, pocketbook diary, a tampon, fountain pen, and credit cards. She returned each item and was about to snap the bag shut when her eyes caught sight of the Victorian brooch. It had been flung from the bag and was on the floor. Jasmine reached down and was suddenly dumbstruck. Within seconds, she was on her knees. On closer scrutiny, she found herself staring dazedly at twenty small pieces of opaque-colored stones.

Her mouth fell open when she realized they were uncut diamonds.

The bastard, her mind screamed. Five minutes later, she was handing over the two new jackets to the store attendant. *So that's what Jax wanted.*

"Any good?" the pretty blonde asked, indicating the jackets.

Jasmine shook her head in the negative.

At street level, she felt unnerved. There was no time to examine the brooch or to sell it. She needed to get home. Jasmine told herself this over and over as she frantically searched the street for any sign of Enrico. It was hard to think. Her mind was working overtime. Devon had told her the brooch was worth more than a few bucks, but now she was to discover that the plunder inside was probably worth millions.

As she was heading back toward the city center, another thought struck her. She had thought Enrico wanted answers for ending their relationship. It was evidently clear this was far from the truth. His only reason for being in England was to get the brooch back. Nothing more. Jasmine wondered how she factored in his equation. Did this man truly seek her hand in marriage or was she someone he had used as a means to an end? She was so startled by this revelation, she failed to see the reemergence of the figure in front of her.

"*Violá!*" Enrico said sarcastically.

Jasmine took a step back.

"Don't run away, please," he implored, in a more mellow tone. Again his hands were carefully raised, and this time Jasmine realized he was suggesting he would not harm her. "I need to know . . ." He paused, almost on a disbelieving breath. "Do you still have the brooch I gave you?"

Jasmine nodded dumbly.

"Oh God," Enrico breathed happily. He intimated with his hands a silent prayer of thanks. "Where is it? Can we go get it? Do you have it with you?"

"Hmm," Jasmine mumbled, stunned.

Mindlessly, she reached into her Fendi bag and took the brooch out. She handed it over without question, without even looking into Enrico's eyes. She could not bear to see how much he had lowered himself. She could not even admit that she had ever found this man adorable in her own eyes. There was so much pain attached to knowing how easy it had been to fall for the wrong man. And Enrico Jax Cajero was such a person, full of charm, magnetism, and style. All the right surface attitude to lure an unsuspecting woman. Jasmine did not know how much she had been in danger with him, only that she was thankful to have left him when she did.

"I'm sorry I have to do this," he apologized, looking amazingly relieved though there was not the slightest bit of shame on his face. "It's just that—"

Jasmine did not want to hear him out. She had nothing to say. Nothing at all. This was how they should end it, with her simply walking away. And that's what she did. She did not look back and Enrico did not follow her. He'd got what he wanted and she was going . . . to church. Gus mentioned she could call there anytime and Jasmine needed somewhere to think. Some place to cry out the last vestiges of what she had felt for Enrico. And she needed to say a quiet prayer for surviving such an emotionally draining ordeal.

She took a bus and later walked into the church forecourt. Jasmine did not know if the church doors would be open. She was thankful to find that they were. In the distance, as she entered and snuck into a pew, she could hear the band playing a hymn she recognized to be a favorite of her grandfather. If only Pastor Henry Charlesworth was with her now, Jasmine mused, before she went down on her knees and took a Kleenex from her jacket pocket. Maybe he could tell her what to do, for no amount of prayers could help her now as she looked up toward heaven, opened her mouth, and spat out twenty small uncut diamonds onto the white tissue laid out in front of her.

"Hi!" a voice suddenly intruded.

Jasmine quickly closed the tissue and turned to find Gus Thompson towering over her. He looked slightly different from when they had last met, but was still very much part of the modern youth culture dressed in a pair of black Fubu jeans, a green sweater, Timberland boots, and sporting a head of fresh cornrows to complement the new style of his multishaven eyebrows.

"*Bonjour,*" she breathed, surprised.

"I thought I heard someone come in," Gus said brightly. "What are you doing here?"

"You said I could stop by anytime and I wanted to see what the place looked like when it's empty," Jasmine explained, quickly planting the tissue into her jacket pocket. "Before he died, my grandfather and I used to visit the church when it was quiet."

"Old Pastor Henry Charlesworth," Gus acknowledged. "Mom told me he was a legend in the church back in his day."

"Yeah," Jasmine agreed, feeling honored. "My grandfather was so good at delivering a sermon, he and my grandmother traveled all over the world at the invitation from several churches who requested him to preside over their congregations."

Gus extended his own invitation. "Why don't you join me out back with the brothers?" he said, helping Jasmine to her feet. "I'm rehearsing with the band."

"I can't stay long," Jasmine accepted. "I should be starting work at the Birmingham Savoy soon."

"How's that going?" Gus probed, while they walked the length of the aisle toward the organ. There was a small space at the back large enough for a band of young black men to practice their music.

"It's going great," she answered, taking a seat on a stool and nodding her greetings to four band members, similarly dressed like Gus and who were taking pride in their musical instruments.

"Guys, I'd like you all to meet Jasmine Charlesworth," Gus introduced. "She's Carmilla Charlesworth's granddaughter. Let's show her what we can do."

It was as though the rehearsal had specially been prepared soley for her. Jasmine was treated to a private showing of what would be offered to the congregation on Sunday. As the hymn seeped into her soul and the vocals spiritually heightened her emotions, she became tearful. Her thoughts reluctantly strayed to Jax Cajero. He was one of the bright-eyed, bushy-tailed men who had put excitement and adventure into her life. It had been one long adrenaline rush. But she could never have married someone like him, bouncing through life on a whim, taking what little of real love he would have to offer.

She never doubted, at one time, Enrico cared for her. However, any attachment from him was meant to be spread thinly like jelly. She could not possibly have taken his marriage proposal seriously. And just when she thought he had come to England to validate his offer of taking her hand into that fine institution of human bonding, Enrico's shallowness was made more clear. His only interest lay in taking back the brooch he had given her.

A sudden sweet memory of being crushed in Devon's arms made Jasmine catch her breath in a shuddering sigh of disappointment. How was she going to explain everything to him? She could not imagine keeping all this from Devon, not when there was a substantial fortune in diamonds hidden in her jacket pocket. Jasmine was still stunned she'd even dared take them. A strange feeling told her it would be wrong to put them back.

Yet she was aware that if Enrico knew they were inside the brooch, it would only be a matter of time before he wanted the diamonds when he found them missing. Jasmine resisted the urge to wilt like a flower and threw a purposeful smile at the church's young men. They were as good as any five-piece male Gospel band on the world stage. The song over, she disguised the turbulence of her emotions and showed marginal enthusiasm with the clapping of her hands.

"Bravo," she heartedly exclaimed. She was still clapping when two newcomers entered the small space, holding trays with mugs of coffee and biscuits.

"Jasmine," Lilian gushed. "We didn't know you were here."

"*Bonjour*," Jasmine greeted. "I'm visiting to hear the band."

"We were helping in the kitchen downstairs," Martha explained, immediately placing a mug of coffee into Jasmine's free hand. "We cook down there on occasion, you know, for the shelter across the street."

"Sounds like very rewarding work," Jasmine said, accepting the mug and watching while Lilian and Martha distributed coffee to the others.

"Are you here with Mr. Rutherford?" Lilian ventured to ask.

Jasmine felt the sudden tremor of awareness at the mention of his name. "No. I—"

"He's in love with you," Gus suddenly blurted out.

Jasmine choked on her coffee.

"He told me," Gus continued, honesty resonating in his tone. The other members of the band suddenly chuckled. "He loved you from the moment he saw you," he added.

Jasmine shook her head vigorously. "Gus, there's no such thing as love at first sight," she insisted cynically, trying not to disparage him in front of his male friends. "Monsieur Rutherford and I have not known each other very long and this is not pleasant, you making up stories."

"I'm not," Gus insisted, wounded. He turned to the other members of the band, nodding for their support. "When a man knows, he knows, right?"

"He mustn't love her," Lilian instantly mouthed out like an old sage about to reveal a bygone prophecy. "He can't."

"Lilian?" Jasmine probed, noting the strenuous high tone in her voice.

But Gus was laughing. "Why can't he?" he drawled, looking boyishly at his friends as though the elderly woman had gone mad. "She's single. He's single. What's the problem?" He shrugged.

"The problem is . . ." Lilian began, hardly daring to confess what she knew. But being a woman who loved to pass on hearsay, she spat it out anyway. "Devon Rutherford is Pastor Henry Charlesworth's grandson."

Gus stepped back in awe. "Way to go, old-timer," he joked in reference to the late pastor.

"It's true," Martha inserted blandly.

"I don't believe you," Jasmine protested in denial, jumping from the stool. "Why are you saying this to me, you . . . you heathens?"

Lilian would not be told otherwise. "It was the biggest scandal to hit the church congregation back in 1953."

"Didn't I tell you that a dead spirit often avenges filthy talk against a loved one?" Jasmine bristled, offended. "You take that back about my grandfather, or else."

"Ask Carmilla about Gracie Manning," Martha expanded, feeling slightly saddened that the whole truth of the matter was now out in the open. "Ask your grandmother who got Gracie pregnant."

On that disclosure, Jasmine dropped the mug.

* * *

Jasmine mulled over the horrible news in her mind like acid sizzling into cold metal as she returned to the house. As she quietly closed the front door and thought she could steal her way upstairs, unseen, she heard a bout of laughter from the living room. A famous Caribbean calypso was playing on the stereo system and her grandmother's voice echoed loudly, indicating she had found her stash of Kentucky bourbon.

"You can't call yourself a West Indian without having heard of Lord Kitchener," Carmilla boomed, amused. "'Sugar Bum Bum' was his biggest hit and the best calypso to ever leave the shores of Jamaica. We used to dance to it like this."

Jasmine could not resist peeping through the door where she glimpsed Carmilla showcasing her dancing talent to Andre and her parents. Her feet shuffled from left to right and the flavor of the music caused Carmilla to dip low and wiggle her bottom in the manner of an old lady lively enough to attempt reliving her youth. A smile creased Jasmine's lips as she watched how well her grandmother moved. At the age of eighty-two, she still possessed grace and agility in every movement. It hardly seemed possible Carmilla could still perform to a calypso so well.

"There you are." A voice suddenly startled her. "I'm leaving for the Savoy in ten minutes. I thought you'd be back sooner."

Jasmine turned and saw Devon walking from the kitchen. "You shouldn't creep up on me like that," she berated him.

"Where have you been?" he asked, reaching out

to take her by the waist, but Jasmine pulled back, and this surprised him. "What's wrong?"

"Can we talk?" she whispered. "In your room?"

Devon didn't like the sound of her voice. "Sure." He made toward the stairs. "Come on."

In the attic, he closed the door. Jasmine nervously perched herself on the edge of his bed. He wanted to reach out to her, tell her that whatever the problem it would be okay, but Devon felt rooted. His brain told him it would be best if he remained standing with his back against the door, barring her escape. He would listen to whatever she wanted to say.

"That night we were in the restaurant," Jasmine began, "and you thought I had something to hide. I did." Her heart was racing. "Jax . . . Enrico Cajero had asked me to marry him."

Devon felt the news hit like a grenade. "And?" he ventured, hoping to dear God he was not about to lose the one woman he felt certain he had fallen in love with.

"I turned him down and that was that. I never thought I'd see him again." Jasmine tried to curtail her voice as she continued. "Then today, I walked right into him."

"He's here?" Devon almost choked. He felt the sudden impact when his heart started racing.

Jasmine nodded forlornly. "I thought he had tracked me down because he wanted to know why I wouldn't marry him, but that wasn't it at all," she said, her voice trembling as the realization hit a second time. "Jax came to England to take back the brooch he had given me."

"Where . . . how . . . ?" Devon hardly knew which question to ask first. "I thought you were going to pawn it."

"I was in the Jewelry Quarter, looking around for a suitable shop to go into, and suddenly he was there," Jasmine explained. Her own heart was racing faster. "He followed me."

"Followed you?"

"I think he was at the club the other night," Jasmine said, moving on. "I thought it was the chandeliers playing tricks with my eyes, but—"

Devon wanted her to cut to the chase. "What happened?"

"I gave him the brooch," she finished.

"That's it?"

"Yes." Jasmine nodded. "Jax took the brooch and left."

Devon's head was filled with relief. A weight suddenly fell from his shoulders. "That's good, isn't it?" he said, breaking into a smile. "You got rid of it. That's what you wanted. It obviously meant something to him or else he wouldn't have traveled all this way to get it back."

"It meant something all right," Jasmine said, nodding and reaching into her jacket pocket. She removed the Kleenex and opened it out to reveal what she had found. "Before I gave him the brooch, I dropped it. It fell open and these were inside."

Devon slowly cut the distance between them until he found himself staring at the small collection of uncut stones. "Je-sus," he drawled out slowly. "The Guerilla Diamonds."

Jasmine looked at him. "What?"

"Oh God." Devon rubbed an exasperated hand across his forehead. "I thought there was something about that brooch. It was an antique Victorian Estruscan Revival cameo in nine-karat rose gold. A 'one of a kind,' I said. Why didn't I pick up on that? The black enamel and scrolled open work at the edges was a dead giveaway. It should never have felt so heavy."

"How . . . how do you know all this?" Jasmine asked, suddenly frightened.

Devon rushed to the pine chest of drawers in his room and pulled out a newspaper clipping. It was an old copy ripped from the *New York Daily News* and reported on a heist at a famous hotel where robbers had successfully gotten away with an undisclosed amount of stones that became nicknamed "the Guerilla Diamonds." He handed the paper to Jasmine, who scanned it at speed. She read about the local African populations who were brutalized, maimed, or drugged into submission and forced to work for rebels in the search for diamonds.

"In Sierra Leone, these are called 'alluvial' diamonds," he told her. "They are found at the bottom of riverbeds and require a lot of digging, shoveling, and mesh-sieving to find them. Cut and polished, they'd be worth around two million. As these are uncut, I'd know them anywhere. I used to work at the distinguished jewelers in that hotel."

Jasmine gasped. "You told me you worked in accountancy."

"That was me, trying to forget my past," Devon replied, apologetic. "I didn't want to go through any of this. I never thought I would *have* to, but—"

"Jax was the general manager at this hotel," she interrupted, pointing at the news clipping. "Did you know that?"

"What?" Devon hollered.

"Devon, I'm scared," Jasmine revealed, thoroughly shaken. She folded the Kleenex and placed it on the bed. "You need to start from the beginning, because this is . . . too bizarre and I'm having a hard time keeping up."

Devon seated himself next to her and began to unfold his old life. He had worked at a jeweler's in the New York hotel. Some diamonds had been deposited there for safekeeping by two African men, but Devon's boss had suspected they were blood diamonds and was duty-bound to report his suspicions. But before the alert, the jewelers were robbed and gunshots had been fired. One man was murdered and Devon witnessed the slaying and agreed to testify.

Threats on his life forced him to be taken into the witness protection program for his own security before the trial. He always thought the robbery was an inside job, but there had never been any evidence to substantiate this, and after the trial, when the murderer was left on death row, he left the jewelry business and started his new life in England. The Guerilla Diamonds had never been found, until now.

"The hotel was supposed to be a haunt for international statesmen, globetrotting businessmen, and foreign politicians," he continued, "but I'd always suspected something else was going on other than it being used for visiting diplomats."

"If I know Jax," Jasmine confessed, "it would also have been a meeting place for international arms dealers and major criminals."

"What are you talking about?" Devon inquired.

"Enrico Cajero had his feet in waters where he should not have been paddling," Jasmine said, feeling a flurry of tears erupting. "He stole the brooch from a guest room and he was probably too stupid to realize there were diamonds hidden inside it. That's what he does. My ex-boyfriend is a thief."

Devon's eyes widened at the revelation. "That means whoever did the robbery was a guest at the hotel," he suddenly surmised, his mind working double time. "They had a custom-made compartment put into the back of the brooch where they could successfully hide the diamonds and leave the hotel without detection. All the guest rooms were searched. The police found nothing. And the robbers were probably just as surprised when they couldn't find their brooch."

Jasmine's tears welled over. "They found Enrico instead and he had to tell them that he gave the brooch—"

"To you," Devon finished.

It was like piecing a tremendous jigsaw puzzle together. "The robbers are here in England," she gasped. "They must be. I'm in trouble." She started to cry.

"Darling!" Devon placed his arm around her shoulder. "You're not alone in this. I'm here." He kissed her at the side of her cheek. "There are people I can call. I can deal with this."

"But Enrico—"

Devon kissed the tip of her nose, noting that Jasmine pulled away from him slightly. "No man is ever worth your tears, and the right man will never make you cry, so don't waste any on Jax Cajero. He's going to get his comeuppances."

"Told you I'd get Mr. Van Phoenix his brooch back," Enrico triumphed, as he returned to the

Hyatt Hotel in central Birmingham and tossed it across the room.

Johnny the Bear caught the brooch like a real trouper and clasped his strong big hand around it. It felt good to have it. For him, the long journey was now over. His only impediment was to tie up the loose ends. He threw a smirk across the room at Enrico Cajero and weighted the brooch in his hand. "Fine work," he said, curious that the brooch felt a touch lighter. "Where's the girl?"

"Back at her grandmother's, I expect," Enrico said, relieved. He perched himself on the edge of one of the room's twin beds and looked at Johnny.

The bear was standing next to the vast curtained window that overlooked the city. The Hyatt was far too plush for them both, though Johnny looked more at home in his new classy suit. Enrico was still wearing the one he had left New York in. At least the hotel's valet had pressed it before he followed Jasmine from her grandmother's house that morning in a rented car.

Enrico had not felt ashamed seeing her again, knowing his only reason was to get the brooch back. And he admired Jasmine's good sense not to verbally slate him, though it surprised him she had kept her mouth shut. That girl had done the right thing leaving him and not taking his proposal of marriage seriously. What was he going to do with a wife anyway? Enrico chuckled to himself at the whimsical prospect.

"You happy now?" Johnny remarked on hearing the chuckle.

"I'm good and I have a great business proposition for you. About them rocks," he opened with the voice of reason. Something eased inside Enrico as his broad I'm-a-good-guy smile lit up. "I figure if they're from Angola or the Democratic Republic of Congo, they must've been used by a rebel group to finance war against their government, which means you can't sell them legally through Antwerp. That's the principal world market for uncut diamonds, right?"

Johnny didn't answer. He weighed the brooch again in the palm of his hand and sensed something was wrong.

"I can help you sell them," Enrico continued. "I also figured that you got them from that hotel robbery that went down at the jeweler's in my hotel, which means the rebel group who wanted to use them as currency to buy weapons from a contact at the hotel is also looking for them rocks. I can be your go-between guy. You'd be surprised what connections I have."

Johnny the Bear flipped open the brooch and stared vacantly. "Where are they?" he demanded weakly.

"I can make a few phone calls when we get back to the States." Enrico's smile widened. "Set up a rendezvous with—"

"Where are the goddamn diamonds?" Johnny grunted like a bull seeing the color red.

A heartbeat later, Enrico asked, "What . . . what did you say?"

"They're not in here." Johnny held up the empty brooch for emphasis.

Enrico rose to his feet, offended. "I . . . I thought you had the combination numbers inside that thing for a safety deposit box back in New York," he voiced in disbelief. "Van Phoenix told me—"

"Forget what he told you," Johnny growled, his

fist tight. He needed to punch something, and Enrico Cajero looked the perfect target. In one swift movement, he cut the distance between them and sent his fist pile-driving into Jax's midsection. Johnny enjoyed his first moment of satisfaction since their awful journey had begun. He watched Enrico curl over in agony, holding his liver down to stop it from jumping out of his throat. "That's for getting me into this shit," he bristled, enraged.

White blinding light flashed before Enrico's eyes. "I didn't know the diamonds were in there," he pleaded, bemoaning the sudden affliction. "I swear."

Johnny hit him again. "And that's for trying to be a smart-ass," he said.

He had a fist like a cinder block. Enrico squealed at the incredible pain. "Don't do me over, please," he begged. "I'll help you get them back. We just need to figure out who has them."

"Your ex-girlfriend, stupid," Johnny snarled, turning to prowl across the hotel room floor like a wildcat. "And we got to play this cool, because if she's gone to the cops—"

"Jasmine's not like that," Enrico interrupted in her defense. A moment of clarity hit him when he realized why she had not said anything on his finding her a second time. She must have had them hidden in her mouth. "If she's found the rocks by accident, she'll be running scared."

Johnny's brows rose speculatively. "Is that right?"

"That's right," Enrico insisted, buying time.

"In that case," Johnny considered, "we can probably avoid more bloodshed."

"What?" Enrico gulped.

"The two rebel group representatives who

brought the diamonds to the hotel to make the exchange with their arms dealer are no longer a
problem," Johnny remarked evilly. "One's on death
row doing time for murdering the other one, who
is dead. They thought a double cross had gone
down with each other when we robbed the hotel
jeweler's and took their stones. And now that you
know what I'm capable of, you'll do as I tell you."

"Yes." Enrico nodded without question.

"That waitress you got sweet on outside the
club where your ex-girlfriend works, what's her
name . . . Petro?"

Enrico gulped. "Petronella."

"You still got her number?"

"I got it."

"Call her now," Johnny ordered on a foul note.
"Ask her if she'd like to earn a fast buck and say
it nicely."

Chapter Twelve

For Jasmine Charlesworth, idyllic family life in Birmingham was approaching paranoia. The weekend rolled by in an unrelenting battery of nerves.

After her amazing confession to Devon about the brooch and its contents, Jasmine felt she had hardly enough brain span left to deal with her family and their endless demands for her attention. Carmilla presented her with a new watch for her birthday. Her parents talked constantly about how twenty-nine years had whirled by in a flurry, and before she departed to work at the Birmingham Savoy, she learned from her father that Jax Cajero had visited him in Paris.

Her father indicated she was to receive a birthday surprise from Enrico, much to the disapproving grunt ejected by her grandmother. Jasmine was almost panicked into admitting that Enrico's visit was already upon her. This made the two-night stretch at the ballroom more hectic. There was the mask she wore to hide the turmoil of having to find a safe haven to place the diamonds in, and there was the fixed smile to appease her parents over breakfast and dinner.

The guest band and the storm they brewed with their music at the Savoy did little to sedate her mood. Though Saturday night proved to be one of the most successful in the short history of the ballroom—which was almost filled to capacity with dancers from all over the country—Jasmine felt sidelined from it all. She could not understand why Devon appeared much more relaxed. He had grown accustomed to the spiral of events. She, on the other hand, was in awe by the coincidences that uncannily bound them together.

By Sunday morning, she hoped the feeling of foreboding would soon be over, but Jasmine had settled into a sort of functioning daze. It didn't help that her grandmother was still grumbling over the news that Jax Cajero had visited her son in Paris. At her usual luncheon after church that morning, when they had all listened attentively to the pastor's chosen words about modern relationships, Carmilla was to take her granddaughter aside and have a few words of her own.

"I thought it was over with you and that boar of a man," she began on a disappointing note. Carmilla was in a yellow Chanel suit with a string of pearls around her neck and had just handed Betty Bately a tray of jerk chicken drumsticks when she cornered Jasmine in the kitchen. "What was he doing in Paris?"

"Looking for me," Jasmine proclaimed, short-lipped. It was not easy talking about him now when she had done so much explaining to Devon. "Papa said he wanted to surprise me for my birthday, but I don't want to ever see Jax Cajero again."

"That's all well and good," Carmilla continued, taking a seat at the kitchen table, "if you can keep your word."

Jasmine raised suspicious brows. She was standing by the kitchen sink, but she gingerly walked toward her grandmother with a look of wide-eyed amazement. "What is that supposed to mean?"

"I told you that you needed a new sense of direction and you agreed," Carmilla reminded her, "yet I am to hear that this . . . boar has been looking for you. And at your age, you needn't be with someone like him. I know it's difficult working with what's out there, confirmed middle-aged bachelors and married men—and you know what they want."

"What do they want, Gran-mama?" Jasmine inquired, feigning ignorance.

"I should not have to spell it out for you," Carmilla quipped. "Men who stray from their wives are seldom truthful."

"Don't I know it?" Jasmine answered, thinking of her late grandfather. "Especially if they hold the office of a pastor."

"Don't attempt to trivialize what I am saying," Carmilla snapped, not detecting the hint in Jasmine's tone. "Did he find you?"

"Who?"

Carmilla was rattled. "You know who."

"No," Jasmine lied. "Really, Gran-mama, you mustn't worry."

"But I do," Carmilla admitted. "I worry that you might be left perched on the shelf like a homing bird on a tree branch, lost because your heart can no longer find its way to the one you love."

"Love," Jasmine snorted, cynically. "I remember when you told me that a woman should only love a man with three-quarters of her heart and keep a quarter back for herself. Hardly logical, is it, when the heart is looking for a home?" It was time to come clean. "Jax Cajero asked to marry me."

"No," Carmilla gasped in shock.

"He knows I could never be the wife of a hustler," Jasmine said seconds later, putting her grandmother's worst fears to rest.

"Of course you couldn't," Carmilla agreed wholeheartedly. "You want to be with someone who needs you, like Devon."

"Who needs me?" The question seemed to hold no answers in Jasmine's mind. Enrico had pleaded how much he needed her once, the day she walked out on him. And Devon had declared that mankind needed her more, the day he took her to the Birmingham Savoy for the first time. Now here was her own grandmother repeating herself on how much Devon needed her. There was no hope . . . there could not possibly be any hope when the very man her grandmother was referring to happened to be her grandson. Jasmine closed her eyes and blinked away the terrible deceit that Carmilla could withhold such information from her. "Devon does not need me," she declared forthrightly.

An inaudible sigh escaped Carmilla's throat. "Your father mentioned you had a boyfriend . . . I thought he was talking about Devon."

"No," Jasmine clarified. "He was talking about Jax when he visited in Paris."

"So you feel nothing for Devon at all?" Carmilla acknowledged.

"No," Jasmine lied a second time. How could she confront Carmilla? She didn't know how. "I think after my parents leave today, I should pack my things and go back to Paris with them when they return for the Independence Day Gala. I'll work out my notice at the Savoy."

"You're leaving?" Carmilla gasped again, but this time in horror.

Jasmine nodded sensibly. "I think it would be for the best."

Carmilla clasped her fingers together. "Have you told Devon?"

"I don't know how to tell him," Jasmine said, lowering her head for fear that her grandmother could see the glistening of tears that glazed the mink color of her eyes. "I was hoping you'd tell him, after I've gone."

"Me?" Carmilla shook her head vigorously. "I shall do no such thing. It's time you faced up to certain responsibilities."

"Like you?" Jasmine accused hotly. "You couldn't even face telling your own son how instrumental you had been in helping Devon set up the Birmingham Savoy from a raw concept into a workable urban ballroom. It was your brainchild and I think my father would've been proud, but you hide so much from him, from me."

"From you?" Carmilla seemed suitably provoked. "You think I don't know about you and Devon? You were hardly here a week when he kissed you. I know because I got out of my bed to tell Devon he'd forgotten to take Betty's breakfast tray from my room and there you both were. I was waiting for one or both of you to tell me."

"Gran-mama, I—"

"It no longer matters." Carmilla shook her head. "You're leaving. You said so yourself, so there is nothing left to say." She rose from her chair. "I wish I could understand you, Jasmine. From when you were a child, you've always been a mystery to me. Someday, I hope you find what you want." And on that declaration, Carmilla left the kitchen.

Jasmine felt weakened as she took a seat at the table. She so much wanted to inquire about Gracie Manning. She wanted to ask her grandmother if the wicked rumors were true, but with the treacherous thoughts of rolling between white sheets with Devon's body up close—ravishing her, kissing her, loving her—splintering through her mind from varying angles, she was left feeling reluctant to be told the truth. And yet Jasmine knew she could not return to Paris without knowing the full story.

It was a horrible conundrum made more unbearable by her discovery of the diamonds that were now safely in the attic. She had told Devon that in Victorian times, mad people were often concealed in the uppermost room of the house. Now the loft had become a place to hide diamonds with the value of two million dollars. She had agreed with Devon to keep them there until he had spoken with someone attached to his case. She did not know whether he had done so because she had kept a cool distance from Devon since leaving his room. It was clear to her that Devon did not understand why.

Even now, as he talked amiably among Carmilla's church guests at the house, she knew at any given moment he would steal away to try and find her. The kitchen seemed the safest place for Jasmine. The warm room provided her a little space to think. It had not been in her plans to have a rumpus with her grandmother, but she was angry.

So much of her late grandfather's life was shrouded by secrets. Secrets that could very well affect her.

She was contemplating just how the news about Carmilla's true status should be revealed to Devon, when the kitchen door silently opened. Jasmine knew it was Devon the moment his tall, muscular body presented itself. She could also not deny the shift of emotions that ran through her body like water trickling over her. All her senses were washed anew with every familiar part of him, from his soul-searching brown eyes to the thin mustache that marked his upper lip. When those very lips curled into a smile at seeing her, Jasmine wanted to cry.

"Are you okay?" Devon asked, taking large strides toward her.

"*Tres bien.*" Jasmine nodded. "Very well," she amended in English.

Devon looked around. He was dressed in faded blue jeans and a white T-shirt and looked casual, if not relaxed, as he walked toward her. "What are you doing in here on your own?"

"I wasn't on my own," Jasmine started, as the leather sandals on his feet slapped against the tiled floor. "Carmilla was in here. I told her . . ." Why delay the moment? she thought. "I told her I would be leaving after the Independence Day Gala at the Savoy. I'm going back to Paris."

"Wait a minute," Devon stalled, now towering over her. He stared down at the one woman he didn't want to lose. To him, Jasmine looked angelic in her pale blue T-shirt and white trousers, with her hair swept up loosely with clips to hold up the brown corkscrew curls dangling at her crown. Only minimal makeup covered her caramel-brown complexion, and he liked that about her. "You can't just leave."

Jasmine strained her neck to glance at him. He was so adorable, her heart felt broken knowing she could never have this man. "I need—"

"You need me." Devon took hold of her wrist and pulled her out of the chair. The last couple of days had not been easy for him, either. It was one thing attempting to function as normal—open the Savoy, introduce the guest band, deal with his staff and the street team distributing new flyers for the forthcoming Gala—quite another to keep body and soul together under the steely gaze of Jasmine's parents. "Is it about the diamonds?"

Jasmine nodded, then buried her head into his chest. She hated feeling so weak. She hated more not being able to tell Devon what Lilian and Martha had disclosed. "I can't stay," she mumbled.

"I called my contact at the Home Office," Devon explained quickly. "Everything's in hand. They've got the same person on watch."

Jasmine raised her head. "What?"

Devon looked into her sweet glistening eyes. He doubted very much Jasmine would believe anything he had to say right now. The way fate had shaped their lives with so much happpenstance was enough to swallow for anyone. He decided he needed to bide his time, at least until Jax Cajero reared his ugly head and shadowed his door. It would only be a matter of time before Enrico wanted the diamonds, and Devon knew that in doing so, the robbers would not be too far behind.

"I told you, everything's going to be just fine," he promised. What worried him now was Jasmine's lack of interest in being swept into his arms. As he tried to pull her closer, she pushed him away. "You've been doing this since your birthday," he noted.

"Doing what?" Jasmine inquired, taking several steps toward the kitchen sink where she turned her back on him and looked out toward her grandmother's garden.

"Pulling away from me," Devon told her. "What is it?"

Jasmine dipped her head. "Carmilla knows about us," she admitted finally. "She's always known."

Devon shrugged, relieved. "So? You told me you suspected she knew." He walked over and put his arms around her waist from behind. "I'm glad. Now I can kiss you without any objections from anyone."

Jasmine felt the soft touch of his lips against her nape. "Devon," she weakly protested, as his kisses sent all the right signals to the space between her legs. "Don't."

"I'm going to keep doing this until you give me your lips," he whispered into her ear.

Jasmine closed her eyes as his voice bounced seductively against her eardrums. To her chagrin, her body instinctively leaned against him. She felt the tremor of his limbs along the spine of her back. He was feeling the effect of touching her. And his mouth did not stop working its nibbling magic along the length of her neck. Jasmine heard the deep sigh of arousal leave her lips like a blast of pure heated energy. She wanted nothing more than to turn into Devon's arms and ravish his lips, but her mind was tormented.

"Devon," she groaned.

His breath brushed the sensitive shell of her ear. "Hmm," he answered, working his hands along her body.

Like a spider, Devon's fingers crawled beneath the pale blue T-shirt Jasmine was wearing. He rubbed softly against her navel before working his way higher to the wire of her lacy white bra. He delved under without hesitation and sought the pinnacle of budding flesh that stood erect waiting for the pressure of his fingers. One gentle rub sent Jasmine propelling toward the kitchen sink as she felt the hardness of Devon behind her, poking softly into the small of her back.

Jasmine wished to damnation she had never met this man. "Devon," she warned on a firmer note, taking one last lustful breath to compose herself. She turned into his arms and saw the fire in his eyes light up into a flame that was meant to consume her. But as Devon dipped his head and Jasmine felt helpless to resist his powerful persuasion, the kitchen door shot open.

"Jasmine!" Her father rushed in, cutting the distance between them with lightning speed. "Your grandmother has just been telling me that she was the brainchild behind the Birmingham Savoy. Is that true?"

Jasmine broke away from Devon instantly. "Yes, it is." She nodded while clearing her throat. "She's told you at last?"

"I didn't believe it," Porter replied, astounded. "Devon, I should thank you," he added, shaking the younger man's hand. "I had no idea you made my mother so happy. She told me if it wasn't for you, she would never have accomplished the dream."

"Has she also told you she is going back to Jamaica?" Jasmine added solemnly.

Her father's face clouded over. "No," he said. "All your grandmother told me is that you would be coming home with us when we return and she was worried that Devon would be left alone. She said nothing about going to Jamaica."

Jasmine felt the cold hand of fate pass over her. Devon alone! It was hard to clarify her emotions when she was also witnessing the beguiled expression on her father's face. She had never seen him look so shell-shocked. It was not so unlike her own scare when Carmilla had delivered to her the same news. Porter Charlesworth was riveted for what seemed like an eternity, though in reality it was a mere few seconds, before he smiled weakly at his daughter. When he excused himself from the room, Jasmine felt her limbs sag.

"I'd better go and see if he's all right," she said.

Devon took her wrist again. "I'd like to know what's going on with us first," he said, delaying her departure. "Why do you keep running from me?"

"I'm not," Jasmine insisted quietly.

"It's him, isn't it? Enrico Cajero?"

"Devon—"

"You're still in love with him, aren't you?" He said this in acceptance rather than as fact.

"I'm not in love with Jax," Jasmine confessed truthfully. "What I shared with that man went from 'hot' to 'not' in no time at all. So please don't think that."

"What am I supposed to think?" Devon shot back, angry that she was refusing to stay. "You've gone from hot to Miss Ice Queen all over again."

Jasmine's blood ran cold. She could not bear the

thought of arguing with Devon right now. "I'm going to go find my parents," she told him. "They'll be leaving for the train station soon for the airport. I'll wait until after the Independence Day Gala before I leave. That will give you time to find my replacement. I have to go."

"Go." Devon let go of her wrist. "Go on," he ordered, seeing Jasmine's hesitation. "Go."

When she left, he leaned against the kitchen sink and stared at the ceiling, lost.

The next morning, Jasmine awoke and made a head start on her packing. She tried to put Devon from her mind, but it was proving difficult.

On driving her parents to the train station, he did nothing but taunt her about her work as an au pair, actually trying to convince her that she would not find returning to it as rewarding as working at the Birmingham Savoy. It did not matter to Devon, it seemed, that her father was upset after talking with Carmilla. That her mother was upset at being parted from her daughter. That Andre had found the conversation repetitive and tiresome. And on the return journey, after he'd kissed her family farewell, his grumpiness had turned into a tantrum.

Still in her nightgown, Jasmine opened up her Louis Vuitton suitcases and began to fling all manner of clothes into them. The first day of August was a bright summer's day, but her mood was positively dreary. With every item she tossed into the air, uncaring which case it landed in, her anger intensified. Jasmine knew that Devon was good for her, so very good. Just weeks ago, she would have thought differently. She knew Devon better now and all her suspicions and ill accusations had been replaced by a warmth and deep affection she had never known in life before. A look from him could turn her on. There was no escaping how he made her feel.

But she knew exactly what was lurking in the well he'd sprung from. Devon might not know it himself, and it was enough for her to make the wisest decision for them both. She did not expect to become angry in the Jeep, yet she could not understand why Devon would bring Enrico's name into the discussion. Wasn't it enough that she had explained everything in the kitchen? Obviously not. When Jasmine left the Jeep and ran toward her bedroom, it was with Devon's parting words echoing behind her.

"He's everything you deserve," he hollered at her jealously.

Jasmine angrily tossed a white blouse into the air. It missed the suitcases altogether and landed the exact moment she was interrupted by a knock at the door. "Come in," she ordered, feeling flustered.

Devon opened the door. There was a tiny frown on his forehead when he ventured in and reached down to the floor. He picked up the blouse at his feet. "We missed you at lunch and breakfast," he said without preamble, closing the door.

"I couldn't face either after last night," Jasmine admitted, turning to face the old mahogany chest of drawers. She didn't dare look at Devon and so kept her back to him as she continued. "That was below the belt, you throwing Enrico into my face on our way back from the train station."

Devon's gaze moved to the open suitcases on the floor. He shrugged, almost helplessly. "I just wanted to know what's going on," he replied. He aimlessly threw her blouse onto the bed. "I thought we were doing fine, but since *he* came back, you've changed. You do know Enrico's going to be implicated with the Guerilla Diamonds when he's caught?"

"I know," Jasmine agreed, fishing a handful of underwear from the top drawer.

"I needed to be sure you're not harboring any deep feelings for him," Devon finished, digging his hands into his black trouser pockets.

"Is that all you wanted to be sure about?" Jasmine challenged, turning to face him. He was dressed in a black suit, white shirt, and silver silk tie, and her senses welcomed every inch of his handsome facade. Her heart yearned to rush into his arms, but there was a wrestling match going on in her head to keep her legs exactly where they were rooted. She saw the noncommittal expression marred across Devon's face that forced her question into another direction. "Were you thinking that I'm packing to run back to New York to post Jax's bail after he's caught?" she asked.

Jasmine wondered what was going to come next, because she hadn't seen Devon look this serious before. "I don't want you working at the Savoy tonight," he answered firmly.

"Why?" she asked, throwing her find onto the bed.

"Take the night off," Devon ordered coldly. He glanced at her suitcases again. "It looks like you'll be needing it."

"No, I'm not taking the night off," Jasmine objected, placing both hands on her hips. It was now one o'clock in the afternoon and she had planned to show up for work in three hours. "If you're punishing me, at least say it."

"All right, I'll say it," Devon said, his voice trembling. "There's something about you that tantalizes me. I don't know what it is, or what to do about it. All I know is that I want this feeling to stay. I thought you would, too. But I'm not going to be chasing you halfway around the world when that . . . hood rat is out there biding his time. And as much as you say he means nothing to you, it hasn't stopped you from leaving. I guess you were right when you told me that you only had enough freedom to share with anyone who doesn't mind partaking of a little of your time."

Jasmine stared with a set look to her face. Her limbs were shaking at his declaration. If only he knew how much she wanted to stay. "Devon." Jasmine tried to touch him, but he pulled away. His very motion forced her into holding back her own heartfelt sentiments about how she was really feeling, too. "I told you about Jax," she reminded him. "I couldn't marry him because he's a very selfish man. His only responsibility is to himself. He doesn't want any other obligations that would provide a yoke around his neck. That was one of his many flaws. He's a very jaded individual and a liar, and I don't know why you keep persisting with this idea that I still want him."

"Because I don't know what's going on," Devon repeated. "Why are you doing this to us . . . leaving like this? Don't you feel like an empty vessel, not knowing which way to steer your ship?"

Tears welled in Jasmine's eyes.

"Why are you turning me away?" Devon pleaded. "You must feel what I feel. I know you do."

Jasmine felt rather than heard the tremor that underlay his tone. "Devon . . ." Her mouth opened, but no further words were formed.

Devon's instincts warned she wasn't about to explain anything. He started toward the door. "Like I said, I want a heart that is alive and beating, not a dead one."

"Wait!" Jasmine breathed, determined she should tell him the real reason and be damned if he chose not to believe her.

He stalled with his hand on the door knob. When he turned, Jasmine hesitated. "What is it?" he demanded.

Her heart started to thud against her breastbone. It was a narrow hope wanting to tell Devon the truth. They had been on the brink of a wonderful experience that contained depth, understanding, and emotion in equal measure. But that hope was false. Their love was tottering on the edge of some impending disaster and it was because of what she knew, and he didn't understand why Jasmine could not allow Devon to make love to her again. She couldn't face what his reaction might be if she were to say something, no matter how much she told herself she could.

"I . . . I . . ." She didn't know where to begin.

"You have nothing to say, do you?" he said, peeved. "Well, let me make it easy for you to leave. You're fired." And with that blunt remark, he left the room.

Jasmine flinched as though a rough blow had landed against her mouth. She took a ragged breath, then rushed out of her bedroom and followed him down the corridor. "You can't fire me," she yelled. But Devon continued walking, sprinting down the stairs like a raging bull. Within seconds, he was out the front door. Jasmine stamped one foot in annoyance. Suddenly, her grandmother was at the bottom of the stairs.

"Jasmine, is that you shouting?" Carmilla inquired.

"*Oui*, Gran-mama," Jasmine replied, staring down at her grandmother, who was in a simple patterned frock that she had, no doubt, tended the garden in earlier.

"Was that Devon leaving?" Carmilla ventured further.

"*Oui*," Jasmine answered, dismally folding her arms beneath her heaving breasts.

"Were you two having words?" she asked, concerned.

"More than words," Jasmine admitted, her eyes blazing. "I was about to reach for his throat and throttle him."

Carmilla chuckled. "Well, do it at the Savoy, not in my house."

Jasmine hesitated. "Gran-mama," she began, alighting on the top step. As she looked down at the eighty-two-year-old woman, with her white Afro hair, maple-syrup complexion, and the slight smile spread across her face, Jasmine felt her confidence slip. It was almost on her lips to confront Carmilla for the truth about Devon's grandmother, to tell her what Lilian and Martha had said, but the words were not forthcoming. "You're right," she agreed, stepping back.

She ran back along the corridor and quickly looked out through the stair window. Jasmine had expected to see Devon stepping into his Jeep parked out front. Instead, she was surprised when she found him talking with a woman standing close by. Jasmine's brows dipped when she realized to whom Devon was speaking. Petronella was outside the house.

Jasmine felt her heart react with a leap of panic. She had not forgotten the relish with which Petronella had spoken at their last standoff in the Savoy's office. Jasmine was also racked with the knowledge that if she was fired, was that to mean Petronella was going to be rehired? As she turned from the window, her blood ran hot. Suddenly, she was running down the stairs.

Jasmine thrust open the front door and felt the cool August breeze ruffle her nightgown. She was not about to have Petronella wade into their lives again. And what was the woman doing here anyway, outside her grandmother's house? Jasmine marched down the six wide steps that led toward the sidewalk in her bare feet. She did not care that her appearance was not up to par, or what Petronella would think on seeing her. All Jasmine knew was that she didn't want this femme fatale anywhere near.

"What are you doing here?" she lashed out, staring directly at the older woman.

"Keep your voice down," Devon warned, mindful of the neighbors. "Petronella's here delivering a message."

"Is that right?" Jasmine snapped.

"Yeah, that's right," Petronella slurred. "From your ex-boyfriend."

Jasmine was stunned. "What?"

Petronella moved on without flinching an eyelid. "He wants his diamonds back. He also wants a time and a place."

"Tell him to go to hell," Jasmine spat out, looking across at Devon. "I'm calling the police."

Devon restrained her immediately. "Jasmine, he says if he doesn't get the diamonds, then he'll have to pay a visit to Carmilla."

"Gran-mama!" Jasmine gasped. She looked across at Petronella. "You're enjoying, this aren't you?"

"I'm the girl who's being paid three hundred bucks to pass on the message," Petronella gloated. "That's all."

"How did you know about the diamonds . . . and about my ex-boyfriend?" she demanded, schooling her eyes in suspicion.

"Let's just say I keep my ears and my eyes wide open," Petronella declared triumphantly. "Now, I suggest Saturday night, ten o'clock."

"That's the Jamaican Independence Day Gala night," Devon said with resistance. "We can't—"

"The busier the better," Petronella said knowingly. "The less likely you are to try anything. That's how Enrico wants it."

"Get the hell off this sidewalk," Jasmine threatened. "You go tell that little weasel of a man that if he wants to give me a message, he should deliver it himself. And if he's sending one, he shouldn't have it delivered by a half-baked, dried-up courier like you with your weave and false eyelashes, nose job, and . . . is that a beard you're wearing under that chin?"

"Shut her up, Devon, or I'll do it for you," Petronella warned sternly.

"Jasmine, go back into the house," he ordered. "I've got this."

"Devon, don't you dare—"

"Go pack your things," he insisted, cutting her dead.

Jasmine stared at him. Devon's soul-searching eyes had clouded over, shutting himself off from her. She was suddenly weakened. He was making it clear that this was his problem and his alone. As far as he was concerned, she was going back to France. The hard sidewalk beneath her feet was what propelled Jasmine to move. Though her legs felt like jelly, she retraced her steps back into the house without saying another word. She turned and found Devon chattering with Petronella again. Maybe this was how it should end, she thought bleakly, closing the door. This was how she would leave Devon's life.

In a few days she would be in Paris and it would be as though they'd never met. Jasmine told herself she would grieve for what might have been, but as she took the stairway toward her bedroom, she could not understand why she felt more determined than ever to be at the Birmingham Savoy on Saturday. And why she would want to pitch herself against Petronella was another question unanswered.

Chapter Thirteen

It was the second time at the popular ballroom that there were paparazzi outside. Forcing her way through the long waiting line outside the Birmingham Savoy, Jasmine paused at the threshold and looked around with some confusion. It only took a few seconds to recognize the few famous faces seen in the world of boxing, the soccer arena, and on large billboards promoting perfume, urban wear, or the latest pop single.

She felt strange being there among them, but under the circumstances, Jasmine told herself that she could not refuse accompanying her parents. It was her great-aunt Helena's charity gala to commemorate Jamaica's Independence Day and she was determined to join the many guests to celebrate the occasion. It was silly of her, she thought, as she walked along the red carpet that led into the nightclub, why she had worried, but she had been dreading coming tonight.

It had also taken her a while to decide what to wear to the black-tie event. Undoubtedly, Devon would be expecting her to be dressed up to the nines. As she glanced around the interior of the ballroom, Jasmine was relieved to note that her pale blue chiffon gown and high-heeled silver sandals, had been the right selection after all. The room was crowded and everyone was dressed in similar good taste.

But it was seeing Devon across the room that suddenly tugged at Jasmine's heartstrings. He looked suave in his black tuxedo and was standing next to Petronella. Seeing them together caused Jasmine the most concern. She repeatedly told herself it was ridiculous to get into a state, because for most of the week Devon had done his downright best to avoid her. It was his way of making it crystal-clear she was no longer of any interest to him. While he had successfully removed her from his life, she, on the contrary, was not as successful in removing his dark presence from her heart and mind.

Jasmine had no idea how it should be done. How does a woman obliterate the feelings of love and gentleness from her soul? Over the past five days, she had tried everything to eradicate her pining emotions for the man she loved. By keeping herself busy during the day—washing and ironing her clothes, neatly repacking her suitcases, even helping her grandmother prune roses in the back garden—she'd thought the battle would soon be over. The nights were something different entirely.

Her body wept for Devon. Hugging her pillow was no compensation for his tall, muscular frame. Having him pressed against her was what she needed most. In truth, even her dreams were filled with images so lurid she had begun reenacting their lovemaking to the point that she had awoken on numerous occasions drenched in sweat and trembling. Jasmine *needed* Devon like she'd never needed a man before.

Her grandmother's words seemed all too real now that she had lost the comfort of his arms. Petronella was destined to fill that gap, she thought, dismally watching them from across the room. Carmilla's mention two days ago that the waitress had been reinstated was the sad thought that dogged her mind. It meant at some point during the evening, Jasmine would find Petronella residing in the restaurant area where her parents had planned for them to eat later.

"I don't think I'm hungry," she immediately told her father, shedding her glum memories in one fell swoop. Having Petronella serve her was not something she wanted to endure. "I think I'll have a drink at the bar."

"You're not going to eat anything?" Patti asked, with motherly concern.

Jasmine smiled at them both to allay any fears. Her parents were dressed for the occasion, and it was the first time she had ever seen her father in a tuxedo. "I'm not hungry, that's all," she said, fleetingly gazing across the room again.

Her heart was beating far too fast when her gaze fell on Devon once again. He hadn't seen her and that felt like a mercy in itself. Jasmine was beginning to feel all too nervous by his presence. It was her first time arriving at the Birmingham Savoy as a guest and she wasn't quite sure whether she should acknowledge his presence or ignore him as he had ignored her for much of the week.

She was amazed to find that the dance floor was almost filled to capacity and yet the time had not reached 9:00 p.m. The Savoy's resident house band was playing that evening and putting out a soft tune with very little percussion to keep the crowd swaying. Before long, that same crowd would be kept busy on their feet with some of the more popular swing tunes of the era. Jasmine imagined seeing the Jitterbug, the Stomp and the Flying Charleston by midnight.

But she kept her gaze fixed on the two people standing near the bar, talking among a group of guests. Petronella seemed relaxed enough, she noted, though there was something about her eyes. Jasmine noticed that the waitress's gaze darted from one direction to the next with such speed it was almost as if she was anticipating something. And then, despite the pool of people swimming around the dance floor, her eyes met Devon's.

Jasmine took a deep, unsteady breath. She saw the glitter of ice in the steady look he gave her, and felt compelled to look away. To her chagrin, she couldn't. Instead, Jasmine's senses absorbed just how devastatingly attractive Devon appeared in his white ruffled shirt and black tie beneath his tuxedo. His freshly shaven face, groomed hair, and neatly trimmed mustache against the roasted chestnut color of his skin made him loom at her more like a powerful pharaoh than a mere mortal who had found the route to her heart.

She ruthlessly swallowed the glimmer of hope that reared its ugly head in that very region of her soul where she felt the most peculiar fluttering sensation. She told herself most of it was fear. She had become afraid of even looking at Devon. She had attached so many feelings to this one man, and now his very loathing of her seemed unreal in her world. But Jasmine fabricated a smile, more for the lay observer than to convince Devon she was happy to be there.

Petronella was seen to whisper something into his ear and Jasmine felt her fingernails dig into the sequined fabric of her pale blue handbag. Regarding her warily beneath black eyelashes, Jasmine came to realize that her grandmother was right. The waitress was dressed in uniform—black skirt and white blouse—indicative that Devon had indeed rehired her. The blow felt like a knock to her head and Jasmine finally tore her eyes away.

"I need a drink," she said, swiftly glancing at the bar where she caught a glimpse of Gibson. "I'll be right back."

"Wait a minute," Porter said, stalling. "Aren't you going to ask your mother and me if we'd like something?"

"*Oui, Papa,*" Jasmine answered, apologetic. She looked at her mother, who appeared almost angelic in an orange and peach silk and georgette off-the-shoulder gown. "Champagne?"

Porter glanced at his beautiful wife and encouraged a nod. "Why not?" He smiled.

Jasmine conceded. "Coming right up."

She crossed the ballroom floor on legs that felt like jelly. Jasmine was certain she was being watched, but refused to let it unsettle her. It was likely Petronella had seen her. It was also possible that Devon might decide to obstruct her before she reached the bar. As Gibson observed her arrival, his brows rose speculatively on his seeing Jasmine dressed as one of the guests. It was not what he expected.

"You look beautiful," he began with a smile. "What'll it be?"

"Three glasses of champagne," Jasmine demanded, trying to force a smile. "I'm here with my parents tonight."

Gibson threw a long gaze across the room. "You have the look of your mother."

"*Merci*," Jasmine acknowledged, wondering whether any rumors had circulated in her absence. She risked looking into Gibson's face and couldn't resist asking, "How's everything been without me?"

"Hard to say," he replied covertly, placing three flute glasses on the bar top. "I don't know why you've not been coming to work, but there's people all over this place like a rash."

Jasmine giggled. "It's an independence day celebration, Gibson. All kinds of people come out of the woodwork when there's a party going down."

"Yeah?" Gibson said, pouring Bollinger champagne. "Is that why Devon's put on extra security?"

Jasmine's antenna lit up immediately. *The diamonds*, her mind screamed. Enrico Cajero was to make the pick up that night. "He doesn't want any trouble," she stuttered, picking up the three glasses and throwing a brief glance across at Devon. His eyes leveled on hers. Jasmine had no idea what he was thinking. "I'll see you later," she told Gibson before departing.

She walked carefully around the perimeter of the dance floor back to her parents. Porter and Patti were doing a twirl to the blare of the jazz trumpet when Jasmine arrived and handed over their drinks. From her vantage point, she could see Freya in the restaurant area, taking the first of the evening's food orders. Gibson had become swamped at the bar. The room was beginning to come alive with the Savoy's regulars, and just when

Jasmine spotted the arrival of Carmilla with her great-aunt Helena and the mayor, they were suddenly beside her.

"Porter," Carmilla began, rushing over. "You remember your aunt Helena and her second husband, Richard, the mayor?"

"Of course," Porter answered politely, before kissing his mother on her left cheek. "How have you both been?" he asked the mayor.

"Wonderful," Helena answered on his behalf. "Naturally, we have been very busy since your uncle Richard became the mayor of Birmingham. My life just hasn't been my own."

The words were soft, but held such poignant meaning of Helena's newly acquired status that Jasmine couldn't resist asking, "Who's taken it?"

Her father stifled a chuckle while sipping champagne.

"Well . . . no one exactly," her great-aunt stuttered, thrown by the remark. "My meaning is that . . . well . . . one has to put in a lot of time and effort into supporting one's husband and such like."

"And there just aren't enough hours in the day for that," Jasmine stated sarcastically, "are there?"

Carmilla shot Jasmine a glare. "I don't know what's wrong with my granddaughter tonight," she apologized, using her brows to signify that Jasmine behave herself. "Why don't you go and find Devon?"

Jasmine refused. "He's with Petronella," she said with a hint of scorn. But no sooner were the words out of her mouth than she suddenly heard a familiar male voice behind her.

"Hello," he exclaimed.

Jasmine swung round. "Monsieur!" she gushed.

"Devon!" Carmilla greeted jovially. They affectionately embraced before Carmilla began the introductions. "You remember Jasmine's parents and the mayor?"

"Yes." He nodded with a smile while shaking Porter's hand.

"And my sister-in-law, Helena Charlesworth-Smith," she added acidly.

"Pleased to meet you . . . again," Devon said, accepting another handshake.

He recalled Helena well. She towered over Carmilla by an inch and was perfectly polished in a chocolate-truffle dress beneath a cream-colored chiffon jacket. With her silver-gray hair relaxed and swept up over her oval-shaped face, and her pale tawny brown complexion enhanced with makeup, she appeared in direct contrast to the simple two-piece rose-pink linen suit that his godmother was wearing. If there was one thing Devon remembered about the woman in her late seventies, it was the boastful way in which Helena spoke of her wealth. Though much of it came through her remarriage, she relished the idea that she was a person of great importance.

"It was kind of you to oblige the mayor and me to hold this momentous event here at the Birmingham Savoy," Helena conceded, flinching slightly. "I should never have tried to preempt your decision and have apologized to Carmilla for behaving—"

"Imprudently," Devon finished.

"I'm sorry," Helena quickly offered, before nervously turning her attention to her own glass and sipping Veuve Clicquot to bolster her stamina.

"What are they talking about?" Porter whispered into his daughter's ear.

"There was a bit of a fuss with Aunt Helena," Jasmine told him conspicuously. "Ask Granmama about it later. Personally, I've never seen her so angry."

Her father nodded as Jasmine returned her attention to the open conversation.

"I'm sure we can all move on," she heard Devon add for closure. "And I hope you have a successful evening here at the Savoy."

"Thank you," Helena accepted on a smile.

"How are your parents enjoying the evening?" Devon asked, quickly glancing at Jasmine.

She almost choked on her drink when she received his undivided attention. She glanced over her head to find them sipping from their champagne flutes, talking quietly among Carmilla, Helena, and the mayor. "As you can see, they are enjoying themselves," Jasmine responded, not daring to look at him. Devon was so close she felt the electric current ripple along her bare arms as pure energy.

"How are you?" he ventured, coldly rephrasing the question.

"*Moi*?" Jasmine asked, surprised that he should even care when he had succeeded in avoiding her all week. "*Tres bien.* You?"

Devon hated when she spoke in French and so responded to her. "*Tres bien.*"

His American accent spoiled the pronunciation and Jasmine recognized the irony of it. "Do you want something?" she implied, knowing full well he would never have crossed the ballroom at all unless he wanted to tell her something.

"No," Devon answered flatly.

His tone knocked her slightly. Jasmine felt as transparent as cellophane film. Devon was aware of it, too. He knew that every part of Jasmine felt exposed. But she forced a smile and reminded herself that the news of Devon's heritage still sat with her, undigested. "To what do I owe your attention?"

"I thought you'd like to know that Jax Cajero's arriving soon and we're going to be handing over the diamonds."

Jasmine's brows rose. "We?"

"The special liaison team that was attached to me on my relocation to England," he replied.

Jasmine loathed the fact she felt compelled to look Devon right in his eyes. She feared he would read her mind in a single glance and uncover their disgrace. But Devon was closed off to her. His every manner remained within the confines of acceptable behavior. He now seemed uncaring to dwell on the main event of his life, which had once been her. Their love was suddenly reduced to one simple question.

"What are you talking about?"

"They're part of the relocation program," Devon explained, "and they're going to apprehend your boyfriend."

"Ex-boyfriend," Jasmine quickly corrected, tossing a disapproving glance at Petronella, who was in a pretty good mood at the other side of the room. "These . . . liaison people, where are they?"

"Around," Devon remarked, while leveling his eyes at her.

Jasmine felt panicked. "Are my parents . . . my family safe?"

"Of course." He nodded. "Everyone's having a

good time. Nobody knows or suspects anything, except you."

"Devon—"

"It'd be a mistake to overreact," he cut in. "The place is covered."

Devon certainly didn't seem intimidated by the prospect of an impending face-off with Enrico, but then it was his past he was dealing with to some extent and perhaps that was why his confidence seemed unshaken. "Are you having a good time?"

I'm not Jasmine's mind screamed with scorn. She felt positively wretched at being unable to fall headlong into Devon's arms. "That'd be difficult," she said, "when Petronella keeps looking at me. It's become quite a habit with her."

Devon briefly glanced over his shoulder before returning his attention to Jasmine. "She's on watch," he expanded.

"It didn't take her long to figure her chances with Enrico, did it?" Jasmine scoffed cuttingly. "What is she, a female piranha, having you and Enrico both? Maybe I should make a play for Gibson, then perhaps she can add him to her pool of men, too. You're a fool rehiring her. That woman's cavorting with the enemy and—"

"I'm reminded that the enemy was *your* man," Devon finished. "So quit taking a dig at Petronella. She's only trying to help."

Jasmine felt sick. "Help!" She almost spat the word out. "Don't make me puke. She took a payoff to lure Enrico here so that you can hand over two million dollars in diamonds. Why would any woman do something like that unless . . ." Jasmine's mouth suddenly dried out. *She's on watch,* he'd said. "Unless . . . she's part of the liaison team." The blind truth knocked her rigid.

"I think we should talk in the office," Devon suggested a few short seconds later. He saw the wide-eyed expression on Jasmine's face and took a hold of her hand. "Come on."

Jasmine walked through the crowd in a daze. It was only when Devon closed the door to the office that her emotions let rip. "Tell me I got that wrong," she pleaded, deep in astonishment.

"Jasmine—"

"Please," she begged, her mouth unhinging. "Is Petronella some kind of . . . cop?" She made several inarticulate angry sounds, before she finally added, "Is she?"

"It's not like that," Devon remarked, walking toward the desk where he perched his bottom on the edge of it. "She's a liaison officer at the Home Office. She and her team were assigned to me because the witness protection program believed I might be a possible target for someone who wanted to locate the diamonds."

Disbelief was rife in Jasmine's tone. "You mean they thought you were involved?"

"No, no." Devon almost grinned at her. "Yeah, I worked for the jeweler's, but I wasn't involved. As it turned out, *you* being the ex-girlfriend of Jax Cajero led the culprits to me anyway. Kinda ironic, isn't it?"

Jasmine's mouth unhinged further. She tried to recover from the shock, but found it a difficult process. It was clear she still could not make heads or tails of the twist in the situation. "I thought you and Petronella—"

"I know," Devon interrupted. "She chose to fit

into my life in a way that would allay any suspicions. Things only became tricky when you came along."

"Me," Jasmine said sadly. "So without knowing it, I've walked into another circumstance of deceit, betrayal, and lies. You gave no thought whatsoever about telling me the truth. Did you ever intend to?"

Devon's soul-searching brown eyes turned into slits of razor-sharp remorse. "You were always so hung up on Petronella, I didn't think you'd believe me," he insisted.

"One of the reasons why I could never have married Enrico is that he was a liar, and I told you that," Jasmine proclaimed breathlessly. "It was bad enough that he was a thief, but his inability to tell me the real facts was equally a problem. I always had to find things out later, mostly after the deed had been accomplished on his part. As someone looking for love and hoping to find it, I knew I could never live my life that way. Now you're behaving as badly as he had done . . . I don't know what to say."

"You can't possibly be putting me in the same ballpark as that hood rat?" Devon murmured, shocked.

"Can't I?" Jasmine bristled.

"I never intended to hurt you," Devon answered sheepishly. "I thought about telling you, believe me, I did."

"When?" she demanded.

"After Gibson told you Petronella had followed me into the men's restroom," Devon reminded her. "We were having a private conversation there when Gibson walked in and so Petronella improvised the moment."

"By kissing you," Jasmine recalled. "The office wasn't private enough?"

"You were in there," Devon said astutely, "on one of your crusades to take over my business. Petronella was beginning to think you could pose a problem and wanted my views on the situation."

"Which were?"

"I wanted you to stay," Devon stated tersely. "I was enjoying watching you try to assert yourself as lady of the Birmingham Savoy, but I wasn't sure how to break to you the news of what was going on because you were yet to learn that the ballroom belonged to me. And when you found that out—"

"Which gave you the ultimate authority to fire me," Jasmine recalled, "and then ignore me all week—"

"You made the choice to return to France," Devon interrupted. "What more could I possibly say after trying to stop you? I was annoyed."

Jasmine felt so sickened by Devon's entire explanation of the unfolding of events that a combination of anger and shame suddenly enveloped her. "You're very good at explaining yourself, aren't you? I'm supposed to accept everything you're saying without question or feeling the tiniest hint of pain. Well, I've got some news for you, too," she said.

Devon folded his arms beneath his chest and raised his brows slightly. "What is it?"

"Your grandmother, Gracie Manning, was a loose woman," she spat out with all the venom of a snake. "She got pregnant with my grandfather's child, so that makes you and me cousins."

Devon's jaw dropped open. "Is this some kind of sick joke to get back at me?"

Jasmine refused to be dislodged. "Your father,

Ralston, and my father, Porter, are half brothers," she added, allowing the poison to seep in. "They were both Pastor Henry Charlesworth's sons."

Devon stared at Jasmine. Hypnotized. Terrified. "You're lying."

He looked awful, stricken, his forehead crossed with worry lines, but Jasmine remained steadfast. "Ask Carmilla," she tossed out scathingly. "As you can see, there's always a price to pay when getting down to the truth, isn't there? I hope you enjoy how it feels." Jasmine left the office before another reaction from Devon rocked her to tears.

The first person she saw on reentering the ballroom was her grandmother, appearing remarkably energetic as if to prove that she intended to outlive them all. Carmilla and her great-aunt Helena were showcasing an elderly dance routine to the delight of the younger dancers who reveled in the two women's slow shuffle to the jazz beat. Her parents had joined in the festivities, circling the dance floor with their own tamed dance steps, while more agile dancers sidestepped around them. They were all laughing, but Jasmine felt limp as she ambled her way over to the bar.

"A lowly paid worker like me isn't valued at all," Gibson complained instantly.

Jasmine's thoughts were lost. "What's that?"

"I should get an annual bonus for the things I see in here," he expanded, referring to the two women in their sunset years putting on a groove.

"You see too much," Jasmine accused, thinking back to everything he had told her. "Just one time, I'd like you to get your facts straight."

Gibson picked up on the sarcasm and waded right in. "So it's like that," he started. "Why don't you check out the two guys that just walked in here? I told you there'd be some bloodletting soon."

Jasmine followed Gibson's stare until she found her eyes landing on a familiar face. The green eyes of a human iguana glared right at her. She felt her heart stop. Enrico Jax Cajero was walking majestically across the ballroom toward her. At his side was a tall, white companion whom Jasmine vaguely recognized as the man who broke monkey nuts on the Savoy dance floor and left the nutshell casings in a mess at his feet. And then, as they came closer, Jasmine saw Petronella.

"Hello there," Petronella announced to the two men, deliberately walking directly into their line of vision.

"Did the girl get our message?" Johnny the Bear inquired.

Jasmine immediately picked up on the nuance in Petronella's behavior and became aware the liaison officer was attempting to remove the two men from the ballroom. It would be unfair to say she wasn't scared, but as Jasmine's gaze fell on Enrico, she felt she ought to assist Petronella by alerting Devon that the men were here. But before she could move, Enrico was suddenly beside her.

"Shall we dance?" he asked, instantly pulling Jasmine onto the maple-wood floor.

She was stunned, but tentatively moved her feet to the tempo of the brass trumpet that was pumping from the house band. Enrico hadn't changed. He was still in the same purple suit, though his face seemed freshly shaven and his hair had regained its sleekness, which indicated he had washed it before pulling it back into his trademark ponytail.

"You gutless little weasel," Jasmine spat out, narrow-

ing her eyes. "How dare you try and threaten me with
my grandmother after giving me something you've
poached from bigger thieves than yourself? Have you
any idea what trouble you're in?" She looked across
the room and realized she had not seen Devon ven-
ture from the Savoy's office since their altercation,
which meant he had no idea what was going on.

Jasmine knew Enrico wouldn't care less if he was
up in a dock explaining to a judge whether he was
culpable or not. In his view, it would simply be a case
that he was down on his luck. For in Enrico's world,
crime paid. He lived by that error of psychology
where if the opportunity presented itself to earn
money by doing nothing, he would be right in there.
He only had to look at the insider traders, the White
House political musketeers who cashed in on their
connections, and the international dealers who prof-
ited from trafficking secrets to know that he was
right. So it was quite a shock to Jasmine when Enrico
came at her from another angle.

"I'm on your side," he whispered one octave
below the music. "They're going to kill me once they
get the diamonds, so I want you to do as I tell you."

Jasmine felt her heart tremor. "They?" she
queried.

"That guy over there." He indicated the one talking with Petronella. "He's Johnny the Bear. He
tagged me until I found you, but he's here with his
boss, Mr. Van Phoenix. Believe me, he's a nasty
piece of work."

"Jax," Jasmine said, panicking, "are they the
ones who want the diamonds back?"

"Don't panic," he ordered, keeping the momentum of the dance. "Just tell me where the
rocks are."

"I don't have them," Jasmine admitted.

Enrico recoiled in shock. "What?"

"I . . . I—"

"Didn't that waitress . . . Petronella give you my message?" he demanded hotly.

"Yes," Jasmine confessed, "but—"

"Je-sus, you went to the police, didn't you?"

"No," Jasmine said emphatically. "Listen, that brooch you gave me . . . the loot inside it, they're known as the Guerilla Diamonds. They were going to be used to buy weapons, but before that could happen, the diamonds were stolen by your guys."

"They are *not* my guys," Enrico amended.

"They were stolen nonetheless," Jasmine went on, "and you've led the robbers here to a team who have been monitoring a witness who saw the murder of one of the African rebels who originally had the diamonds. His partner, who thought there had been a double cross, did the shooting and is now in prison."

"Oh my God, I'm dead," Enrico wailed quietly. "Johnny the Bear and Mr. Van Phoenix think you have the stones."

"I gave them to someone," Jasmine whispered. "He doesn't know you're here, but Petronella knows and she's part of the monitoring team."

"What . . . that waitress?" Enrico asked, aghast. He stopped the dance instantly and pulled away from her. "She's some kind of cop?"

"She's attached to the Home Office," Jasmine explained, trying not to look conspicuous. "I don't know if she has the power to arrest, but she works in liaison with the witness protection and relocation program in New York and her team is possibly watching us right now."

Enrico instantly panicked. He left Jasmine's side and suddenly began to march across the dance floor away from Johnny. Unknown to Jasmine, Mr. Van Phoenix had already arrived at the Savoy. He was standing across the ballroom, observing what was going on. He immediately suspected that the woman Enrico had been dancing with was Jasmine Charlesworth. In his mind, he was one step closer to the diamonds.

As he took one step forward, he caught sight of Enrico trying to escape the ballroom. Van Phoenix indicated with a nod of his head at Johnny to follow, and that was when the Puerto Rican ran. Enrico darted through the traffic of people like a rat scurrying for cover. Within seconds, Johnny was in quick pursuit. As Petronella gave the order with her right hand to several security men on watch to deal with the situation and they all gave chase, Van Phoenix came up behind Jasmine and pushed a hard metal object into her back.

"Take me to my diamonds, Miss Charlesworth," he ordered on a steely note.

Jasmine felt the knife's edge and suddenly lost the feeling in her legs. "Don't hurt me," she begged.

"You're not going to get hurt," Van Phoenix said sternly, "if you give me what I came here for."

"They're in the office," she told the tall, rigid frame of the man standing behind her.

"Lead the way," he snarled into her left ear.

Jasmine began the slow walk from the dance floor toward the corridor that led to where she had last seen Devon. It seemed to take aeons to get there. The heels of her silver shoes almost slid with each reluctant step she made. Jasmine's only hope was that Devon would be alert enough to take action, though after what she had told him, there was no telling what mood he would be in. With a stranger holding a knife to her back, Devon would probably welcome whatever just deserts should come her way for her outrageous disclosure.

They reached the office door and she opened it slowly. The knife's edge ripped slightly into the fabric of her dress when she ventured forward. Devon was pacing the floor like a dangerous black panther when he turned and saw her entrance. He opened his mouth and was about to speak when he saw the Dutchman behind her. Devon knew he had seen this face before. The man was a familiar at the hotel jeweler's as a supplier of bracelets and brooches.

"Mr. Van Phoenix, I might have known," Devon admonished, suddenly enlightened. "They thought it was an inside job, but no one is going to suspect a supplier of goods."

Van Phoenix closed the door behind him. "Well deducted," he answered, pushing Jasmine three steps forward. "Now where are my diamonds?"

Devon thought about stalling for time. He glanced at Jasmine, who was doing her level best to stay focused, though the urge to burst into tears was not far from her. He threw a brief, comforting smile her way. *I love you*, he mouthed out without sound before returning his gaze to one of the two robbers who had stolen the diamonds from the jeweler's safe. But Van Phoenix did not miss the heartfelt gesture.

"How sweet," he bristled, softly stroking Jasmine's neck. "Two lovers destined to die together."

Devon watched as Jasmine squeezed her eyes

shut and decided he needed to do something.
"Wait," he warned.

"Are you stalling me?" Van Phoenix challenged.

"I have your diamonds," Devon confessed suddenly. "Just let the girl go. This is between you and
me."

"I think not," Van Phoenix remarked firmly.
"She's my insurance to get out of here."

"Take me," Devon surrendered. "Me, you, and
the diamonds. We walk right out of here, together."

"An interesting proposition," Van Phoenix announced. "There's just one problem."

Devon raised suspicious brows. "Whatever it's,
we can straighten it out."

"The girl is much prettier and I have my ego to
think about. Now where are my stones?"

Devon hesitated on a long breath. "Van Phoenix,
I can't let you do this."

"Do what?" Van Phoenix laughed as he held
the knife over Jasmine's face and tilted the blade
until he saw the reflection of her pulsing red lips.
"Just get me the diamonds and I'll think about
whether I'm going to let this girl live long enough
to give you a kiss."

Devon didn't waste any more time. He slowly
reached into his tuxedo pocket and removed a
small white envelope. Van Phoenix's eyes lit up immediately. Finally, his search was over. He lowered the knife slowly and kept his gaze fixed,
nodding with a slight inclination of his head to in-
struct Devon to move forward. Five steps closed the
distance between them before he called a halt.

"Stay right there," Van Phoenix ordered. He
briefly threw a devilish grin at Jasmine, unmoved
by the tears he saw running down her cheeks. "I

might just let you two live happily ever after," he said, sneering, "if you do as I tell you and take the envelope."

Jasmine silently nodded and looked across at Devon. His own eyes were glazed with tears. He had already refused to believe anything she had told him. Since her leaving the office, Devon had paced almost every square inch of the room rolling over in his head the awful lie she had obviously been told. That's what it was to him. A lie. It had to be. Carmilla would never have allowed him to fall in love with her granddaughter if such a thing as Henry Charlesworth being his own grandfather were true. There had to be a story behind the misunderstanding. This was the final conclusion he had arrived at before Jasmine made her untimely intrusion with Van Phoenix.

He held Jasmine's gaze. He felt the strong bond of trust and love linger between them. There was no escaping his feelings for her. Devon could never be rid of such a wonderful woman. He would do whatever it would take to save her from the evil grasp she was under, and that was when he craftily tilted the envelope. Holding it into the air, he slowly offered it to Jasmine.

"Careful," Van Phoenix warned.

Jasmine reached for it. Her hand was shaking so badly she was forced to retract it and try again. Her heart was racing so much that she feared a repeat. But she kept her nerve and thought of nothing but surviving the ordeal. She even promised herself she would be a kinder and more forgiving person. After it was all over, she would accept that she had loved and lost. She would no longer duel with her heart about how much she loved Devon.

In time, she would even learn that by losing him she had gained a cousin.

"That's it," Van Phoenix encouraged, watching the handing over of the diamonds. "Careful."

Jasmine took the small white envelope and searched Devon's eyes. Without fully understanding the motion, she read them with the instinct of a woman in love. In one swift moment, she tilted the envelope and sensed the tiny droplets of uncut diamonds gravitating to the floor. Van Phoenix was instantly immobilized. His body shook at the horror of two million dollars falling through the air.

But Devon did not waste his opportunity. Within seconds, he had knocked the knife from Van Phoenix's hand. As a much younger and taller man, Devon had the advantage. As the two men fought, Jasmine was free to rush from the room and get help. She found Petronella immediately at the end of the corridor and could hardly control herself when the words tumbled out in a flurry of tearful, frightened emotions.

"In there." She pointed.

Three security men leaped into action. By the time Jasmine found herself back in the Savoy's nerve center, Van Phoenix was in handcuffs. She quickly searched for Devon. Her heart raced when his tall, muscular frame failed to materialize among the cluster of men. Then suddenly, he was there in front of her. She saw blood in the palm of his hand and felt weak with worry.

"Devon . . ."

"I'm all right." He stepped forward and hugged her. "It's just a small cut where the knife got me, but I'm fine."

Jasmine pressed her cheek into his chest and closed her eyes. "I thought—"

"Shhh," Devon said. He kissed her forehead.

"Take him away," Petronella's voice blared. When the activity in the room began to thin, she smiled at Devon. "You're very brave, just like your god-mother."

Jasmine raised her head from the haven of Devon's warm body. "My grandmother?"

"If it wasn't for her, we wouldn't have caught Mr. Enrico Cajero and his accomplice." Petronella smiled. "Carmilla caught him weaving his way through the guests to get out of the club and tripped him with her foot. She has a nasty bruise on her ankle, but she'll be fine. We got the other man, too. Security explained to the guests that they were both a couple of troublemakers and removed them from the building. Don't worry, the party's still going strong."

"Where's my grandmother now?" Jasmine asked, concerned.

"She's been taken to the hospital with her son and daughter-in-law," Petronella declared. "And on behalf of my team, we should be thanking you, too. I hope you have no hard feelings. I was just doing my job."

Condolences and sisterhood were not what Jasmine needed right now, especially from a woman who had presented her with so many obstacles. "I must go to her," she said tearfully, wiping her eyes. She looked up into Devon's face. "I have to see Gran-mama."

"No," he protested, restraining her with a light hold of her wrist. "We'll wait until your grandmother gets home, because she's got some talking to do. The rest of our life depends on Carmilla."

Suddenly there was a commotion at the door. It was Gibson. He rushed into the room like a burst of steam and observed the opaque stone pieces beneath his feet. He looked at Jasmine. "What are those on the floor?"

"Two million dollars in uncut diamonds," she answered. "Devon's just foiled the master criminal with a knife."

He caught sight of Devon's hand. His eyes rolled heavenward and he made a barely audible sound. Squirming at the sight of blood, Gibson fainted.

Chapter Fourteen

In spite of catching only a few hours of sleep, Jasmine was awake at dawn. She rose from her crumpled bed, where she had tossed and turned for most of the early hours, and glimpsed at her wretched reflection in the bathroom mirror. Seconds later, she turned on the shower. She could not see out into the world through the bathroom window, but Jasmine knew that the day would be grim because she could detect the charcoal night sky paling to the blue morning through the opaque glass.

Her heart dropped when she stepped beneath the shower spray and allowed the warm water to wash over her. She was frightened by the prospect of facing Carmilla. The black misery that had hung over her head for most of the night since leaving the Birmingham Savoy was still with her, too. That had to be one night she would not forget in a hurry. Right at this very minute, it was likely that Enrico was undergoing a grilling and papers were being prepared to extradite him and the two foreign men who were instrumental in the

Guerilla Diamonds heist back to the United States for a judicial hearing.

But that was not a worry to her now. Her own case was yet to be prepared in front of the one woman who had the authority to explain everything about her grandfather. As she reached for the shower gel and began to sponge her body, Jasmine felt her throat dry out. Devon was convinced that the story about him and his grandmother was a pack of lies. She, on the other hand, was unnerved by the fact of its being true.

After all, Lilian and Martha knew of her grandmother and Pastor Henry Charlesworth for many years, she decided. They were old ladies themselves, perhaps not as old as her grandmother, but longtime congregants of the church. But if Gibson was a person to measure gossip by, there was margin enough for error because he was always getting hearsay wrong. Perhaps Lilian's and Martha's story had traveled from so many mouths it had become tainted with plausible lies.

Jasmine worked the lather into her caramel-brown limbs and reworked the problem in her mind. She should have talked to Carmilla sooner, she told herself. Having done so, she could now have saved herself the embarrassment of causing Devon's involvement. But she just hadn't been able to talk to her grandmother. Carmilla had been so distraught over the tremors of her last relationship with Enrico Cajero that Jasmine felt, in part, a semblance of shame presenting her with further troubles.

But Devon was Carmilla's godson. It was inevitable that Carmilla would have some inclusion in the end. Only she could now explain the truth

behind Gracie Manning's pregnancy. No doubt it
had been referred to, at times, while Gracie had
lived in England. Obliquely perhaps by stalwart
friends, congregational members, or others close
to her. And as wife to the pastor, Carmilla must've
heard something, whether it be enough to share
her anguish with someone else.

Jasmine rinsed the soapy bubbles from her body
and closed her eyes to feel a sense of control
within herself. She should not panic. She should
wait until her grandmother had awoken from her
bed and was ready to face the day. Carmilla had arrived home with a bandaged foot from the hospital in the early hours of the morning by taxi with
her parents. It wasn't serious and was just as
Petronella had said. Carmilla had suffered a nasty
bruise when she purposely tripped Enrico in his
haste to escape the ballroom, causing him to take
a fall. A few days of bed rest with no weight on her
foot was advised, her mother had explained, before
they all bade Carmilla a good night and departed
to their rooms.

But now the thought of talking plainly and seriously with her about Devon's true heritage was
sending her haywire. Jasmine tilted her head in
front of the shower and allowed the needle spray
of water to wash her face. She was restless standing beneath the downpour with her arms wrapped
around her body as she hugged herself tightly
and felt the warm flow trickle over her. But Jasmine
willed herself to remain calm until she heard
Carmilla out.

When she returned to her bedroom, her packed
luggage loomed in front of her. The four Louis
Vuitton cases were in the middle of the floor, just

as they had been weeks before when Devon had helped her carry them to her room. Jasmine felt a tremor run along her body at the thought of taking the cases to the top of the long, winding staircase. Devon would probably offer to take them down. He might even imagine her heartless, leaving when Carmilla had bruised her ankle.

Jasmine envisaged she might be required to stay for a few more days, though she knew that Carmilla was in the capable hands of Devon and Mrs. Bately. And, of course, she had promised her parents she would join them on the return flight to France. Suddenly, her life seemed complicated again. It had been one thing after another since meeting Devon, finding that her brooch contained stolen uncut diamonds, seeing Enrico again, and discovering that Devon's life was enshrouded with Home Office officials. And there was Petronella, the woman assigned personally to him.

Jasmine roughly toweled herself as a flash of anger ripped through her. Petronella may've been an official of sorts, but her position did not give her any right to taunt her as she did. Admittedly, Jasmine now knew the whole facade had been part of the setup. Petronella had not wanted a hint of suspicion to fall upon herself, and given that there were the likes of Gibson running loose, Jasmine understood to some degree that a little playacting went with the job. But she strongly resented Petronella. In her opinion, the Home Office official had gone too far with her fixation on Devon. Fiction or fact, her affection toward him overran the borders of professional conduct in Jasmine's mind, and a part of her still refused to forgive the manner of her behavior.

It was all over now, she mused, taking her thoughts back to her present predicament. There was one final hurdle she had to jump. Jasmine did not know whether she had the legs for it. If Lilian and Martha's story *was* true, what then? Would she and her parents take the news badly? Would the church congregation need to know? How would Devon take the blow? These were all questions in Jasmine's mind as she threw back the curtains.

From her bedroom window, she could see the blue rivulets in the sky. They were edged in silver and black where the old day was dawning into the new. As Jasmine began to dress in a pair of jeans and a yellow jersey, her thoughts strayed to Devon. She imagined his soul-searching brown eyes, the trim of his mustache, the neat cut of his black Afro hair, and the smile she had grown accustomed to and wondered what he was thinking.

The day itself was a good one to confront Carmilla. Devon could hardly imagine her attempting to visit church that morning with her bruised ankle, which meant he would not be pressured into driving the Jeep. He contemplated washing it instead to calm himself, but it had been hard to sleep since his return to the house with Jasmine. They dared not speak on the journey home about what Carmilla might say in case the sleight hand of fate were to work against them. Instead, the silence was one of reflection and hope.

He felt encouraged that the story of his being Carmilla's husband's grandson could not be true. He deliberated his past and could not recall any single incident where his parents talked of Pastor Henry as being someone more than he was to the family. With this in mind, he felt more anxious

that Carmilla should allay all Jasmine's worries
than his own. Only then could he reveal how
much he loved her.

As he turned in his bed, still reluctant to pull his
tall, muscular limbs from beneath the layer of
sheeting, Devon decided he needed to ask Jasmine to stay in England. The whole horrible mess
he thought he'd left behind in New York was now
well and truly behind him. The robbers of the
hotel jeweler's where he'd worked were now
caught, the uncut diamonds were found, and all
three men were likely to face criminal charges
and jail terms. Though a part of him was rattled
by the fact that Jasmine was a fringe involvement
in the whole affair, Devon was not swayed from his
decision at attempting to keep her in his life.

No woman had ever affected him in the way
she did. Since his meeting her, his every awaken-
ing hour was riddled with his obsessing about her.
It was an inward mechanism at work that was not
seen by Carmilla, his colleagues, or even Jasmine
herself. Devon was certain he had displayed no
outward show of his feelings to anyone. He still did
not know how Carmilla came to realize his involvement with her granddaughter, only that Jasmine had told him she knew. It did not worry
Devon unduly. Carmilla was approving of the situation, which made him certain more than ever
that the rumors about Pastor Henry Charlesworth
were unfounded.

As he turned further under the covers, Devon
smelled the scent of Jasmine on his pillow. She was
right there in his bed. He could almost imagine
tasting her lips. His hands yearned to touch her
body and trace every contour—the outline of her

breasts, the shape of her hips, the angle of her chin—even the knowledge that she would forever be a fascination to him. He wanted to satisfy her again.

There was something about Jasmine Charlesworth that made him feel intensely male. He liked the way she responded beneath his fingers. Even now, he felt his muscles contract as the soft noise that erupted from her mouth when he had taken her to the highest mountain of desire filled his subconscious mind. Devon turned his head and growled into his pillow as his lust for Jasmine began to build.

Damn those false rumors and lies, he seethed, forcing himself with supreme effort to control his desire. He was in love with Jasmine. This was something very real to Devon. The feelings that were running riot through him were far too strong to mean anything else. He needed her. He needed her now. He could not allow her to go back to France without at least giving her hope she could return to him. And that was something he could not achieve until they had both spoken to Carmilla.

The importance of that discussion suddenly propelled its way into his mind. Devon jumped from his bed in an instant. It was imperative that he talked and talked now. Within seconds, he had thrown on his clothes—a pair of brown khaki trousers with an olive-hued jersey—and hurriedly left the room with bare feet. He needed to know the truth about his grandmother. Why she left England and came to live in America with his grandfather. He had known there was an enormous age gap between his grandparents and that was an enigma he wanted solved. And why did his own parents keep in touch with Carmilla Charlesworth? Was there indeed a family secret that had been kept hidden from him for many years? Devon was not only intrigued, he felt that his own life and his very love for Jasmine were hanging by a thread.

He hurried along the stairs that led down to the second floor and along the corridor that would take him to Carmilla's bedroom. Devon did not care what time of day it was. He suspected his godmother would be in bed, still nursing her bruised ankle from the night before. She might not even attend church that morning after breakfast, which she would probably take in her room. But her usual afternoon luncheon was still likely to go ahead, for she had no prior time to cancel that.

Still, given the workings of Carmilla's schedule for the day, Devon needed answers. As he came closer to the room, he saw Jasmine about to knock on Carmilla's bedroom door. To him, the sight of her was amazing. Dressed in jeans and a yellow jersey, with her corkscrew brown hair pulled back and her face bare of all makeup, she looked as fresh as the flowers in the back garden.

"Jasmine!" Devon whispered, making his way over to her, on the verge of taking a kiss.

"Devon!" Jasmine wanted to fall into his arms and be told that everything was going to be all right, but restrained herself from doing so. "I was just about to—"

"Me too," he finished.

"Are you all right?"

"I think so." Jasmine nodded, even knowing this was the one hurdle they both had to face. "I'm nervous."

"I'm feeling the same way," Devon admitted, "but I need to get this over with. I need to know so that we can get on with the rest of our lives."

"Do you think she'll be awake?" Jasmine asked.

"She'd better be," he said, hopeful. It was the only way he could look forward to the new life that was beckoning in Jasmine's eyes. He held her hand and squeezed it tight. It was an act of togetherness where one's very sanity felt at stake. "C'mon. Let's do this." Two firm raps with his right knuckle and Devon quietly pushed the bedroom door open.

Jasmine heard the portable radio and knew instantly that her grandmother was up. "Granmama?" she whispered loudly on entering.

"Jasmine, good morning," Carmilla uttered, raising her head from her pillow. She saw Devon poke his head round the door. "Devon, my boy, come in." With a smile on her face, Carmilla propped herself up, concerned that her granddaughter and godson should be disturbing her so early. "I was just listening to the seven o'clock news. Is everything all right?"

"Gran-mama, we need to ask you something," Jasmine began, venturing into the room with Devon at her side. "It's about the past and it's very important."

"Oh?" Carmilla acknowledged, positioning herself comfortably in her bed. Her white Afro hair was tied back with a silk scarf and she was wearing a patterned blue cotton nightgown. "You'd better sit down."

Jasmine perched herself against the edge of the bed while Devon took the adjacent chair opposite and faced Carmilla. "It's about my grandmother,

Gracie Manning," he began softly. "We've heard a rumor—"

"A rumor!" Carmilla interrupted, clearly alarmed.

"At the church," Jasmine continued, amazed that without her teeth, her grandmother appeared much older.

"I'd like to know about my grandmother," Devon waded in. "How she got pregnant and came to live in New York with Pastor Erskine Rutherford, my grandfather."

Carmilla caught the look of desperation in Devon's eyes and breathed a heavy sigh. "What happened all those years ago is not something I like to talk about," she said almost bitterly. "My reputation and that of my husband were at stake."

"Gran-mama, please," Jasmine implored her.

"It was your grandfather Henry's fault, that's how it all started," Carmilla suddenly spat out, recalling she'd said this before. "It happened the year we bought the house—1953."

"I'm listening." Devon nodded, nervously rubbing his fingers.

"Everyone said that Gracie Manning had been . . . raped," Carmilla said, slowly, ignoring her granddaughter's gasp. "There were wicked people saying that my husband had done it, but that wasn't the truth at all." Carmilla swallowed bitterly. "When she came to England, Gracie was already four months pregnant, but nobody knew of it. Henry had visited New York to see another pastor, his friend Erskin Rutherford, and Gracie came back with him because she wanted to be with her mother, the organ player at our church. She needed some place to live and we put her up at the house. That's when we found out about Gracie's condition and naturally everyone decided it was Henry's baby, even though we had a little boy of our own, only six years old. Because my husband was a much older and married man, they suspected rape. It was very ugly."

"Oh, Gran-mama," Jasmine gulped, seeing the tearful hurt behind her grandmother's hazel-colored eyes.

"I begged Henry not to get us involved. It wasn't our business, but as pastor of his congregation and with her being the organ player's daughter, he saw it as his responsibility to sort the matter out and protect his reputation. Henry talked with Gracie and then flew back to New York to confront Pastor Erskin Rutherford. His poor wife had to live through the shame of it. Pastor Erskin Rutherford was the father of Gracie's unborn child."

Devon ejected a loud sound of relief. "What happened then?" he asked solemnly, still twisting his fingers.

"Pastor Rutherford's wife divorced him, of course, which was a rarity in my day, and Erskin married Gracie," Carmilla continued. "Well, he was an old man by then, nearly sixty years old, when Ralston, your father, was born. Ralston was eleven years old when Pastor Erskin died. That was when Henry and I took it upon ourselves to help Gracie. We visited often, especially Easter and Christmas when Henry was invited to preside as guest pastor over a congregation, and we sent money, too. You see, Henry was Ralston's godfather. He grew up, married your mother, Juanita, and had you, their only child. But then, you know the tragedy of what happened afterward."

Devon glanced across at Jasmine, his eyes light-

ing up. "We thought . . . we heard that Pastor
Henry was . . . my grandfather and—"

"What!" Carmilla exclaimed, clearly hurt. "That old
rumor died over fifty years ago."

"We thought—"

"That you'd committed an unspeakable act by
loving each other?" Carmilla cut in, annoyed.
"How could you think such a thing?"

Jasmine dipped her head. "I'm really sorry,
Gran-mama," she said, regretful she had not found
the courage to speak to her sooner. "I didn't know
how to talk to you about it. I was so scared of it
being true."

Carmilla looked directly at Devon. "Pastor Henry
Charlesworth is not your grandfather," she confirmed. "But he wanted you to have the best of
everything in life. He respected your grandmother
a great deal for her courage in telling him the
truth, even in her hour of shame. In my day, it was
never easy to admit to carrying a baby and to
being unwed. Gracie had to be strong to tell Pastor
Henry what had happened to her. She was young
and in love with a married man. She was always
going to be his and had she not gotten pregnant,
he would never have been hers. Those were shameful days and shameful times, but Henry was prepared to make something good of a bad situation.
He was determined that your father be born in
wedlock. Pastor Erskin's four children were already grown adults and married and so it seemed
the best thing that he divorce Mary and marry
Gracie."

"Mary?" Devon probed deeper. "She was my
grandfather's first wife?"

Carmilla nodded. "Yes, Mary gave in quietly.

She accepted her fate with all the sadness and dignity of a woman who'd been disrespected by her husband. I admired her a great deal because she kept her pride and did not make a fuss."

"What happened to her?" he asked further, immersed in the entire story.

"As I understand it, Mary went to live with one of her children," Carmilla went on. "I do not know of what became of her afterward."

"I haven't met any of my grandfather's family or his children," Devon said sadly. "Until now, I did not know of their existence."

"That was one thing Mary did have control of," Carmilla explained quietly. "She kept Pastor Erskin from his older children until the day he died. You have an aunt and three uncles somewhere in America and Ralston, your father, had a sister and three brothers he never knew."

Devon took a long breath. "I don't want to look back in the past, but someday I'd like to find them."

"Of course you would," Carmilla agreed. "But until then, you have a life to lead here, in England, if you decide to stay."

"Stay?" he asked, confused.

"I'm assuming you may like to go back to New York now that your life is no longer in any danger?" Carmilla queried solemnly. "You'll probably want to headhunt a manager to run the Birmingham Savoy?"

Devon glanced at Jasmine. "That'd be up to your granddaughter," he answered, hopeful. His deep brown eyes searched hers. "I'm in love with her and just want the opportunity to make her happy, if she'll have me."

Carmilla smiled at her granddaughter. "Well, Jasmine?" she asked.

Jasmine's eyes flickered as she tried to fight back the tears. "I . . . I . . ." she stuttered, overwhelmed. Through a haze of tears, she looked at Devon and felt the flooding of emotions run along her body, making her light-headed as hope surged deep inside.

"Jasmine?" her grandmother prompted a second time.

"I was thinking," Jasmine finally answered, holding Devon's gaze. "A woman reaches a certain age and suddenly she begins to understand what the feelings a man gives her mean."

"And what are your feelings?" Carmilla probed.

"I feel like my attention is something Devon values and that his attention is something I want to receive, always."

"Forever," Devon added with an earnest smile.

"Yes," Jasmine agreed, her senses reeling, especially when she caught the dark, compelling gaze that was hidden deep in Devon's eyes as he willed her to believe him.

"Anything else?" Carmilla asked.

Jasmine had a revelation of light and realized it was just that easy. "I'm in love," she said in awe. She loved Devon and he loved her.

"Of course you are." Carmilla laughed as she watched Devon reach out to squeeze her granddaughter's fingers. "You both are. That is how it was with your grandfather. I felt the same way, too."

"You did?" Jasmine chuckled as her gaze shifted from Devon's tearful expression to Carmilla's.

"Love is the truest feeling you will ever find to

treasure forever," Carmilla explained. "I know. And that is what you feel."

"And the quarter I need to hold back for myself?" Jasmine reminded her with a tearful chuckle.

Carmilla laughed as she saw the glimpse of concern on Devon's face. "That is the twenty-five percent you will need for keeping your spirit nourished," she explained. "As selfish as that may seem, it is what the soul requires to gain strength through the good times and the bad. Devon's love for you will do the rest."

Carmilla seemed so certain about everything that Jasmine knew she was listening to the wisdom of an old lady who had once been in love and was now of an age to know all the many emotional facets attached to such a simple word. And when she looked into Devon's face and felt the love that only his lustful gaze could give her, Jasmine knew this was the man she was destined to be with.

Her whole body tensed for one long moment before she leaned forward and felt Devon's arms fold around her. They hugged, enjoying the endless relief of being told the truth by Carmilla, putting to rest the ugly rumor of what Lilian and Martha had told her. There was also the mitigating relief that the recent drama in their lives, which had trailed them both from New York, was now over. Devon planted a kiss on Jasmine's forehead in the comfort of having found each other in true love. That was the lasting impression on Jasmine's mind before Devon dipped his head and kissed her, long, hard, and desperate.

"Perhaps you two would like to be alone?"

Carmilla suggested, ejecting a shallow cough to intrude on the couple.

Jasmine pulled away. "*Je suis désolé*," she hurriedly said in French, apologetic at their show of affection.

"We'll be skipping breakfast," Devon advised, standing from his chair while gently pulling Jasmine to her feet with him.

"I'll be sure to tell Porter and Patti." Carmilla smiled knowingly. "Now go and find each other and leave me to try and get some more sleep. I have a bruised ankle, remember? It requires restful mending."

Devon gave a low seductive laugh that made Jasmine feel heady and renewed with desire. "Come on," he cajoled, squeezing her fingers tighter. Outside Carmilla's bedroom door, he pulled Jasmine closer. "I love you," he whispered into her left ear. "And I need you."

"I need you, too," Jasmine admitted.

Devon smiled and laced his fingers through hers as he led the way toward the attic. "You should've seen your face when you told Carmilla that you're in love," he said, giggling like a teenager. "I thought you were going to cry."

"You should've seen yours when you wondered 'if she'll have me,'" Jasmine repeated. "I'm glad it's all over," she added seriously. "I expect you thought I'd reject you."

"And you didn't."

"I didn't," Jasmine agreed. "What do we do about Gibson, Martha, and Lilian?"

At the stairwell, she was caught in his arms again, feeling as though she'd been touched by magic. "We show them just how much we are in love and that nothing is going to make our hearts battle with one another again," Devon told her, moments before their mouths sealed that promise with a long, passionate kiss.

It sent all the right shock waves running through Jasmine's body. "Whatever you say," she whispered as she paused on a heady breath.

Their eyes met. Her breathing stopped.

His mouth was velvety slick and hot when he retook her lips. The sensual touch was skillful and intent, speaking volumes of what was going to happen next. Jasmine was hardly aware of the small lustful moans that escaped her throat. It was only when Devon slightly parted her lips in a symbolic gesture of what they both needed and skimmed the tip of his tongue along her own that she felt the strong reaction within her.

Ten minutes later, they were in the attic, naked in Devon's bed.

Devon was . . . pure heaven. Delicious. Fluid. Sweet. A deep warmth spread throughout Jasmine's limbs as he repeated his torturous routine of plunging his tongue between the portals of her legs. Each repetition was slightly more intense than the last. Every time his dewy tongue ventured deeper, Jasmine shook with delight as Devon played with each tender fold.

She moaned and he pressed the invasion a little harder. Her breathing increased and seemingly forced his fervent need to please her further. Devon was deliberate in his pulsing rhythm, keeping the tempo with each flick of his tongue. Jasmine quivered like a leaf on a tree. It was an obvious response to the expert way in which Devon was wooing the secret core of her soul.

Soon, he would conquer her, in the way a man in love with a woman would.

But for now, his mouth kept the intention of capturing her. Devon's hands moved along the length of her thighs, working a magical sensation that ran in tandem with his tongue. When he dipped into her for another endless taste, Jasmine's eyes rolled heavenward and her fingers took hold of the sheeting. She felt the pressure build within her as her spine molded itself to Devon's bed.

She became ever more hungry for the pleasure of his creative lips. Her legs widened to allow him all the access he required. Devon did not wait for permission. He delved right in and licked his way up and down in a purposeful slow motion that left Jasmine almost screaming. Instead a guttural moan left her throat. Devon lifted his head and examined her face. Jasmine's eyes were closed and her breathing ragged. He enjoyed the way she looked at that precise moment.

But he was not done.

Something moved in him. A flame that burned every vein and pulse point. Scorching his very soul. It was very intense. He wanted Jasmine more now than when they had last made love. In the time they had been apart, he felt deprived of playing with her in this way. He had felt like a man lost, being unable to act out the very primitive urges that were born within him to love a woman. Now this woman did something to him he could not explain.

Devon's lips crept upward toward her navel, where he began to plant kisses, but he pressed his thumb purposefully along the folds of her core, completely opening her for him. His finger plunged firmly inside, in ardent possession. Jasmine's hips lurched forward in primal surrender. She clung to the sheets, tighter, overwhelmed by his sense of knowing how to keep her going.

As his lips moved upward toward her breasts, Jasmine felt like putty in his hands. Dazed, she licked her lips, while Devon continued in his knowledge of knowing exactly what to do with her. His powerful lips dropped kisses softly against her chest. Her mind disappeared into oblivion the moment he found the twin pinnacles that reached out, hard and sensitized, ready for his claiming of them.

Jasmine's palms brushed against the sleek hair on Devon's back as his mouth sucked ardently on each nipple in turn. She could feel him now, all around her as she worked her hands from his back to his neck. With her eyes still closed, Jasmine enjoyed the intimate moment of pure bliss. Devon lazily took his time, knowing that his woman was completely beholden to his every touch.

And then he moved upward toward her neck. Each kiss he planted against the soft caramel brown of her skin was to signify how much he loved her. When Jasmine's eyes opened, Devon's soul-searching gaze was filled with desire. She had never seen his face look so . . . *burning* with passion. He lowered his head to her with an intense, erotic expression that softened seconds before he hovered over her lips.

"Baby . . . you feel so *good*," he whispered quietly.

"Hmm," she murmured, rubbing her fingers up and down his back.

And then he reclaimed her lips. Jasmine melted. She felt a frisson right down to her toes. The kiss was coaxing her further into accepting him. With Devon already positioned between her legs, where she could now feel the hardened rod of his need for her, Jasmine was already feeling ready for him. But there was one thing missing and he knew it, too. Devon's lips softened and he pulled away.

"I'll be right back . . . sugar."

He threw her a long, lingering look before he jumped from the bed. Jasmine felt tortured waiting for him. She watched with lustful eyes as Devon walked naked to the cane chest of drawers and pulled from it the protection he needed. She heard the packet rip open, sensed him applying the latex, and almost wriggled with impatience as he hurried back to her.

Jasmine reached for him immediately. She felt strength in every part of Devon's body as her arms circled around his neck. His arms enveloped her, the roasted chestnut color of his taut skin smooth as silk over rock-hard muscles. He drew her closer. Their lips met for another sharing of emotions. When his tongue invaded her mouth, Jasmine yearned to be conquered.

Her legs instinctively opened to accept him. Devon's body was hot. Very hot. She felt the heat from him sear her senses. His teeth scraped a pulse point at the tip of her nipple, and Jasmine clenched her own as her hands boldly grabbed Devon's buttocks and guided him toward the one place she needed him most. His powerful thighs brushed against hers and she felt the soft curls of Devon's hair rub against the smooth satiny part of her inner thigh.

Their eyes locked. The commanding gaze he threw her told Jasmine to raise her hips forward.

Devon turned her slightly to maximize the pleasure and gently took her inch by inch. A groan left
his throat seconds before she wrapped her legs
around him. Jasmine had never seen such a sultry
expression than when Devon began to build the
tempo between them. His handsome face was lost
in the depth of feeling she was giving him.

His momentum was as old as when Adam took
Eve. Hard, throbbing, and incredibly surreal. And
Jasmine displayed the feminine action of a woman
who was in pure ecstasy, given by the man inside
her. Every movement, every inward and outward
motion pushed her one step further to the blinding clashing of emotions she had experienced
the last time they were together.

Jasmine slipped into a lustful coma as her heart
went along with the feelings erupting inside her. The
energy level between her and Devon had risen to another plane. They both seemed equal in their drive
to test the spectrum of desire that tugged back and
forth with each thrusting of Devon's hips. Somewhere in the back of his mind, Devon knew Jasmine
had him in her grips. This woman was whipping him
silly and he had no intention of pulling from her.
He didn't want this to end. She was fit and he was
going to keep the pace.

Jasmine's little cries of passion burned his soul.
The choking sounds from his own throat spurred
her further. Their body temperature soared higher
and higher. Jasmine could hardly believe this man
had once considered her an ice queen, unable to
be thawed out. He was doing a pretty good job
keeping her wet and sweaty.

Devon's hands slid under her bottom and raised
her to him. His head dropped between her full

breasts as Jasmine's fingernails gently grazed his back. She inched him in deeper, felt his rod graze a sensitive point that made her inhale from her gut and breathe through her mouth like a mad animal. Her heart was pounding. Her limbs were shaking. Jasmine was now well ignited and was scorching like a fire that had lost control.

There was no taming her now. There was no restraining Devon either. Both of them were lost in the moment. Jasmine's arms fastened securely around Devon's neck and imprisoned him to her body. She was not going to let go until they were done. Everything that was infinitely female demanded her to hold on. The craving to experience the release that was rushing to the fore was just too strong.

She was relentless in mirroring his every action. He rocked, she swayed. He thrust, she yanked. As wild as that of two panthers, the primal lovemaking became insatiable. Jasmine had never felt so alive. Devon had never felt so much like a man. When the spasms came, the very ones Jasmine knew would come soon enough because she had waited for them, her mind was made up. Devon was her fate just as Carmilla had always intimated.

When her wet and limp body fell helpless to the bed, a satisfied smile creased along her lips. She could not imagine what her late grandfather would have said, but were she to guess, a picture of Pastor Henry Charlesworth officiating over the wedding of his granddaughter was not too far from her mind.

Chapter Fifteen

Negril, Jamaica

The rhythm of the Caribbean waves was the most refreshing and soothing sound Jasmine had ever known. It was different from the pounding of the Great Barrier Reef, north of Brisbane in Australia, where she had once worked. It was also distinct from the noisy shores of the Mediterranean, south of Greece, where she had spent a wonderful time with a family whose three young boys who were under her care.

Lying on her back, under a large umbrella that shielded her and Carmilla from the baking sun, Jasmine glanced through her Moschino shades at the tall, muscular man coming out of the clear blue water. While she had been wrapped in her own aura of peace and warmth, listening to the hush of the ocean waves with the morning newspaper on her lap, Devon was immersed waist level, displaying his recently toned biceps to the local tourists.

She had heard the distant voices of the other people sharing the white sweep of beach just a stone's throw from the house Carmilla had now made her home. Entirely built from wood, with all modern utilities installed, the three-bedroom accommodation was another perfect honeymoon haunt, and Jasmine did not want to miss the opportunity of seeing her grandmother again.

It had been a year since she met Devon and began working with him at the Birmingham Savoy. No one, except maybe Dame Carmilla Charlesworth, expected their relationship to end in marriage after the turbulence they had gone through. Jasmine may have fancied the idea, but not even she could have envisioned Devon's proposal, especially when she considered that there was still much to resolve in her own mind about her disastrous love life.

But here she was, twelve months later, a married woman and wearing a very expensive gold band on her left ring finger.

"Don't you think Devon's putting on a little weight?" Carmilla said with a quizzical look, as they both watched him make his way over.

Jasmine dipped her shades and observed the tall man running through the sand. She sucked in her breath instantly. Wearing two-toned yellow and orange Speedo shorts, with a symphony of chestnut-brown muscles washed in seawater, Devon never looked so good. The past few days of swimming and long walks along the beach had already seen an inch disappear from his midriff, though Jasmine had to admit, their dining out had a lot to do with any excess weight in his bearing.

"He's looking just fine, Gran-mama," she answered, mindful of his masculinity concealed beneath his shorts.

Their honeymoon had started five days ago with

their arrival at Sangster International Airport in Montego Bay. Three nights were spent at the Buccaneer Beach Hotel before they journeyed by taxi through the Great Morass along Norman Manley Boulevard. As soon as she saw Carmilla again, Jasmine felt even happier. The last time they had occasion to meet was at her wedding in Paris.

"What he needs is more fruit," Carmilla continued, "not all this restaurant food you both have been eating. We should cook tonight."

"*Oui*," Jasmine said absently as her husband made his approach.

"How're the two ladies in my life?" He smiled, dipping to first kiss Carmilla on her cheek and then planting a kiss on his wife's lips.

"I was just saying," Carmilla began, fixing the multiprint sarong around the blue one-piece bathing costume she was wearing. A head scarf was wrapped around her head, showing no sign of her white Afro hair. "We should—"

"Eat at the Sugar Mill Restaurant tonight," Jasmine interrupted softly. "Remember, Gran-mama? We'll be staying at the Sandals Resort tomorrow until our honeymoon is over. Devon and I have booked nine days alone together before flying back to England, so tonight will be our last evening with you."

"The time just flies," Carmilla breathed, assessing the smoldering gaze in Devon's eyes. He was already committing to memory the beautiful curves of her granddaughter beneath her yellow Gucci bikini, and she had noted from the moment he had awakened that he had not taken his eyes of her. "I feel so blessed you two got married. If only Henry could've been here to see it. When I think of those lies that nearly tore you two apart—"

"Lilian and Martha didn't know any better," Jasmine interrupted, in a bid to put the whole matter to rest. They had already gone through it all, the apologies and the pain, days after the truth became known. "It's like you once said, Gran-mama. Sometimes it's best not to hold malice with people who cannot help themselves. They did try and make amends by bringing you that beautiful decorative decanter on your going away party before you came out to live here. Now you are a Caribbean madame, living a life of leisure, just like I imagined you would."

"That is true," Carmilla relented, touching her heart. She watched Devon take a seat in the deck chair beside her recliner. "Has Porter sold the house?"

"He's still thinking about it," Devon replied, twisting the wedding ring on his left finger. "But like you said, as long as Jasmine and I are staying there, I doubt he'll do anything."

"How are things at the club?" Carmilla pressed on.

"Very busy," Devon admitted, while reaching for a towel at the back of his chair. Drying himself, he added, "Jasmine thinks we should open up another club in Nottingham or Manchester."

"Are you planning to?"

"We're still talking about it." He threw Jasmine a devilish grin.

"I told him I'd like to be lady of at least three Savoys." She chuckled as a slow, ironic smile tugged at her lips.

"You have your whole life ahead of you to plan all manner of things," Carmilla enthused. "I was eighteen when I got married. Had I thought more about it then, I would've done some things differently."

Jasmine's brows rose. "Really?" she asked. "Like what?"

"Had more children, perhaps," Carmilla said flatly. "Porter should never have been an only child. Your grandfather and I were always traveling. Being pastor of a church had its rewards, but there were many sacrifices, too. I don't expect he would complain if he were with me now, but I have my regrets."

She spoke in the manner that only an eighty-three-year-old woman could, and Jasmine picked up on the nuance in her grandmother's tone. "Devon and I want to have a bunch of kids. In fact, we're working on it."

"That's wonderful." Carmilla smiled. "You're thirty years old now. It's time you were ready."

"I know," Jasmine agreed. "And I want to thank you for everything, Gran-mama. Helping me and my mother choose the wedding dress and the cake. And checking all those invitations."

"Nonsense," Carmilla said, unabashed. "It's the one day I've always yearned for, to see Porter take his daughter down the aisle."

"I still can't believe Mr. and Mrs. Pepperton came all the way from Australia to my wedding in Paris," Jasmine said, moving on. "Her boys have grown."

"A testament on how well you looked after them, which is why they remembered you," Carmilla remarked proudly. "I'm sure you'll be a good mother."

"I hope so." Jasmine smiled, throwing a swift gaze at the newspaper in her hand. "Oh my God," she gasped suddenly. "There's a commentary about Enrico Cajero."

"That . . . boar," Carmilla chimed instantly.

"What does it say?" Devon inquired, leaning his body forward to catch a glimpse of his wife beneath the umbrella shade. He sighted the caramel-brown of her long shapely legs and a flash of the newspaper she was reading, but that was all. He knew he would not be able to wait too long before he had to be with her again.

"He's written a book," Jasmine exclaimed in surprise. "It's called *The Confessions of an International Thief*, and . . . I don't believe this. It's a best seller." She tossed the paper onto the sand. "He's cashing in on his criminal celebrity."

"He got off lightly," Devon said, wading in, as he recalled reading news of the trial in *U.S.A. Today*, which reported Enrico receiving a two-year custodial sentence, though there was no mention of his connection with the Guerilla Diamonds, or the two foreign men associated with them. "None of those hotel guests he stole from will ever recover what he took from them."

"As long as he's out of my granddaughter's life," Carmilla said quite happily. "I am curious though. Whatever became of those diamonds you told me about?"

The space was a narrow room, dissected at equal intervals by tables. Each table contained two cutting wheels. The polishers, almost all of them Hasidic Jews from Tel Aviv, were seated on benches with their wheels spinning continuously. They were like robotic machines, hardly making a sound. One cutter among them would monitor sixteen stones at a time, mostly "cookie cutter" stones, but these were not what Petronella had brought with her.

She walked past a table toward a bare wall, broken only by a small mirror and a framed photograph of the "Marker." He was an old African man with a coffee-brown face, piercing gray eyes, and a wild white, flowing Afro beard. His appearance was like that of a witch doctor from a remote tribal village. The Marker was a man who, with the naked eye, could study an uncut stone, detect its location, and evaluate each internal flaw. With this skill, he would know which point of entry would bring the greatest number of blemishes to the surface before the stone was cut and polished.

Petronella caught her reflection in the mirror and studied it dispassionately. Her long weave was now replaced with a hairstyle that was braided into tiny plaits. The dark eyes that looked at her were gutsy with the bravado of an African warrior princess, but she was a very different woman from the one she had known a year ago. She turned from the mirror and ran an index finger along one of the tables. Minute speckles of diamond dust covered her finger. She rubbed the debris between her thumb and forefinger, quietly humming to herself.

Suddenly, a figure emerged from behind her. He was wearing a white overall and holding a clipboard and pen. "Her Majesty's Treasury has seen a sizeable boost to its coffers this year," he noted, while signing the sheets of paper attached to the clipboard. "Another confiscation at Heathrow Airport through customs and excise, was it?"

"No," Petronella admitted soberly. "These diamonds brought two people together."

"Where are they now?" the man asked, ripping two sheets from the clipboard.

"On their honeymoon in the Caribbean," she answered, retrieving her signed copies. "I should be so lucky." Her file on the man she'd been assigned to was now closed.

"You will find love, one day," the man assured her. "Good-bye, Miss Johnson."

"I don't know what Petronella did with the diamonds," Devon answered his godmother. "But I'm sure they're in good hands, just like my wife." He got out of his deck chair and felt his wet feet dig into the hot sand as he snuggled beneath the umbrella.

Jasmine giggled when Devon planted himself next to her on the sand. Lying with her back on a towel, she propped herself up on one elbow and gave him a kiss. "I told you one day, you'd be answerable to me," she said, chuckling.

"And I told you, in the end, you'd be responsible to me," Devon teased, his gaze moving down the velvety skin of her body.

He liked the added luster of her skin, smoothed all over with after-sun oil to protect from overexposure to the sun. Not a trace of fat was on Jasmine's slim frame, and from his viewpoint, her trim bottom, lovely back that gleamed with the coating of oil, slender neck, and firm hips were all of interest to him. This honeymoon was putting a fine gloss on her physique and the tug at his heartstrings was strong.

"Can I take you into the beach house?" he whispered hotly.

Jasmine giggled. "It's the afternoon."

"I know," Devon said, wriggling his eyebrows in provocation.

Jasmine felt her heart strings flutter. Devon was certainly all man. What woman could possibly resist being ravaged by his lovemaking? She looked into his handsome face, noting that beneath half-closed lids, his soul-searching eyes betrayed the sparkling flame that was already igniting in his rising passion for her. When their lips met and she answered his persuasion with all the love of a woman, Jasmine knew she had made the right decision. Devon was always going to be her fate. And whatever the future, they would walk the journey together.

ABOUT THE AUTHOR

Sonia Icilyn was born in Sheffield, England, where she still lives with her daughter in a small village that she describes as "typically British, quiet and where the old money is." She graduated with a distinction-level private secretary's certificate in business and commerce and also has a master's degree in writing. *Significant Other,* her first romance novel, was published in 1993. Since then, she has added eight titles to her name. She has been featured in *Black Elegance, Today's Black Woman, Woman 2 Woman,* and *New Nation,* and her work has appeared on the *Ebony* recommended-books-to-read list. Sonia is the founder and organizer of the African Arts and Culture Expo and the British Black Expo in Great Britain. She is also CEO of the Peacock Company. She loves to travel and realistically depicts her characters from the fine tapestry of the African diaspora. *Roses Are Red* was her first title for Arabesque, followed by *Island Romance, Violets Are Blue,* the sequel, *Infatuation, Possession, Smitten, Valentine's Bliss* (an anthology), and *One More Chance.* She would love to hear from her readers at:

P.O. Box 438
Sheffield S1 4YX
England

Or e-mail her by visiting her Web site at:
www.soniaicilyn.com

BOOK YOUR PLACE ON OUR WEBSITE AND MAKE THE ARABESQUE ROMANCE CONNECTION!

We've created a customized website just for our very special Arabesque readers, where you can get the inside scoop on everything that's going on with Arabesque romance novels.

When you come online, you'll have the exciting opportunity to:

- View covers of upcoming books

- Learn about our future publishing schedule (listed by publication month and author)

- Find out when your favorite authors will be visiting a city near you

- Search for and order backlist books

- Check out author bios and background information

- Send e-mail to your favorite authors

- Join us in weekly chats with authors, readers and other guests

- Get writing guidelines

- AND MUCH MORE!

Visit our website at
http://www.arabesquebooks.com